Her Mother's Daughter

Jackie Walsh lives in Dublin with her husband Paul. She's a member of the Irish Writers Centre, The Irish Crime writers group, and loves to travel to writing festivals including Harrogate and Bristol.

Also by Jackie Walsh

The Secrets He Kept
Five Little Words
Her White Lie
Her Mother's Daughter

HER **MOTHER'S** DAUGHTER

JACKIE WALSH

hera

First published in the United Kingdom in 2019 by Hera Books as *Familiar Strangers*

This edition published in the United Kingdom in 2023 by

Hera Books
Unit 9 (Canelo), 5th Floor
Cargo Works, 1-2 Hatfields
London SE1 9PG
United Kingdom

A CIP catalogue record for this book is available from the British Library.

Print ISBN 978 1 80436 515 1
Ebook ISBN 978 1 80436 516 8

Printed and bound in Great Britain by Clays Ltd, Elcograf S.p.A.

1

To Phyllis and Denis

Prologue

The light is dimming now, casting shadows all around, but I continue to dig. Dragging up soil, tossing it aside, digging out more. Lifting my hand, I rub the water from my eyes. Rain? Tears? I no longer know. Sirens whine in the distance, getting louder, closer. I have to find it, take it from the ground. It's what she wanted, what she asked for.

Rain blurs my vision, seeping through my t-shirt and soaking my skin, running down my front, down my back, filling my shoes.

I glance up at the house looming in the darkness. A gust of wind catches the broken guttering, banging it against the wall. Bang-bang-bang.

I'm alone here, which is what I want.

The hole is already filling with water so I work quicker, making it wider, wishing the gathering pool away. To my right I see a plant pot caught below a plank of wood. It cracks when I pull it free. Sweeping the pools of water into the pot, I pour it to the side but the more I bail, the quicker it fills up again.

My eyes burn as I look up at the sky and feel the rain sting my face. I think I see Him in the shapes created by the dark menacing clouds rolling past, hiding the stars, hiding the moon. Help me, God. Please, help me.

I dig again, harder and harder, grabbing at the earth until finally my fingers catch on something hard. My breathing stops. Tugging and pulling, I haul the box out of the ground and open it. Removing the bundle from inside, I lay it on the grass, let the rain wash it clean.

The bag is badly worn and torn in places, but it's still pretty much intact. With one finger I press on its hard contents. My hand reaches to my forehead, painting a mud cross on my face. The storm rages on around me but now I feel calm inside, more at peace than I have ever felt before.

Stretching out my hand, I place it on top of the bundle and gently press down on the tiny skeleton.

Chapter One

I hate walking through these doors. Failing bodies shuffling past the white walls and cheerful pictures, struggling to get their feet to take them wherever it is they want to go. The dining room, the TV room, the family room. There's not a lot of choice.

When I get to Mom's door I take a deep breath and cross my fingers. Will she know me? The gentle music humming in the background does nothing to ease my tension. My heart is beating a little faster, my stomach twisting into a knot. This is not how it was supposed to be. I try to put a smile on my face but it's hard. Hard when I know that what's behind this door will crush me as it does every time. Mom lying on her sanitized bed, surrounded by photos, flowers, a beaker with some Disney character smiling on it, unaware of anything. Reduced to the package she came in; a body that is also beginning to fade.

The doctors say her breathing is becoming more labored, her swallow weakening, her legs no longer able to hold her up. The little things she could do, like hold a spoon, or run a brush through her hair, have all disappeared over the past few weeks. Getting her mouth to open is the new goal. When that goes, we're all in trouble.

–

A nurse stands with her back to me when I enter the room, blocking my view of Mom and glancing around when she hears the door. For a brief moment I pause, waiting for her reaction. If everything is okay, the nurse will have a smile and a big hello. If things are bad today, she will whisper gently. I know these signs off by heart now.

Holding my breath, I wait while she presses the controller on the bed, moving Mom into a raised position. When she is lying flat she looks like a corpse and it scares the hell out of me.

'Hello Rebecca,' the nurse says, nice and loud and cheery, easing my stress and letting Mom know that I have arrived.

'Nancy, Rebecca is here.' I tilt my head to see Mom but there's no response. Her glossy eyes are locked on the nurse, looking at her like she's trying to figure out what she is.

'Your daughter is here… Rebecca is here.' I fix my eyes on Mom, willing a reaction. *Know me, Mom. Please. Know me.* Her lips pinch together. Slowly she moves her head in my direction, lifting my heart in the process. A smile moves the corners of her sagging face, releasing the chains that grip my body. I want to jump around the room and shout out loud. *She knows me. She knows me.*

'You look lovely today, Mom,' I lie. The tide has gone out on my mother's eyes. They were the first thing I saw each morning when I was a little girl, those eyes, the color of the sea. 'Good morning, baby,' she would say.

Pulling the chair in closer to the bed I sit to talk to her, telling her day-to-day stuff, about work; how I'm settling into my apartment; the new shoes I bought the other day in the mall. But it's painful watching her struggle to understand what I'm saying. I tell her about Joanna, my brother Danny's wife, expecting the baby. She has been told this a hundred times but I have to keep talking, anything to dull the awful reality of this silence.

After a few minutes of me babbling on my mother interrupts.

'Becca,' she murmurs, through the small gap her lips will allow. Delighted to hear her say my name, I pull the chair in as close as possible to the bed.

'I better start the supper,' she says. 'Your father be home soon.'

This often happens, her mind going back to days long spent, to moments that revisit her as if they are happening now.

'I'll help you,' I say, in my best 'play along with her' voice. But I don't get an answer. Mom is someplace else now, somewhere only she recognizes.

Her hand slowly reaches out trying to grab something from the air. There is nothing there, nothing I can see. Hopelessness surges through my veins; this is desperate. How much more of this can I handle? Tears sting my eyes asking me to cry, but I won't cry. Not in front of her. Instead I stand up and tuck the sheets in at the side of the bed.

Another few minutes pass with my mother's slow, swaying hand clearing the air. It's only when the nurse returns that she stops.

'Are you staying to feed Nancy?' the nurse says, placing a tray on a trolley by the end of the bed.

'Yes, if that's okay,' I say, watching the nurse press the bed controller and move Mom, like a robot, into a fully upright position. We have been told how important it is that the food goes straight down. Very important, they said, especially with Mom's swallow weakening. If particles of food are inhaled into her lungs she could get pneumonia. And that, they said, would be the end of her. We were also told that eventually her brain will forget how to swallow altogether and Mom's life will be preserved by a plastic tube. I'm dreading it.

'This looks lovely,' I lie again, pulling the tray closer to me, opening the napkin while the nurse makes my mother comfortable, fluffing up the pillows at her back.

'Your daughter is going to feed you today, Nancy. Aren't you a lucky woman?' Then the nurse walks out of the room, leaving a pile of mush on a plate that looks like someone has already had a go at eating it. The greyish goo makes me want to gag, but I better not. Taking the spoon in my hand I scoop up a tiny piece and lift it towards the *lucky* woman's lips, but Mom moves her head away from it.

'You're not my daughter,' she says.

'Mom, it's me, Becca.'

'I know it's you, Becca. You're not my daughter.' Grabbing my arm, her bony fingers wrap around my wrist.

'You're not my daughter,' she repeats and although she's freaking me out, I laugh. I can't help it. Things can be very funny in this hopeless situation.

'Of course I'm your daughter Mom, I'm Rebecca.' She tugs at my wrist, wanting me to move closer to her, so I do.

'Put Rover in the ground, Danny… don't cry Danny… Rover's gone to heaven.' Now she's worrying me. Her face has turned an even paler shade of white than I have become used to and she is getting very agitated. Her eyes are filled with fear, staring at me, scaring me. 'Stop, Mom,' but her grip is tightening, shaking my arm.

'It's Rebecca, Mom, I'm here beside you,' I say, willing her to relax, to take her mind someplace else, anywhere else. And even though her words have turned to meaningless sounds now, fear is still carved all over her face.

Then it stops. She lets go of her grip and sags back into the pillows, her eyes wet with tears. Slowly she lifts her hand to stroke my hair, taking me back to when I was that little girl, the one she cared for. I move my face closer to hers, to where her warm breath heats my skin, comforting me. Then Mom jerks her head up from the pillow and I jump back in the chair. Her eyes are open wide, staring at me, staring through me. Her usually lifeless eyes are alive with a fear so intense it's scaring me. I want to cry, to tell her she'll be okay but she is desperately trying to tell me something. I know it. Taking her hand, I squeeze it gently but she continues to stare, to scare.

'What is it, Mom?' What are you trying to tell me?

'I took you, Becca. You're not my daughter.'

Chapter Two

The parking lot is empty when I step outside, unlike my head which is about to explode. What did she mean? Why did she say she took me? For over an hour I sat there trying to get her to explain, to drag her mind back to where it was when she said those words: *I took you, Becca.* But it was a complete waste of time. Her thoughts had moved on to whatever dream, hallucination or flashback had decided to visit her. Turning the key in the ignition, I drive the expressway, watching the dark clouds gather in the distance above Boston city. What I'd really like to do is go to the nearest liquor store, get the biggest bottle of red wine I can find and saturate my anxiety. Maybe later, when I finish my shift.

I go through the shadow of the Hancock Tower and negotiate the tight space that leads to the underground parking lot of my very expensive one bed apartment. 'It's the location,' the realtor announced when my face couldn't hide the shock at the rent. 'By the river, Fenway Park just a short stroll away, and the famous *Cheers* bar,' which for some reason he felt important to mention, 'just a few blocks to the left.' If it wasn't for my second job, working behind the bar at Mattie's a couple of nights a week, I'd never be able to afford it.

–

After parking my car, I stand in the lobby waiting on the elevator to arrive. Jeff, the guy who lives for free in an apartment a few doors up from mine, comes rushing in. He's house sitting for his sister, an environmental lawyer who is currently living in Europe and needs someone to feed her rabbits. Nice work if you can get it.

'Hi Becca,' he says, his long, lean body towering over me. 'Are you in Mattie's tonight?'

'Sure am. Are you coming down?'

The elevator screeches to a halt and we step inside. Jeff punches the button for the tenth floor.

'Not tonight, sorry. Big date.'

Jeff always has a big date. Fit and tanned, his black hair shaved tight around the edges but dangling like a cocker's ears on top, he goes through women like he's testing them out for someone else. Which means I shouldn't really like him, but I do. We met the day I moved in when the bottom fell out of the box I was carrying, scattering my privacy across the floor in the lobby. Jeff arrived at the scene, helped me gather up my belongings and carry them to my apartment. Later that day he called in with a bottle of wine and we've been friends since. Just friends. Jeff is one of the few people I speak to in this building. Ms. Cannister is another – an old lady, who hasn't realized it yet.

'Call me Sophie,' she demands when I address her as 'Ms. Cannister.' Her wardrobe is more exciting than my own and she carries an iPhone with her at all times that no one has ever seen her use. Her age is a closely guarded secret, but the maintenance guy reckons she had a sister who died five years ago, aged ninety.

The lift jolts to a halt. Jeff rushes down the corridor, all systems go, leaving me strolling behind.

'Good luck with the date,' I shout before crossing to my apartment and letting myself in.

22A is a small space, but it has a floor to ceiling window that makes my world look a lot bigger than it actually is. Sometimes I sit in front of that window for hours, staring out at the tall grey buildings beyond, wondering about the lives of those strangers who come and go, come and go. Below me the street is quiet; most people who work around here empty out to the suburbs once six o'clock arrives.

In between the two tallest buildings a narrow sighting of Boston Common hangs like nature's clock; browns, yellows, reds. In the summer it's green. A few blocks down to my right the great Charles River flows, unhindered by market value. If I get right up against the glass and crane my neck, I can see the water glisten in the sunlight. Below the moon, it's like black oil.

–

I drop my bag onto the coffee table, switch on the light and straightaway know something is wrong.

Someone has been in here.

I tiptoe into the middle of the room, my heart bouncing in my chest. There doesn't seem to be anything out of place, everything seems okay. Holding my breath, I listen for the sound of someone moving, someone breathing. But there is no sound of life, just the usual clank from the archaic heating system.

The bedroom door is open so I stick my head in – just my head, I'm not going in alone. There's no one there. Mom's words must have me on edge.

Relax, Becca. Take a deep breath, make a strong cup of coffee.

The kitchen area is about four feet long and two feet wide, with everything squashed into it, including the kitchen sink. To make any kind of a decent meal I would have to be an especially dedicated member of Cirque du Soleil – which I'm not. Boiling water and reheating takeaways is about as much as I can pull off without doing myself damage.

Slipping off my jacket, I make for the kettle when I notice the pile of clothes neatly stacked on the floor beside the cabinet. What the…? Those clothes were on top of it when I left this morning. Someone *was* here. Someone searched the cabinet. My heart races as I sprint down the corridor, banging on Jeff's door.

'Jeff? Jeff!'

'What's wrong?' he says, when he finally answers, tucking in the top of a towel he has wrapped around his waist. He runs his hands through dripping hair, pushing it away from his face.

'I think someone broke into my apartment.'

'Seriously?' he says, already pulling his door closed behind him, following me down the corridor. Back in my apartment, Jeff looks around, then at me. He was expecting chaos, I guess. To his eyes, I know, it all looks as it should, or maybe even a bit cleaner than usual.

'I don't get it,' he says.

'That pile of laundry, Jeff. I left it on top of the cabinet.'

'No way,' he grins. 'Someone broke in and moved your clothes. We better call the FBI.'

'You're not listening, Jeff. I left those clothes on the cabinet. Someone's been in here.'

'You're sure?'

'I'm certain.'

The grin slips away. 'Is anything missing?' he says, walking around, leaving damp footprints, one hand gripping his towel, which for a brief moment, I imagine him dropping.

'I don't know. I haven't had time to check.'

'But you're certain that's where the clothes were when you left?'

I nod.

'Maybe they fell down,' he says.

'Into a neat pile and in the same order they were in before?'

He shrugs, slides me another grin, the kind you use when what you really want to do is growl. Jeff doesn't believe me. He thinks I've simply forgotten I moved them, and he doesn't want to waste any more time in my apartment when he's already under pressure to get to his, no doubt, extremely hot date.

'You want to ring the cops?' he says with a sigh.

'No,' I say, 'that's okay. Maybe you're right, I must have moved them and forgot about it.' I give him a push. 'You go, get ready. And thanks.'

'No problem.'

After I lock the door behind him I investigate more thoroughly, but there doesn't seem to be anything missing. It's not long before I find myself wondering if Jeff was right. *Did* I move the laundry?

No, I didn't. I know I didn't. Why would I move it to the floor?

Then I see it. I'm in the bedroom when I notice the photo, face down on the bedside cabinet. Someone was in here. That photo is always standing. My eyes open to it every morning searching out her smile. I place the frame upright and a chill runs down my spine. I'm icy cold.

Looking around I see nothing else has been touched, just this photo. Why? Who? And how did they get in? The spare key is out at my dad's house and I doubt Dad even knows how to find my place.

There's Lenny, of course. Lenny the concierge. Lenny the security guy. He's got a bunch of keys, one for each apartment in the building. Would Lenny have handed over my key? Or could someone have swiped the keys from behind Lenny's desk in the lobby? Ms. Cannister is always complaining about Lenny falling asleep on the job, says he spends more time counting sheep than counting visitors.

I'll ask him on my way out. Now I have to get ready for my shift at Mattie's.

–

Heading for the bathroom the apartment feels different, somehow. As if it has betrayed me. Everything looks okay, but the silence is eerie, so I switch on the TV and leave it playing in the background.

After a quick shower, make-up, clothes and shoes, I'm ready. But just as I'm about to walk out the door, TV remote already in hand, I get distracted by the face on the screen. A woman is missing, apparently. Katie Collins. According to the anchor, she hasn't been in contact with her family for days and they are all very concerned. Taking a step closer to the screen, I scan the young woman's features. Blonde hair, pulled tightly into a braid. Blue eyes, gleaming above a slight smile and skin that mustn't welcome the sun – it's as pale as my own.

Katie Collins looks familiar.

Chapter Three

Mattie's is a place of dim lighting and threadbare velvet, pocked wooden stools and sprung sofas, pre-owned air and Zeppelin blasting from the speakers, all of it infused with a tingling anticipation that anything might happen.

I pass Al and Don who stand by the entrance door every night, each of them with that seen-it-all-before expression nailed to his face. I've never seen them dressed other than they are tonight: black leather jackets, iconic band t-shirts and Al in jeans that he somehow, magically, manages to close over his bulging beer belly.

Mattie's gets an older crowd, so Al and Don don't often need to flex their muscles; checking ID is their main job. The clients, which is how Matt insists we refer to them, come to listen to the music. To nod along to bass riffs and guitar solos, gaping in awe at the finger hopping Wally executes on the fender.

I drop my bag in the changing room and head out to the bar. Mattie's is renowned for two things. Once a famous baseball player, Mattie broke his neck sliding into home base seven years ago and now runs his business from an ergonomic wheelchair, as seen on *Dr Phil.* And Aerosmith played here a couple of years back. A couple of decades back, to be precise, long before Matt Henley bought the place, but that didn't stop him putting a big sign on the wall making sure everyone knows Boston's Bad Boys once darkened these doors.

-

The night drags on until Brian, the head barman, tells me I can finish early. The bar is not as busy as usual.

In the changing room, I strip off the black shirt with Mattie's logo stitched onto the left breast pocket and slip into a plain white t-shirt. The anxiety is already creeping back, prickling under my skin. What did Mom mean? Who was in my apartment? Passing the storeroom on the way back to the bar I almost trip over a cardboard box outside the door. I peek inside to see if it's empty. It isn't. Seven bottles, all gin. After a quick glance around, I take one of the bottles and tuck it into the bottom of my bag. Then I head through to the bar, where Brian asks if I'm having a drink. I think about it, not sure if I should add poison to anxiety, but I tell him I will, just the one.

'Everything okay?' Brian says as he sets down the vodka and soda.

'Fine, yeah. Do I not look okay?'

'Terrific, honey, as always. I just thought you were a bit quiet tonight.'

There's a surprise. I didn't know Brian paid any attention to me.

'I'm fine, Brian, really. Bit of a rough day is all.'

'I hear that,' he says, pushing the vodka closer. 'Get that into you.'

I do. Then I do it again. And again. Soon my mood is mellowing out, the bar and its bustle fading in the background. Then Stephen Black walks in the door.

I am so not in the mood for this. With more confidence than a three-year-old drawing a picture, Stephen Black thinks every woman is just dying to sleep with him. Some probably are – not me though. I don't go for married men. From the far side of the bar I can deal with his advances, laughing, pretending to be flattered. It's not a good idea to burst your boss's bubble when you're a month away from being made permanent. But I don't know how to deal with him from this side. Maybe he'll behave like he does in the office. Mr Nice Guy. Showing respect for everyone as he waits to be made partner. With the alcohol swimming through my veins, Mom's words drilling through my brain. I'm not sure I care.

'Hey, Becca,' he says, leaning against the counter with a big grin. He introduces the two guys with him but I don't catch their names. If they're not drunk they're well on the way. Stephen orders a round, including me in the order.

Should I stay or go?

I stay. Soon I'm even enjoying the attention. The vodka working its magic. Now his hand is on my back, sending a warmth through me. This is good, this is how I want to feel, although I do find myself wondering, which hand is on my back… the one with the wedding ring?

Don't do it, Becca. Walk away.

I know, but…

But what?

Don't I deserve a bit of fun? After the day I've had?

Fun, sure, but this guy's married.

Then Stephen leans in and suggests we go someplace else, whispering in my ear, his warm breath starting the party. Ignoring the old Becca, the strong Becca, the one who seems to be losing control more and more, I agree.

–

Back at my apartment *Now That's What I Call Music 77* plays on the tinny stereo that cost a hundred bucks in a Music Depot flash sale. It came with two free CDs. The only CDs I have. Stephen is spread out over the sofa, watching me pour us both a glass from the bottle of gin. It doesn't take him long to make his move.

Within minutes we are both naked on the bed. My head is spinning, my heart is swelling, my body vibrates. Ignoring how wrong it all is, I continue making love, or whatever it's called when you're fucking someone else's husband. But, I tell myself, just don't get caught and no one will get hurt. It's that simple. For me, anyway. I don't have to go home and lie to the love of my life about where I've been and what I've done. How will Stephen do that? Does he worry he might get caught? I don't think so. It doesn't seem to bother him at all. Hot and all as the guy might be, he is cold enough to be able to detach himself from what he is doing. I'm glad he's not my husband.

–

A couple of hours pass before Stephen glances at the fancy gold watch on his wrist and shuffles out of the bed. I imagine it's worth a lot of money, that watch.

'I'll have to go soon,' he says, turning and bumping into the photo that he knocks off the nightstand. Watching his lean, naked body bend down to pick it up, I lie there, feeling content and awful at the same time. What did I just do?

Stephen is holding the photo in his hand, scanning the faces peering back at him.

'Who are all these?'

'My family.' I'm not comfortable with Stephen meeting my family like this. 'Mom and Dad, and that's Danny.' I feel sad when I say 'Mom'. It doesn't sound right. Should I say that *was* my mom?

In the picture she's standing by my side, her face wreathed in a smile. Long, dark hair hangs loosely around her face, shiny red lipstick vibrant on her lips. There is happiness in Mom's smile, real happiness, not the Kodak type. In fact, we all look happier in that captured second than we do now. Photos can do that, make you think life was better years ago, that things were simpler in the past.

For the people in that photo, they were.

'You don't look like your mother,' Stephen observes. He puts the photo back on the nightstand and walks out the door, cool as ice cream on a winter's day. The bang of the door closing behind him sounds extra loud.

I lie still on the bed, staring at the ceiling, wondering why his words made me feel afraid. His casual comment surges through me as if I've been injected with panic. Why *wouldn't* I look like my mother? Bolting upright, I take some deep breaths. *Relax, Becca, relax*. Then I let my eyes slowly move to the picture on the nightstand, to the mother who looks like me. Does she?

Chapter Four

The next day I head for Dad's with a terrible headache. He likes to have us all around the same table for Sunday lunch, the way we used to before Mom went away. It takes me twenty minutes to get to Dorchester and pull up outside the blue wooden house with the white porch where I grew up. I see Danny and Joanna's people carrier hogging the driveway, leaving me to park on the street. They bought the big car because the baby is on the way. Always prepared for what life has in store. I hope it stays that way. For Danny's sake, especially; he's not good with changes to the script. Everything has to be mapped out and planned to perfection. Not like me, I never know what's on the next page.

I finally squeeze into a tight space between two cars. I see Bert in his yard, leaning on a rake, and I wave over to him.

'Hi Bert. How's Edith?'

'She's fine. She'd be better for seeing you, though.'

'I'll be over as soon as lunch is finished.'

'She'll be happy to hear that.'

Except Edith won't hear that. Edith is old, older than Bert, and things are slowly breaking down on her. Her hearing was the first gift to be taken back, almost two years ago now. But she's in the hands of a good man who carries on like nothing has changed.

Bert shuffles off and I step up onto the front porch of my family home. Or what used to be a home, when Mom still lived here. Before the big hole appeared at the heart of it. Not a hole you can see. One you can feel.

–

At first it was all a joke, passing comments no one paid any heed to. 'Oh, I can't remember what I came in here for.' Or, 'Do I want a cup of tea or did I just have one?' Then she would laugh and let it go. Until one day the local store rang to say my mother was in the manager's office because she had forgotten how to get home.

I remember that moment like it is happening now. The fear that gripped me, tossing me into a place I never want to go back to. My father coming through the kitchen door, whistling, a rope and a hammer in his hand, then seeing my face and dropping the tools, rushing to my side.

'What's wrong, Becca?'

We are still getting the answer to that question. It comes in dribs and drabs from week to week, month to month, slowly torturing us, feeding us death through a drip.

'Here she is,' Joanna says, her voice traveling out through the open window.

Here she is. Not 'Hi, Becca' or 'How are you, Becca?' *Here she is*, implying everyone was discussing why I'm late. Oblivious to my paranoia, my father walks in from the back yard. His face is pale and he is ageing at a rapid pace. There are swollen bags beneath his sad eyes and his hair is now completely grey.

'How's my favorite daughter?' he says, giving me a hug before trudging back out to the yard. Through the window I can see him watching Danny, who is fixing something near the shed at the bottom of the yard. The pride never leaves my Dad's stare as he watches him. I know what he is thinking; my son; big strong Danny, with all his degrees and important job in the tall glass building. Not to mention his beautiful wife and eco friendly home the size of a small hotel that he's about to garnish with a baby. I imagine all Dad's friends down the pub are sick of hearing him talking about himself, Nicholas Wall, the mechanic, whose son is making it big in the corporate world. But it keeps Dad happy. He needs something to be happy about. Maybe I'll make him happy some day.

Mom was different. She never cared for suits and breakfast meetings. Having us around, healthy and happy was enough for her. She told me. Mom harbored no dreams for me that I didn't dream for myself. She loved Danny but she super loved me.

Danny lifts his head. There are times I think he's growing into my Dad – that same jawline jutting out, same square head. He sees me watching, nods and smiles. If he knew I'd slept with my boss last night, I would not be seeing that smile.

Rummaging in the kitchen dresser for some hangover relief, I find a packet of Advil and take two out of the pack.

'How's Nancy?' Joanna says, her false eyelashes lined up like synchronized swimmers preparing to dive into her eyes.

'Fine, the same as usual,' I say, filling a glass with water. I don't want to get into the details of what my mother said, not with Joanna.

After swallowing the tablets, I unzip my jacket and fling it onto the closest chair. *Please let her move on to the next subject, I can't handle this today, not with this blinding headache and burning guilt.*

'Poor Nancy,' she says, 'it's so sad seeing her like that.' She pauses for a moment, giving me a flicker of hope. But no, here she comes again. 'Have you ever thought about getting tested for the gene?' she says just as Danny walks in the door.

'Not really,' I say.

'It's just, with your mom having gotten it so young, you should maybe think about it.'

It kills me to admit it, but Joanna has a point. My mom is one of the youngest ever to be diagnosed with Alzheimer's at the Mass General Hospital. Early-onset Familial Alzheimer's Disease, to be exact, or eFAD, which is different to the more common one that older people get, LOAD. Which means Mom has a fifty-five-year-old heart in what looks like a hundred-and-five-year-old body, with a less than a five-second memory. Nowadays they know a lot more about the gene that carries the possibility of this elongated death sentence.

Sure, there is a possibility that I may have inherited the gene, so I will think about getting tested. Whenever I have spare money. Or top tier health insurance like Danny. I just don't want to discuss it now, not with Joanna, and definitely not with Danny.

'What are you talking about?' Danny says, washing his hands. Danny is a lot taller than me, keeps himself fit, and has parted his hair the exact same way for as long as I can remember. His clothes always sport an expensive logo, so they'll do his boasting for him. And he is always doing something, anything; he just can't sit down or keep still.

'Nothing much,' Joanna says, handing him a paper towel. 'I was just asking Becca if she'd thought about getting tested for the Alzheimer's gene.'

'And why would she want to do that?' he says, drying his hands a little too vigorously.

'I just thought...' Joanna says, turning away.

'Well, don't. Becca has no interest in getting tested.' Then, for her sake or mine, or his, I can't really be sure, he turns to me. 'Do you, Becca?'

'Does she what?' says Dad, walking in.

'Get tested,' Danny says.

'It's no big deal,' Joanna says. 'I only asked Becca if she'd considered getting tested for the eFAD gene.'

'And what did she say?' Dad says. It's like I'm not even here.

'That she's not sure,' Joanna says, turning to look at me.

'You're not sure?' Dad says.

I stare back blankly, and shrug, hoping it will quieten them. But no, in jumps Danny with my answer all prepared for me.

'Becca won't be getting tested for any gene,' he says. 'Why the hell would she want to know if that nightmare was waiting for her?' He puts an arm around Joanna, pulling her close and wrapping his hands around the baby bump. 'Maybe when she has kids, okay, maybe then she'll change her mind and get tested.'

Well fuck you, Danny. Why do you care if I get tested or not? You got tested and didn't ask anyone's opinion or permission.

Grabbing my jacket, I stomp for the door, saying, 'You know what? Maybe I'll do whatever I want.'

The kitchen door makes a bigger bang than I meant it to as I storm out, but I don't care if the house falls down.

I'm sick of Danny trying to run my life, judging me and telling me how to do everything better.

A brown paper bag on the hall table catches my eye. Opening it, I inhale the warm smell of freshly baked muffins. Cinnamon, blueberries, warm sugar, a bouquet of calories. Joanna must have baked them for my father. Taking the bag with me, I slam the front door closed.

Chapter Five

A soft breeze plays on my face when I step outside. Tall trees line both sides of the street; a palette of fall colors. I take a few deep breaths to calm myself, then cross the street to Bert and Edith's.

From nowhere Stephen Black jumps into my mind. I just slept with my boss. Shit, what am I going to do? There's no way I can face him tomorrow. Maybe I'll ring in sick, or just not show up, or move job. Or move city.

Bert's yard is bare, with dusky grey soil where green grass flourished before the summer sun scorched it. After ringing the doorbell, I hear the shuffle of Bert's footsteps and pray the Advil starts working soon.

Bert opens the door, a smile tugging at his sagging face. He has one of those funny smiles where only one corner of his lips curls up. He steps back to let me in, calling out to Edith to let her know I've arrived. Habit, I guess. She won't hear him.

The strong smell, of yesterday's fried chicken, makes me want to gag. It's never like that at Dad's. Joanna always has some scent of the month destroying the ozone layer. I used to call it Mom's, I don't know when that changed. But it did. Everything did. There are no more messages on my phone. No more trips to the mall on a Thursday evening for coffee in Bakers Beans, where we would chat about everything and anything. She always had something for me; a t-shirt, my favorite shampoo, a hat in winter. It was like she could never give me enough. I miss it. Not the stuff. Her.

-

Following Bert down the hallway is like traveling back in time. The wallpaper, with big yellow flowers on a grey background, has probably been back in fashion twice since they bought it. A carpet of blurred diamond shaped colors with a pathway worn into it leads us to the back room, the good room, where Edith sits in a chair by a blazing fire. The house is warm, so I'm surprised to see her wrapped in a blanket. Bert glances at me, shaking his head briefly, before I walk over and kneel down by her side.

'Hi Edith,' I say, speaking close to her good ear.

'Hello Becca,' she smiles. Her hand shakes as she attempts to grip mine. She looks about ten years older than she did two weeks ago. Her face has diminished to skin stretched on bone. Her sunken eyes are glass stones in quicksand. Just lifting her head seems to take every ounce of energy she has.

'I baked you some muffins.' I open the bag so she can see inside.

'They look lovely, Becca. You shouldn't have bothered.' She gasps for air between every word.

'It was a pleasure, Edith. You can have them with a coffee.'

'I'll put them in the pantry for later,' Bert says loudly. He beckons for me to follow him. Taking the walking stick that's resting on the back of Edith's chair, he leads me into the kitchen.

'What's going on, Bert? How come she's wrapped up like that?'

'We had a bit of bad news this week, Becca.'

When I called in two weeks ago, Edith was going into the hospital the following day for some tests.

'How bad?' I say.

'Six to eight weeks, they say.' Tears are gathering in the corner of his eyes. He lifts a frail hand to wipe them away. Six to eight weeks is such short notice.

I think about Mom and her endless departure and wonder which is easier.

'Does Edith know?'

'She knows she's sick, that she's not getting better.'

'Is there anything I can do? I feel like…' But I can't finish the sentence.

Placing his trembling hand on my shoulder, Bert sighs.

'No, everything is being taken care of. The palliative care team are great, and I'll do what I can to make it as pleasant a journey for her as possible.'

'You're a good man, Bert. She's a lucky woman to have you.'

He smiles, pleased to hear that someone might think him a good man. That someone might think Edith a lucky woman to have him. But I've always had a soft spot for Bert. He always had so much time for me, never forgetting my birthday, always taking an interest in what I was doing. Mom said he was a weirdo; that he was trying to play daddy because he had no kids of his own. I didn't buy it then and I don't buy it now. Bert is just one of the good guys.

–

Edith has fallen asleep by the time we go back in, her head hanging over the side of the chair. Bert rushes over to pull the cushion into place. My heart is not strong enough for this kind of pain, for the sight of old people struggling just to put the day in.

Leaning over Edith, I kiss her papery cheek and tuck the blanket around her shoulders. Something surges through me like an electric current. Mom is lying in a bed ten miles from here with no one to kiss her goodnight. I need to get back to her. Need to see her, to touch my lips to her cheek. Bert sees my face change.

'Are you alright, Becca?'

I turn to hug him, to hold him tight to stop me falling. As frail as he is, he keeps me upright.

'Don't be so sad,' he says. 'Edith's had a good life.'

'I know,' I sniffle, stepping back out of his arms, 'but Mom is only fifty-five and she's dying too.'

He puts his hands on my shoulders, holds me at arm's length, that sad smile tugging down the corner of his lips.

'Becca,' he says gently, 'your mother is already dead.'

'What?' Did I just hear right? How *dare* he? Mom might have Alzheimer's, her memory and her sense of self so faded that if *I* told her she was dead she'd probably smile, but she's still alive, still breathing, still *my mom*.

I'm already opening my mouth to say all this when it occurs to me to wonder if Bert is entirely himself. If the stress of caring for Edith, of nursing his own broken heart, isn't taking its toll.

I watch him, bent over at the fireplace, struggling to stoke the fire, keeping the room warm so Edith can decay in peace. This is not a room for confrontation. Let it go.

'Goodbye, Edith,' I say. 'Take care, Bert.'

'When will you be back?' he says, leaving his post by the fireplace to walk me to the door.

'Probably next week, Bert. I'll do my best.'

'Good. She gets very lonely, does Edith.'

–

Dad is out on his front porch, waiting for me.

'Becca? Dinner is getting cold.'

He likes to keep the peace, my Dad, hates any sort of row, which can be hard when Danny is around. And I don't want to upset him, he has enough to be worrying about. So I smile and hurry across the street. It's only right I go back and have the dinner Joanna has made, for my dad's sake. Also, I'm hungover, starving, barely hanging in here.

If anyone brings up the gene test again, I'm out of there, hungry or not.

Chapter Six

Behind the bar I'm praying for my break to arrive so I can drop another couple of Advil. The hangover is still torturing me, punishing me for my night of debauchery. I wonder if Stephen Black has a hangover. Is he thinking of me? Sorry for what he did, or still savoring the pleasure? Picturing the deed with a discreet smile simmering on his face?

From the corner of my eye I see a woman and man making their way towards the bar, conspicuous in their suits. They're not wearing the usual black t-shirts, leather jackets or anything to suggest that they are faithful rockers. They won't stay long.

Oh my God, she has a gun! Her jacket sways and I see the black, heavy-looking piece on her hip. Cops. Something is going down.

I try to pull a beer but I can't stop watching them. They're at the far end of bar now, speaking to Brian. The male cop is showing him something. He looks younger than his female colleague and must be over six feet tall because he's towering over everyone, even Brian. Brian's looking at whatever he's being shown and shaking his head, calling another bar staff member over. Now he's shaking his head too. Then the female cop points up at me. Does she want to talk to me too? I hope not. Cops I can do without right now. I've enough going on in my head, what with having to face Stephen Black and figure out what Mom was ranting about.

Slipping out from behind the bar, gin-scented sweat dripping from every pore, I head to the changing room, searching my bag for some Advil. Please be here. Rummaging through the contents, my fingers eventually locating the pills, I hear a knock on the door.

'Detective Ivy Turner,' the female cop says while shoving her ID card in my face. 'I wonder if I could have a moment of your time.'

'Sure,' I say, standing back to let them in. Beer barrels are the only places to sit in the room, so they remain standing.

Turner stares at me, freaking me out, until eventually she asks my name and how long I've worked at Mattie's. Then she shows me a photo.

'Do you know this woman?' she says, her eyes focused on mine.

'No. But isn't she the woman I saw on the news?'

'Has she ever made contact with you?'

'No, I've never seen her before.'

'Are you sure?'

'I'm certain.'

'Facebook, Twitter, anything like that?'

'No, just the news.' Shaking my head, I move towards the door. 'Listen,' I say, 'I have to get back behind the bar, why do you think I'd know her?'

'We're asking the questions.'

'And we're not finished, miss,' the male cop says.

'But I have to get back to work, sorry, I have to run.'

I hurry down the hallway with my heart pounding louder than the band on stage. I probably shouldn't have bailed like that, but I've never been questioned by cops before, and it made me nervous. Why would they think I know Katie Collins?

Back pulling pints, I see the cops moving through the crowd, showing the photo around. Every now and then Turner looks over at me, making it hard to concentrate. When I get the chance, I make straight for Brian.

'She just asked me if I'd seen the woman in the photo,' he says when I finally get him alone.

'Did she say anything about me?'

Brian stops pouring, looks at me sideways. 'Why would she say anything about you?'

'No reason. I'm just trying to figure out why she questioned me.'

'She questioned everyone, Becca,' he says, walking away with his drinks. 'No need to be paranoid.'

Well, at least that's something. Or it is until I hear Turner's voice in my ear, dead, as if coming through a device that removes any evidence of personality.

'A quick word before you go,' Turner says.

'About what?' Fuck, why won't she leave me alone?

She flicks through her notebook, stops, and nods to herself.

'Rebecca, right?'

I nod.

'Okay, Rebecca, I need you to really think about this. It's very important. Are you certain Katie Collins didn't get in contact with you?'

Her staring is making me nervous. Like she's trying to see behind my eyes, into my head. I'm not getting why I'm being questioned for a second time.

'No, she didn't. I'm certain.'

She hands me a card with her name and number on it.

'Rebecca, I need you to go home and check all your social media accounts. Contact me when you've done it.'

'I don't get it,' I say. 'Why would you think she'd get in touch with me?'

'Because she was trying to contact a woman who works in the bar in this club. And you're the only female working in this bar. She came to Boston looking for you.'

Chapter Seven

I'm awake all night. No chance of sleep. All kind of crazy ideas going through my head. Is it possible Turner is right, that Katie Collins *is* looking for me? But if so, why hasn't she found me? I'm not that difficult to locate. And where is she now?

And now, totally paranoid and sleepless, when the last thing I need is more grief, I hear Mom's voice, whispering: *I took you, Becca.* What if she is telling the truth? If Mom did take me I wouldn't have a birth certificate, or photos of her holding me after giving birth at the hospital. But what if?

Standing by the window in one of Mom's old t-shirts, I watch the world pass by below. People going about their normal daily grind, heading to offices, shops, cafes. Well, I won't be heading to the office today. The idea of facing Stephen Black is just too much.

And here it comes again, the guilt, flushing through my body, torturing my conscience. Why did I sleep with someone else's husband? What if his wife finds out? Oh my God, his poor wife. Bit late now! Mom always told me to find a gentleman. 'Someone who will treat you right, Becca, that's all you need, someone who makes you feel you are the queen of their world. Someone to love you.' Someone to love me, if only she knew. She would not be happy.

I wonder, *is* she happy? Is she anything? Happy? Sad? Scared? Scared was the worst part of the diagnosis. For me, anyway. The tears that flowed when she remembered she had forgotten. The panic, the terror in her eyes. Gasping like she was drowning, knowing there was only one direction this diagnosis was going. It seems like all we did was cry in those early days.

-

The first time she didn't recognize me, I was devastated. She'd sent me to the store for tomatoes but when I came back she just looked blankly at me and smiled politely as if I was a stranger. 'Hello,' she said, before walking out of the kitchen. At first I thought she was joking. She joked a lot when I was a kid. But then she came back into the kitchen and said, 'Ah, there you are. I didn't hear you come in. Did you get the tomatoes?' Unable to answer, I dropped the bag and hurried upstairs to my bedroom, where I cried for an hour. I wasn't supposed to leave her alone with the cooker, but I was boiling my own fears. Coming to terms with Mom switching on and off, like a bad internet connection. I didn't want to see it. No Service. But I did, more and more.

Having settled on skipping work because of all the conflict swirling around in my brain, I open my laptop and scan my social media sites as Turner requested. Nothing, not a sign of Katie Collins. Not a clue as to why she looks familiar. I knew there wouldn't be. If anyone had tried to contact me on Facebook or Twitter, I'd expect a band to be playing instead of a beep. No one is ever looking for me. But then again, was someone in my apartment?

I call Turner but I don't get an answer so I hang up and try again. Still no answer. I leave a message. This whole saga is draining me. My body wants to go back to bed and sleep, but my mind is restless. I need to find out about what Mom said. First thing I'll do is go to my Dad's and find my birth cert. The proof. That should put my mind at rest. I check the time, it's eleven a.m., Dad will be at the nursing home now.

–

When I get to Dad's I park around the corner in case Bert sees my car and wants to delay me. Sneaking in the side entrance I find the key for the back door that Dad hides under one of the broken laths at the side of the decking. Once inside I almost break my neck tripping over a brown cardboard box with Dad's name on it – more tools I guess – left sitting right inside the door.

'Dad? Are you home?' I call out. No answer. It's just me here now, alone with the past. Taking the steps two at a time I head upstairs to Mom's bedroom.

–

Mom was fussy about a lot of things, especially her *papers*. Her papers consisted of anything she thought worth keeping: insurance policies, birth certs, school reports, photos, and even certificates of compliance for various pieces of equipment she purchased over the years. Nothing fancy, my Mom had no weakness for the unnecessary, only documents for essential equipment – washing machines, microwaves, dishwashers. Nothing that would have you wondering what she wanted *that* for.

Everyone knew the leather bag that held all this vital material. It was old, made of crocodile skin and hidden behind a pile of gloves and scarves in her wardrobe.

Amongst the papers sits one of her prize possessions: a medal my grandfather was presented with after the war. I'm not sure which war, but my mother has a medal to prove he was there and worth his uniform. I'm guessing that went down well with my Dad when they first met, because Dad was also in the army. He spent a whole year away from his family, starting when I was just three days old. That must have been hard, fighting off the enemy by day, dreaming about his family by night. I remember none of it and neither does Danny, even though he pretends he does. He goes on about how he helped Mom with all the chores when he was just four years old. Talks about Dad's absence like he sat by the window each night waiting for him to return. All bullshit. Honorable, caring, endearing even, but still bullshit. We indulge him. I guess you need to with family, allow them their weirdness. Otherwise we'd all kill one another.

To tell the truth, I'm happy to listen to Danny babble on about what never happened. It's something to listen to, now Mom isn't here to fill in the blanks.

In the wardrobe, behind the pile of gloves and scarves, I find the bag. Turning the metal clip on the flap, I open the strap and smell the importance, the age, the scent of the serious. My heart is racing. Silly of me, I know, to think the writing on my birth certificate would read differently all of a sudden, all of a lot of suddens. But I need to see it. I need to know I am me.

And I am. The certificate in my hand was issued by the Registry of Vital Records and Statistics, Dorchester. Rebecca Sarah Wall, Sarah after my grandma. Born on the 13th of March 1991. Mother: Nancy Wall. Father: Nicholas Wall. I read it over a second time, then place it back in the bag. I am my mother's daughter. I have the paperwork to prove it. I feel like a fool for allowing her words play with my head. I remind myself, *your Mom has Alzheimer's, Becca*.

After putting everything back where I found it, I sit down on the bed. I don't think I have been here on my own since the day Mom was taken to the care home. The worst day of my life. I cried and cried, watching her sit in the wheelchair by the end of the bed while I packed the clothes I felt she would need. Once those clothes left they were not coming back. Blouses, dresses, pants, jumpers, all held up for her to choose from. She smiled, saying 'Ooh,' and 'Lovely,' before gazing again at the wall. Packing for her long goodbye broke me. I was so sad I wanted to get sick, but who else would do it? Who else could reduce my mom's existence to one small suitcase and a shoulder bag, which was what we had been instructed to do. I couldn't ask Dad. He was standing out on the deck, drowning, Danny's arms wrapped around him, helping him survive the torment. It was torture hearing the howls of pain break through his tears. The house was soaking in agony, and my mother played with a necklace.

At first Mom didn't know what was going on, but that quickly changed. When Danny wheeled her out to Dad's car, and she saw her case put into the trunk, her hands started shaking. She gripped the side of the chair and tried to stand. She wanted to go back inside to her own home but she hadn't the strength. The fear I saw in her eyes that day will haunt me forever. She cried, sobbed, screamed. And we still put her in the car.

The care home had left instructions that only one of us should go along with Dad, so Danny went. We decided he'd be stronger for Dad when it came to leaving Mom behind. I would have cracked up.

Watching the car drive away down the street, knowing in my head that Mom would never be coming home, destroyed me. It was a whole new kind of pain. The kind only a daughter could have for her mother.

When the car turned out of sight I went back into the house. Everything looked different, empty, pointless. Even the clock on the wall didn't chime that day. Though I think it might have been broken.

That was two years ago. It feels like only yesterday, and forever, at the same time.

Chapter Eight

Back downstairs I nearly fall over the big box again so I push it over beside the wall. Dad could easily trip over it. His concentration seems to drift with the breeze these days. I look out the window in the hope that the coast is clear but Bert is in his yard, leaning against the gate, looking this way. My God, he must have a sixth sense. I know he's waiting for me but he can't see my car from over there. *Go back inside Bert. I'm in a hurry.* Except for my Dad, who can come and go as he pleases, visiting hours at Oakridge are pretty strict. The rest of us are expected to stick with the program. So I'll have to leave now if I'm going to get there in time.

I check the time on my phone. No calls. Not from Detective Turner and not from Stephen Black. Maybe Turner is satisfied with my message, and I won't hear from her again. I doubt it, though. Something is tapping at my psyche, warning me, this is only the beginning.

Eventually Bert goes inside and I make my escape through the side gate. It's not too far a drive from Dad's to Oakridge. Mom won't be expecting me today.

Then again, is she ever?

–

The lobby is peaceful. Time moves at a slower pace here. Chopin, or one of those guys, plays softly from the two small speakers hanging from either corner of the papered wall. Below my feet, thick carpet offers more comfort. It's all about the comfort, the peace, the illusion. I make my way to the reception desk to sign the visitor's book.

'Rebecca Wall?' the woman behind the desk says, looking up at me through red framed glasses. She smiles and stands up.

'Yes?'

'Would you mind waiting here for a minute? Doctor Reilly left a message here, she wants to speak with you whenever you come in.'

Lifting the phone, she pushes a button and tells whoever is on the other end that I am here.

'What's this about?' I say.

'She'll be along in a… Oh, here she is now.'

Dr. Reilly is young. She wears Van sneakers, tight jeans and a hairstyle that wouldn't be out of place at the Oscars. Pulled back off her face, the hair sits in ringlets on top of her head, a diamond brooch holding it all in place. Without thinking, I run my hands through my own hair, pushing it back behind my ears. I'm pretty sure I didn't even run a brush through it this morning.

'Rebecca Wall?' she says. 'I'm Dr. Josie Reilly.'

She holds out her hand. I shake it, wondering what she might want. She doesn't look familiar. Maybe she's a new member of Mom's medical team.

'Can I have a quick word in my office? I know you're eager to see your mother, so I won't keep you long.'

'I'm not about to discuss Mom's treatment without my father present,' I say, stalling her speedy progress down the corridor.

'Oh this is not about your mother's treatment,' she says, continuing to walk to her office. 'This is about you.'

Now I'm really confused. I feel obliged to follow her even though I haven't actually agreed to talk to her.

'And how is your mother?' she says while punching a code into the keypad beside her office door. One-nine-nine-one, the year I was born. Please don't tell me this doctor is only twenty-five years old. What the hell have I been doing with my life?

'She's okay,' I say, because what else is there to say about Mom? Surely a doctor knows more than me.

'Good, good.'

Slipping in behind her oak desk, she sits down and indicates that I should do the same.

'Rebecca, I'll come straight to the point. We're looking for volunteers to take part in a clinical trial.'

A clinical trial? Should I know what that's supposed to mean? Will I sound stupid if I ask?

'And we're looking for the children of people suffering from early-onset Alzheimer's to participate,' she says.

'You're asking *me* to take part?'

'Well, yes.'

'But…'

Is this woman for real? I really do not need any more drama in my life right now, and even though I'd never admit it to him, Danny is right. I don't want to know if I'm at risk of developing Alzheimer's, not yet anyway.

'Let me assure you,' she says, 'it will all be very discreet and you don't need to receive the results if you don't want to. They can be used anonymously for the trial.'

'Erm…' *Jesus, Becca, don't just sit here with your mouth open, say something.* 'What would I have to do?'

'Very little,' she says. 'Give a blood sample to get started. There will be an information meeting to explain everything and to answer any questions you have. Don't worry, Rebecca, you can pull out at any time if you feel you don't want to continue. It's a terrible disease, but these trials help us make progress for the next generation, whom we hope won't have to endure what your mother and family are.'

Well, she certainly knows how to blackmail a girl.

Handing me a clipboard, to which is clipped a questionnaire, Dr. Reilly continues talking, telling me about the origin of the disease, how it can be traced back to certain countries. Finland, for one. I've never met anybody from Finland, don't know what they're like. And yet it's possible my great-great-great and not-so-great ancestors arrived from there. Or Colombia. There is a town in Colombia, Yarumal, where more of its inhabitants have the 'foolishness', as they call it, than not. Mom never liked coffee so I'm guessing we're more likely to have hailed from one of the Scandinavian countries. It's too late to ask her now. Come to think of it, Mom never spoke about our ancestry. Who was in our family's past? Where do I come from?

Filling in the questionnaire, I answer what I can. Name, date of birth, health questions, lots of health questions. I realize I'm very healthy. Lucky me. The family history boxes I leave blank. Knowing my grandfather had a medal from the war is not going to help anyone studying gene mutations.

When she asks to take a sample of blood, I buckle a bit. So soon, and with no notice. Not wanting to appear weak, I swallow my fear and roll up my sleeve. This is it. The one that will tell all. Does Rebecca Wall carry danger in her veins? Will she be doomed to the same fate as her mother and half of Yarumal?

After she's finished, I head for Mom's room, wondering, yet again, what I've let myself in for.

–

Mom doesn't know me today. I've been sitting here by her bed watching her play with the lace at the edge of her nightgown. Pulling it and laughing, pulling and laughing. How much more of this can I take? My heart cries just looking at her. And what if I'm carrying the gene? What if this is my destiny? Shit, maybe I shouldn't have joined that trial. I'll tell them to keep the results away from me. Or will I? If I'm not carrying the gene, I don't want to spend the rest of my life worrying about it.

My cell rings. More trouble, no doubt. Rooting in my bag, I locate the phone and answer without checking the incoming number.

'Hello?'

'Rebecca Wall?'

'Yes?'

'Detective Turner. We need you to come down to the station.'

Chapter Nine

The precinct looks just like a police station does in the movies, except there are no hookers hanging around. My head feels dizzy, nerves drilling through my skull. What does Turner want now?

I thought about asking Jeff to come with me, but decided against it. I also thought about asking Danny, but he'd try to run the show, tell the cop how to do her job. So no, not a good idea. Dad would have come if I'd asked him, but he has enough on his plate with his wife slowly dying. The last thing he needs to know is that the cops are questioning his daughter.

Turner finally arrives. 'Thanks for coming in so promptly, Rebecca. Come this way.'

I follow her through a set of steel doors and down a corridor. Turner directs me into an interview room. There's a table, four chairs, and a glass window for people to observe from the other side. Turner sits down on the other side of the table. The blunt fringe drawing a black line across her forehead makes her look harsh. Christ, why am I here? What does she think I've done?

Taking the photo of Katie Collins out of a file, she places it on the desk in front of me, then moves her hand to the left and without even looking, presses a button on the recording machine. Her dreary voice informs the machine of the day, date, time, and my name. It all seems very official, like I'm a suspect. I wasn't expecting this. Maybe I should have an attorney with me. *Fuck.*

'Rebecca,' she says, shaking her head slightly, her fringe landing back into the straight line, 'when we last spoke you told me you had never seen Katie Collins except on the TV.' Her fingers are resting on Katie Collins' blonde hair. I nod. Pointing at the machine, she asks me to speak up.

'That's correct,' I say.

'Never heard from her or made contact with her.'

I nod again. Oh shit, the machine. 'Yes. I mean, no. I've never heard from her.'

'Is that still your statement, Rebecca?'

'It is.'

The file on the desk is open and she is moving her head from left to right, left to right, scanning the page in front of her. My mouth is as dry as burnt toast.

'Ms. Wall,' she says. When did I become Ms. Wall? 'Katie Collins' husband told us that during his last conversation with his wife, when she rang him from Boston, she told him she had sent you a note, which you replied to. She said she was going to meet you on Saturday night, which was last Saturday night.'

'I don't know what you're talking about. I never heard, saw, or spoke to this woman.'

'Did you get the note?'

'I didn't get any note.'

'She told her husband she left it at your home, addressed to you. That you then texted the number she left and arranged to meet her.'

I can feel the blood rushing to my head, flushing my face, which I'm sure, makes me look guilty.

'I never got any note,' I say.

Should I ask for an attorney? But that would make me look like I have something to hide. Christ, is this a nightmare? *Wake up, Becca. Wake up.*

No, I'm awake for sure, this is real. Somehow I have become a suspect in the disappearance of a woman I know nothing about.

'Why me?' I say. 'I don't understand. How come Katie Collins is looking for me? I'm entitled to know.'

Turner sits back in her chair, staring me down again, her eyes covering every inch of my face.

'You have no idea, do you?' she says.

'None.'

–

I still have no idea by the time I leave. Too late, all the questions I wanted to ask but didn't, come rushing into my head. As if they were hiding behind my nerves while I was in there. It's the same at the doctors. I never go home from a doctor's visit satisfied. It's always, I should have asked this, I should have mentioned that.

Anyway, the bitch wouldn't tell me why Katie Collins is looking for me. Gave me some bull about it being an ongoing case, then wrapped up the interview by saying I was to contact her if I heard from the mysterious, missing woman.

Same old, same old, and I am none the wiser.

The sun blinds my vision as I leave the precinct. Should I go back and tell Turner about the break-in at my apartment? How the note could have been taken? No. She'll think I'm making it up, especially as I didn't report it at the time. Well, how could I? 'Hello, 911? Someone moved my clothes and disturbed a photo.' Even Jeff thought I was losing it.

There is only one thing to do. Find out everything I can about Katie Collins.

Chapter Ten

Stephen Black is a bastard who is going to be a daddy. I know this because his wife is standing beside me in the elevator, pregnant. I try to ignore her, but the beautiful Grace Black has other ideas.

'Rebecca, isn't it? How are you getting on working with Stephen, I hope he's being nice to you?' If only she knew how nice he's being to me. Her perfect skin glows like she just stepped out of an ad for L'Oréal, because she's worth it.

How does she even know my name? Oh God, I knew I shouldn't have come back into work today. I'm going to be sick.

I've only ever spoken to the woman once, just for a minute at an office party. I remember how fabulous she looked, slim and groomed. But how do I say hello to a pregnant woman whose husband I just screwed? It would be hard enough even if she wasn't pregnant. I didn't expect to ever meet her again, or at least not so soon. The word 'fool' must be engraved on my destiny.

'Hi,' I say without making eye contact. Should I mention the bump? I'd better – she's holding it with both hands, as if she's afraid it might fall off. 'Congratulations, by the way.'

'Thank you.' She sounds calm and happy, like nothing could ruin her day. I bet *I* could.

'When is the baby due?'

'Two weeks.'

Two weeks? Is she for real? That's got to be the smallest bump ever. Joanna looks like an elephant by comparison. The elevator door will not open quick enough – *open, please, open.* I've just found out I cheated on a baby. I'm going to hell.

When we finally step out of the elevator, the man of the moment is walking down the corridor towards us. His eyes are focused on his beautiful wife. Not me, the bit on the side. I doubt he even sees me.

Hoping to avoid the happy couple's embrace, I quickly turn and walk the opposite way. My head is spinning. I'm the worst person in the world. *What happened to your standards, Becca?* I berate myself. *Are you going to let your mom's illness ruin you completely?*

At my desk, I open the computer and hope my face doesn't look as guilty as I feel. Keep your head down, Becca. Don't look up. Just do your job.

-

When I first started working here, my position was described as 'assistant to the assistants'. Anyone can ask me to do anything. Which means everyone in this vast, open-plan field of dark suits and bright teeth is more important than me.

A lot of Bridgeway and King's clients are insurance companies. So some of the things I get asked to do can be interesting. Like searching social media sites to see if a person taking a case against one of our clients is telling the truth about their injuries. Sleazy, isn't it, stalking sites. But it suits me, and anyway I'm under instruction from the more important. I have no say in the matter, no need to get in touch with my conscience.

Last week I discovered a video of a young man gliding with the grace of a Russian ballet dancer down the slopes in Aspen. The video had been uploaded to his friend's website two days after he was wheeled out of our negotiations office, with a date stamp on the video showing it was recorded *after* the accident. The guy is not going to enjoy the next *soirée* at settlement room number two. I hope he arrives in his wheelchair. Can't wait for the miracle to unfold. With a bit of luck, I'll be in the room. I'm often called on to bring in some water or coffee or a can of WD40.

Another, but more boring, part of my job is data entry, which is basically updating client files with the latest information that the important people receive at a rate of $350 per half-hour. That's $700 dollars per hour, which is... well, I can't work it out right now, but it's a hell of a lot of money for a day's work. Imagine earning that sort of money. I can only think of one part time job that could compete with that.

–

A crowd has gathered outside the door of Stephen's office. Stephen has a door with its own office. That's how important he is. They are all wishing the pregnant couple the best of luck. Smiles, pats on backs, giggles and hugs for the princess. She doesn't come into the office often. In fact, I think it's only the second time she has been here since I took up my role as assistant's assistant.

Peeking over, I notice him looking my way. Is he nervous? Does he think I'll say something, tell someone else about our night together? He needn't worry about that. I have no intention of letting anyone know what I did. It's nothing to brag about, screwing your married boss. Looking away, I stare at my computer and decide to distract myself by Googling Katie Collins. I need to find out who she is and why the cops think she sent me a note.

According to Google, there is a Katie Collins for everything, from photography to baking, keeping fit to planting flowers. If I knew what the woman was interested in, I might be able to narrow down the search a bit. Entering 'New Orleans', which is where the news report said she came from, doesn't help either. I still can't find a Katie Collins that matches my girl.

After a few more searches my phone starts flashing. Pushing a bunch of files to the side, I see the number on the screen. Shit, it's him. Stephen Black. What to do? Should I go to his office? When I glance in his direction I see the crowd has dispersed. Stephen is standing alone now, staring out the window. Staring at me.

Damn it, what will I do? I feel everyone is looking at me, that I have a sign on my back saying, 'I slept with the boss.'

But no one is looking at me. They are all sitting at their desks, tapping keys, swiping screens, communicating with the digital world. Ignoring the real one.

Tucking a folder under my arm, I head for his office. I'd rather he was going to berate me for being absent a couple of days, but this is about Saturday night. I know what he'll say. 'I'm sorry.' 'I didn't know what I was doing.' 'I was drunk.' The usual bullshit that seems to come so easy to cheaters. They must all have the same back up file loaded onto their little brains for easy access.

–

Lines are etched into Stephen's forehead when I step inside the door. He must be feeling as nervous as I am. Well, it's something I guess, that he's showing stress, experiencing guilt. This relaxes me a bit, until he opens his mouth.

'No need to sit, this won't take long.'

Stepping away from the chair I grip the folder in my shaking hand.

'Under no circumstances are you to utter a word about what happened on Saturday night,' he says, his dark eyes squinting, staring through me.

I feel punched in the stomach, unable to reply. My mouth opens, but nothing comes out.

'I'm sure you'd like to keep your job,' he adds, breaking his stare and turning his attention to something on his desk. 'That'll be all.'

–

What just happened? Did I hear right? Did Stephen Black just threaten me? It sounded like it. Afraid that sleeping with the assistant to the assistants could ruin his chances of making partnership, not to mention what would happen if his pregnant wife found out. *Keep your head down, Becca, give him no reason to fear you.*

I drag myself to the door and walk out into the main office, where all my colleagues sit staring into screens unaware they're working for a complete prick. The water cooler beckons from the corner so I make my way over still in shock at what just happened. His words echo in my head. 'I'm sure you'd like to keep your job.' Really, Stephen? Well, I'm sure you'd like to keep your wife.

Chapter Eleven

The rest of the day passes in a haze of deep breaths and shaking limbs. When I finally get home I decide to forget about Stephen Black. Let it go; nothing more will happen there. I can't let him distract me from my mission. Pushing his threat to the back of my mind, I open my laptop and continue searching for Katie Collins.

Facebook. Katie Collins. New Orleans. For a moment I get excited when I see a young woman with blonde hair. But on closer examination I see it's not her, not the face on TV. I try Twitter. Instagram. Once or twice I see a face that resembles hers but when I search further it yields nothing. Is it possible she has no online presence other than the news reports, which are not saying much except that her worried husband's name is Thomas Collins? What if I contact him? He might be able to tell me something of use. But how do I do that? How do I get a number for Thomas Collins? Turner isn't going to give it to me, but there must be some other way. Facebook. Twitter. Instagram. Nothing. Resting my head against the cushion, I stretch out on the couch and fall into a deep sleep.

–

The room is dark when I wake. It's after midnight. I've slept for over three hours and missed three calls. Two from Dad, one from Danny. Oh God. Something must be wrong with Mom. My fingers quiver pressing the voice message button. Dad's voice sounds weak; my mother had a bad turn but everything is okay now. Of course he is going to say that everything is okay. I need to see her for myself.

The night sky is completely clear, stars twinkling as I drive out to Oakridge nursing home. The gas gauge needle hovers on the red line, making me wonder if I'll be able to cover the thirty miles to Braintree and back. I never think to check it. Other than visiting Mom or Dad my car usually sits in the underground car park most of the time because the Bridgeway and King offices are not far from my apartment. Walking gets me there quicker than driving, and anyway I don't have a parking place. They're kept for the people on the top floor, who are at the top of their game. The ones with their own offices, own clients, own mistresses. They are not for the mistresses. I wonder if the women in the top floor offices have affairs with the boys in the mailing room. I hope they do. I'd hate to think we have come this far and buckle under the strain of morality.

The journey seems endless as I replay Dad's message in my head. 'There's nothing to worry about, Becca,' he'd said, 'but I just thought you should know. No need to come rushing out here. She's sleeping now, and the doctor says she's doing fine.'

I have never had any reason to disbelieve Dad, but something in his voice is unsettling me lately. It sounds flat, without any emotion, almost as if he is giving up.

–

The doors of the nursing home are locked when I arrive. I should have expected that at one in the morning but suddenly I'm panicking, banging on anything that will make a noise in the hope of alerting someone on the other side.

When Mom first took this step towards her demise, we were given contacts and emergency numbers, a whole brochure full of anything we would need. I never even looked at it.

I could ring my dad but that wouldn't be fair, not at this hour. Danny, on the other hand, I don't care about waking at this hour. It will be good practice for him for when the baby arrives. As I filter down my phone contacts I hear a jingle of keys on the other side of the door.

'I have to see my mother,' I shout at the man behind the glass. He's wearing a brown security uniform with cream piping, the tag 'Barry' stitched onto the breast pocket. He's tall and round and I can tell by Barry's kind eyes that I'm begging a decent person. There is hope.

'I have to see my mom,' I repeat when he opens the door slightly. 'She took a turn earlier this evening, and I need to see her.'

'Well, we can't have you standing out there. Come on inside.'

He sounds like Morgan Freeman, a voice that is dusky, dark and on my side. I know he is going to give me a spiel about Oakridge's policy, how they can't have people in the building outside visiting hours when patients are asleep. Actually, they don't call them patients. It's 'clients,' as if people actually want what they are selling here. But I'm wrong. This man is even wiser than Morgan Freeman.

'I'm guessing you didn't come out here in the middle of the night unless it was really important,' he says, ushering me over towards the reception desk. 'What's your mother's name?'

'Nancy Wall,' I answer, watching him take forever to lift the visitor's book from below the counter.

'I'll have to get you to sign in.'

'Rebecca, I'm Rebecca Wall.'

'Okay, Rebecca.' He is flicking through the pages, looking for the current one. 'Sorry about this, but for fire safety we have to know exactly who is on the premises no matter what time of the day or night.'

Fine, just hurry up.

'I understand,' I say, thinking I might be quicker getting in if I just waited until I qualified as a client.

'Here we are,' he says.

'Wait a sec,' I say. Did I just see…? 'Go back a page.'

'Back where?' he says.

'Not that page, the page before.'

Leaning in, I flick the page back. It's done before Barry has a choice in the matter. 'There,' I say, moving around to Barry's side to get a closer look.

The page gives the date. It lists the time of entrance and exit. The name of the person visiting, and the person they are visiting.

I'm looking at Friday. The day before I last visited my mother.

I'm looking at a signature that shouldn't be there.

Signed by someone who has no reason to visit my mother.

A signature that looks a lot like *Katie Collins*.

Chapter Twelve

Oakridge is a lot calmer than I imagined the middle of the night in a hellhole to be. I thought it would be a chorus of snores and roars, tears and fears. Old people calling out to the shadows, missing the people they love, crying to go home to them. Hurting on the inside, hurting on the outside.

But I'm wrong, and I'm glad to be wrong. Everything is peaceful, everyone is sleeping happily. Everyone is drugged.

Barry insists on taking me to Mom's room. When I get to see her, my world slows down. I won't wake her, I just need to see for myself she is okay. As okay as my failing mother can be. Comfortable, that's how high our bar is raised. What we settle for now. 'Your mother was comfortable today.' Wow, isn't she the lucky woman?

I move over to her bedside and sit on the chair. Tears fall down my face and I let them. I'm sick of hiding them. I *want* to cry.

Mom's hair, brushed back from her face, is in need of a wash. That's what Friday's are for here. Having your hair blow-dried. A young girl comes in from one of the local salons and makes a fuss of her, asking questions, getting no answers, but treating Mom like she is a regular client. On Thursday someone comes in and massages her feet; Wednesdays, her nails get painted. Monday and Tuesday,

I don't know, but I'm sure something gets groomed. Of course Mom never remembers any of it. She is far too young for this. Some of the other 'clients' are almost twice her age, wonderful strong people who once ruled the world but are now unable to do anything for themselves. Playing with their memory might just be nature's greatest gift to them.

I lean in close to feel her breath on my face. Her eyelids twitch, making me wonder if she's dreaming. Is she dreaming of me? Does she recognize me in her dreams? Does she remember the things we did and the places we went to, the things we liked? Mint ice cream. Ketchup on my omelet, and not just a little bit, loads. 'The biggest squirt ever,' I'd say when she asked. Does she remember that? Or socks with no lace trimmings; if they had lace trimmings I would refuse to wear them. I kicked up such a fuss once, refusing to wear the socks my grandma bought.

'Just this once,' Mom begged, but I screamed like I was walking barefoot across shards of my own broken heart. Eventually Mom gave in.

'I'm sorry I didn't wear the socks, Mom.' I place my hand on top of hers, pressing down so she can feel it. 'I'm sorry I didn't tidy my room, Mom. I'm sorry I didn't do my homework. I'm sorry, I'm sorry, I'm sorry.'

Sobbing now, I rest my head on her pillow, thinking of all the times I could have been a better daughter, could have done what she asked. My eyes feel heavy, so I let them close.

A noise in the corridor wakes me. It takes a few seconds before I realize where I am. My head is muzzy, eyes stinging from the tears. Four a.m., time to go home. Kissing Mom's head, I hold my palm to her cheek and stare at her, her twitching eyelids, her shrinking face and parched lips. I want to believe she looks happier than when I first arrived. I know I'm happier than when I first arrived. Tiptoeing out, I make my way back down to the reception where Barry is back behind his desk.

'Everything okay?' he says. 'You were quite a while.'

'She's fine. I must have nodded off for a bit.'

'It must be lovely to have a daughter like you, willing to drop everything in the middle of the night to come and see her mother.'

Lovely to have a daughter like me. Little does Barry know. I fake a grateful smile, then say, 'Can I ask you a question, Barry?'

'Ask away.'

'Are there security cameras recording who comes and goes?'

'Of course,' he says. 'Archived on a weekly basis. Do you need to check something? Has something gone missing?'

'Say it had, and I wanted to check the camera footage.'

'Well, you would need to fill in a request form. That would go to the board and they would decide whether to grant access. It usually takes a couple of weeks.'

'Isn't there a quicker way?'

'If it was an emergency, yes. Is this an emergency?'

'I think someone visited my mom last week, someone who shouldn't have been here.'

Barry has the visitors' book open on the desk. 'This Katie Collins?' he says.

'Maybe.'

'It doesn't say here she was visiting your mother.'

'Then who was she visiting?'

'It doesn't say.'

'Isn't it supposed to?'

'Sure, but not everyone has the time to fill in every blank every time they come.'

'Could you check it for me? It'd really put my mind at rest.'

'You're not getting into trouble here, are you?'

No, I tell him, no trouble. It might even be true. All I know is that someone called Katie Collins visited an Oakridge client last Friday. I know nothing else.

Chapter Thirteen

It will take a day or two, Barry tells me. Once he has the CCTV coverage we can go through it together. There's no way he's letting me take the disc away.

But what then? If *Katie Collins* is the missing Katie Collins, why was she visiting Oakridge? Was it my mom she was searching for all along, and not me?

I can only imagine the look on her face when she finally located Mom and discovered she didn't even know her own name. Should I tell Detective Turner? No, I want to see the CCTV footage first.

Outside, the parking lot is dead silent. The only thing disturbing the peace is the crunch of gravel under my feet. Surrounded by tall oak trees that provide a shield against the outside world, this parking lot in the early hours of the morning is a perfect place to get mugged.

Suddenly I'm certain I'm being watched. When I go to open the car I drop my keys, and sense a presence behind me when I stoop to pick them up. Then a squirrel scurries past, a little grey, rat-like thing. Trying to escape from me, probably. Two seconds later it's halfway up one of the oaks.

False alarm, Becca. Relax.

It's hard to relax when you feel everything around you is on fire and you're the only one with a hose, but this search is going nowhere if I frighten too easy. I need to be strong. 'Toughen up, Becca,' Mom would say when I came in from the street, crying again. 'You can't have Danny fight all your battles for you.' But I did. And something tells me that, as much as I don't want to, I'm going to be knocking on his door again.

The interstate is quiet, not much traffic at this hour. After a couple of minutes, I notice a car behind me. A white SUV, I think. Its headlight beams are very strong, blinding me when I glance in the rear-view. My hands grip the steering wheel like it's trying to escape. I slow down, but it's still behind me. Is this guy following me? *Remember Becca; relax*. I take the turn off the interstate and on towards the city. The SUV does the same. Fear comes squirming through my gut. I look in the mirror, trying to catch a glimpse of the face behind the wheel, but I can't even make out a shape through the bright light. Who the hell is it? Should I stop?

No, don't stop Becca, it could be anyone. Someone dangerous, it's definitely not a squirrel this time. With the steering wheel slippery from my sweating palms, I ease my foot off the accelerator. If I slow down again, maybe they will pass by me. If it's Katie Collins, she will pull up beside me and let me see her.

Fuck, they're still behind, they've slowed down too. What will I do? Where's my phone? Shit. Where's my bag?

It's in the trunk. It's in the trunk because I always put it there for safety in case someone smashes the window and grabs it. Which, right now, sounds like a much better nightmare.

I know what I'll do; I'll stay in the car until I see a police station and pull up there. They wouldn't be stupid enough to attack me outside a cop station. Unless it *is* a cop, Turner having me followed, trying to catch me meeting Katie Collins.

My imagination just won't let up.

I keep driving towards the bright lights and tall buildings until signs of life begin to appear. There are more cars now, people on sidewalks, trying to hail a cab after stumbling out of a nightclub. *That's* what I'll do. I'll drive to Mattie's. Al and Don should still be there, standing at the door.

Taking the next right turn, I pass the Boston Public Library and I head for Mattie's. Soon I'm driving down the awkwardly narrow road flanked by tall buildings that leads to the parking lot at Mattie's Club. Normally I hate that road, it's too easy to scrape the car on the vehicles parked either side. But tonight I speed down there like it's the Indy 500.

I see Al in the distance, pushing the bolt on the big red door, Don beside him, hands in his pockets, watching Al do the work. I have never been happier to see these two guys. Pulling up beside them, I watch the entrance to the lot, heart thumping, hands still gripping the steering wheel.

The SUV is nowhere to be seen.

Chapter Fourteen

Al came back with me to the apartment and waited until I was safely inside before leaving. He told me not to worry, that the SUV was probably just going in the same direction as I was. But I don't think so. It was following me, I know it. But who would want to follow me? And why?

The room seems full of shadows. Creepy little reminders of ghosts and dangers hanging around. I double-check that the lock on the door is securely bolted, then close the curtains before switching on the light.

I used to feel safe here. Not anymore.

There's no hope of sleep. I lie in my bed staring into the darkness and let my worries fill the room. There is only one thing for it. I'll have to tell Danny what's going on. He'll freak out, find some way to blame me. But I'll have to put up with that. I need my brother by my side. He makes me feel safer. Ever since my first day in school when Ellen Griffin pushed me down the slide before I was ready to go. I cried with shock, but somehow Danny arrived on the scene, wiped my eyes and gave Ellen Griffin a look that made her squirm to the back of the playground. She never bothered me again. I'm not sure how long Danny waited in the wings in those early days, but I always felt he was there if I needed him. Now, I need him.

-

I wake up completely exhausted. The sound of traffic wafts up from the street below, letting me know the day has started without me.

I'm late. I'm supposed to be in work already. But I'm not going in. I can't and I don't care. A week ago I would have been a nervous wreck about skipping work. It would have been the biggest deal in the world. But that was before I slept with Stephen Black, before I found out a stranger was searching for me. Before my mother told me she took me. Before a detective started harassing me about Katie Collins.

I ring Bridgeway and King and tell the girl on the other end I won't be in today, that I ate something bad or I'm down with stomach flu, I don't know which. The girl says she'll pass the message on to my manager, but Stephen Black will know it's a lie, that I just don't want to face him. I don't care, he isn't my biggest worry anymore.

In the shower the steaming hot water has a calming effect. The small Band-Aid the nurse applied after taking my blood sample is peeling away, so I grip its edge and rip it off, feel the sting bite into my skin. I wonder what the results will show?

The thought of ending up like Mom terrifies me. Lying motionless in a bed with my memories floating high above, unable to reach them. Knowing nobody as I smile at all the familiar strangers who come to visit. Will I be happy? Or will I be praying for death to hurry up and take me?

A knock on the door disturbs my thoughts. Shit, who could that be? Grabbing a towel, I step out of the shower. It must be Jeff. No one ever calls here except Jeff. Dad has never made the trip. He hates coming into the city unless it's absolutely necessary. Danny and Joanna came to approve when I first moved in. But they haven't been back. There's no need, when I see them every Sunday at Dad's.

Another knock, louder this time. 'I'm coming,' I shout while pulling on a robe. *Please, God, don't let it be that detective, Ivy Turner.*

'Who is it?' I say, with my hand resting on the lock.

'The coffee guy,' Jeff says.

I breathe a sigh of relief and turn the handle. Jeff bustles in, smiling and holding two takeout lattes.

'Heard your shower on my way out,' he says. 'Thought you might need one of these.'

I open my mouth to say thanks but before I can utter the words I'm crying, tears pouring down my face as if some tank inside has overflowed. Jeff puts his coffee down and rushes over, guiding me to the couch.

'Hey,' he says. 'What's happened? Is it your mom?'

Slowly, with much hiccupping and gulping, I tell Jeff about my unfolding nightmare. He doesn't seem to know what to say, this man who is never quiet. Taking a deep breath, he sits back in the chair and pushes his fringe back off his forehead.

Please don't look so helpless, Jeff. Say something. Maybe tell me what I should do?

'And your dad and Danny know nothing about this?' he says.

'Not yet. I don't know whether to tell them, especially with Mom the way she is. Dad is in an awful state.'

I can feel my insides shaking. My teeth chatter. A chill passes through my body, making me clutch myself. I can only imagine what I look like, sitting here with wet hair and a red blotchy face in a sad old bathroom robe. Jeff must think I'm crazy. He's probably sorry he knocked on the door now.

'Why won't the cop tell you why this Katie Collins is looking for you?'

'I don't know, Jeff. She won't tell me anything.'

'What about her husband? Is he looking for her too?'

'I don't know. According to the news they have a baby girl, so he's probably looking after her.'

Jeff looks out the window as if pondering my situation. Or maybe he's just wondering how he can get the hell out of here without looking bad.

'If the cop won't tell you, I think we need to talk to the husband,' he says. 'But how do we do that?'

The relief surges through my bloodstream. The room seems to get brighter. It's like someone has turned my life to the next page.

Jeff said *we*.

Jeff's also got a plan. I retreat to the bedroom and shove on some makeup to cover the red blotches and disguise the trouble in my eyes. The clothes scattered on the floor by my bed are called on to do another shift. My hair is still wet so I run the hairdryer over it and tie it up in a braid. When I get back, Jeff has already located Thomas Collins on my laptop.

'He's an army man,' he says. 'Stationed in Belle Chasse, which is a naval base… I don't see a contact number for him here, but we could always try the army camp, give them a ring.'

I'm feeling nervous again. As Jeff continues his search on the laptop, it all becomes more real. We are actually going to do this. For some reason I feel stronger and weaker at the same time.

When I feel ready, I sit down beside him. He's now Googling Katie Collins' home town, a place called Algiers, a little island in New Orleans you can only reach by ferry. Katie Collins left her one-year-old baby to travel over a thousand miles in search of me. One thousand miles. Now that deserves a ballad.

'That's a long way to come to talk to someone,' I say.

'She must have something very important to tell you,' Jeff says, without taking his eyes off the screen. He finds the number for the naval base and turns his big green eyes on mine. I can do without the distraction. He smells good too, Armani, I think. Taking a deep breath, I say, 'Shall I ring it?'

'Can't do any harm, though I doubt he's on duty if his wife is missing,' he says, lifting the phone and dialing the number before I have a chance to.

After a few seconds he gets an answer. Sitting forward, I bite my nails.

'What are they saying?' I whisper. Jeff waves his hand at me and stands up, but the call doesn't last long.

'Well?' I say.

'No joy. He would not give me Collins' number or tell me where he lives.'

I slump back into the sofa, drained.

'But there has to be a way to get the information,' he says. 'Leave it with me, I'll be back later.'

It's only when he's gone that I realize how happy I am that Jeff is helping me. Pushing me to take action. I never expected to open up to him like that, sharing my deepest fears. Well, maybe not my deepest. I haven't yet told him what Mom said.

Chapter Fifteen

The back door onto the deck is open when I arrive at Dad's but there's no one home. No dinner cooking, either, which is disappointing, because I'm starving. Outside, the deck creaks beneath my feet. A gust of wind reminds me that things can change course at any time. I look up at the clear blue sky and feel the sun's warmth on my face. *I wish you were here, Mom.*

I can see her as I cross the yard, passing the overgrown plants that struggle to impress. I picture her kneeling on an old newspaper, wearing a floral skirt and yellow t-shirt, her dark hair tied back. 'Hi sweetie,' she says. 'Do you want to help me plant some tomatoes? Her smile brighter than the sun, her blue eyes bigger than the sky.

No tomato planting today, or ever again. I continue on, heading for the shed which leans in against the back wall, the oak tree branches overhead stretching out across its roof as if it is trying to hug its old wooden friend. There's a cross behind the shed, between the wall and the oak's trunk, which Danny paints white every year. Why he wants to paint his dead dog's marker every year is beyond me, but he can be weird like that, not caring if the decking is crumbling to pieces or that the front door hasn't been touched up in years, yet the dog's grave marker is kept pristine. Maybe if it had been my dog I'd feel differently, but I never had a dog, or knew Danny's dog either. He died when I was a baby, when Dad was off fighting his war. I asked Mom about it once; what Danny's dog was like, why he regularly painted the cross. But she didn't answer. Something of interest had come on the TV and she upped the volume. I remember it well because it came as a bit of a shock, Mom ignoring me.

I'm almost at the shed when I hear the sound of someone crying. Oh God, it's Dad. This must be where he goes to allow his pain to seep out. I don't want to see him like this, weakened to tears, sadness in his heart. But a good daughter would do what she could to help, so I open the shed door, dragging the words from my mouth.

'Dad?' As my eyes adjust to the dim light I see him sitting on a bench, head in his hands. I lay my hand on his shoulder and gently squeeze. 'Is everything okay, Dad?'

When he looks up his eyes are so red it's like they've been dipped in wine.

'It's nothing, love,' he says, shaking his head. 'I was just thinking about your mom, missing your mom.'

Now my own eyes are filling with tears but I rub at them, hoping to keep the floodgates closed. I cannot do this, sit and cry in a shed with my Dad.

'It'll be alright, Dad. Mom isn't going to get better, but if we stick together and do what we can for her, we will get through this.'

My father loves me. Every time he looks into my eyes I can tell.

'I don't know what I would do without you,' he says, wrapping his arms around me and squeezing me in a hug.

'You don't have to worry about that, Dad. You know I'll always be here for you.'

Linking his arm, I lead him out of the shed and back up to the house.

'Where's Danny and Joanna?' I say when we get back indoors.

'You didn't hear?'

'Hear what?'

'Joanna was at the hospital all night. A scare of some sort with the baby. Danny called and said everything was fine, they're home now but they're too tired to come over.'

'But she's okay?'

'As far as I know. Danny said there's nothing to worry about.'

Making a mental note to ring Danny later, I do my best to distract my Dad from his sadness.

'Nothing to worry about?' I say. 'I'm starving over here, and there's nothing in the fridge, nothing cooking.'

My father looks at me for a second, then laughs.

'I have some steaks we can throw on the grill if you like,' he says.

I don't like, so I don't answer, waiting for the next offer.

'Or we could pop down to Benny's Bistro.'

That sounds better. Benny's isn't the greatest, but I think Dad likes to go there because of the memories. The birthday parties. The four of us around the wooden table. Red and white napkins. Mom smiling. Dad smiling. Danny's face covered in barbecue sauce. And me thinking I'm the luckiest girl in the world when the waitress puts the knickerbocker glory down in front of me. I don't eat them anymore.

–

Leaving Benny's full of steak and cheesecake, I notice that Maxwell's Bakery is open, so I go in and buy a pecan pie for Bert and Elsie. This time I won't be able to pretend

I baked it. The baker has stickers on the box proclaiming ownership of the recipe, and anyway, it's quite a leap from Joanna's buns. They would never believe me.

When we get back home Dad decides to go to the Sam's bar down the road, where a couple of his friends gather most evenings to discuss how the Red Sox should be playing. Ever since Mom went into care it's been his only break from the grim reality of his empty home. Waving him off, I cross the street and knock on Bert's door.

The pecan pie is a big hit. Pecan is Elsie's favorite, apparently. I pretend I knew this all along, and went especially to Maxwell's bakery, because they make the best pecan pies in town. Elsie was really impressed by my thoughtfulness. It made her happy, so I didn't mind the lie.

Then I get an update from Bert. Things are still the same. Elsie is comfortable enough to stay in her own home, and for that Bert is grateful. All his sadness and anger is nothing compared to this one consolation; that Elsie is still at home. Lucky Bert.

'I saw a young woman at the Wall's' during the week.' Bert says, when I stand to leave. He always calls our house 'the Wall's'. Not 'your parents' house', or 'your house', or anything like that. Just 'the Wall's', as if the rest of my family have nothing to do with me.

'Really?' I say.

'She looked like you; same build, same color hair.'

What do I do now? I can't tell Bert I sneaked in the side entrance because I didn't want to see him.

'That was me, Bert. I forgot my key and had to go round the back of the house.'

'No, it wasn't you. You were there on Monday. This was the previous Friday. I wouldn't normally notice who was visiting who, only I was out in the yard at the time.'

A woman who looked like me?

'She was probably just selling something,' I say. 'Was Dad in?'

'If he was, he didn't answer. Besides, she was looking for you.'

'Me? How do you know?'

'Because she came across when no one answered. Asking if I knew a Rebecca Wall, saying that she needed to speak to you.'

There is only one conclusion I can jump to here. Katie Collins was at my house.

'That's odd,' I say.

'She didn't find you?'

'Not yet, Bert. If it's important enough, she'll track me down.'

My heart is beating a little faster. Now seems like a good time to pop around to Danny. I'll say I came to see how Joanna is after her night in hospital. And maybe, while I'm there, ask him if he knows anything about Katie Collins. After all, if she called at Dad's house, she may have called at Danny's. Though I'm sure Danny would have been straight on to me if she had. Wouldn't he?

Chapter Sixteen

Danny stands in the kitchen in running shorts and nothing else. His hair is unaware he has company. It sticks out in every direction, framing a grumpy-looking face with swollen, half closed eyes.

'Didn't get much sleep last night?' I say, taking up position on a high stool beside the island counter.

Danny's house is the total opposite to Bert's. It's all mod cons here. Everything is controlled by a keypad, with a button for music, another for closing curtains or adjusting the temperature, and lots more.

'I did sleep,' he says, 'for about ten minutes.'

'Anyway, I came to see how Joanna is, not you.'

'She's fine, the baby's fine, we're all fine. Tired but fine.'

'Good.' I look around the room until he realizes that I have something else I want to ask.

'Is there something wrong, Becca?'

But now I'm fumbling with the zip on my hoodie, wondering if I'm doing the right thing mentioning Katie Collins.

'What is it?' he says. His eyes are wide open now.

'It's about that girl, the one who's missing.'

'What missing girl?' he says, walking over to the refrigerator. He opens the door and reaches for the orange juice, and is about to start drinking straight from the carton when I say, 'Katie Collins.'

Orange juice goes spilling down his hairy chest. It'll get sticky if he doesn't get rid of it quickly.

'Fuck,' he says.

I stand up to find some napkins but I can't see any, can't find the button, and by then he's walking out the door towards the bathroom. After a few minutes he comes back, wearing a t-shirt and jeans.

'Sorry,' he says. 'What was it you were saying? Some missing girl, was it?'

He pulls out a stool and sits opposite me.

'Katie Collins,' I say.

'What about her?'

'Well, the cops seem to think she's looking for me.'

Danny stares. 'Why would they think that, Becca?'

'I don't know. I'd never heard of her until I saw her on TV; they were saying she was missing. Next thing I know the cops are in Mattie's, telling me she was looking for me before she vanished.'

I'm waiting for Danny to take charge, like he always does, but he only stares straight at me. Then he gets up and walks over to the glass doors, slides one open, and stands there gazing out over his yard.

'Danny?'

He doesn't turn. 'What?' he says.

'What do you think I should do?'

He's already shaking his head as he looks back over his shoulder. 'There isn't anything you can do,' he says. Then he goes back to staring at the apple tree at the bottom of the yard. Losing sleep does not suit Danny. He is going to be a royal pain in the ass when the baby arrives. 'Did the cops say why she was looking for you?' he says.

'No. Just that she's missing and they think she is looking for me, and if she gets in touch I'm to let them know.'

'Who's looking for you?' Joanna says, bustling into the kitchen. I fill her in. Joanna seems a lot more interested than Danny does. Then again, she's had a good night's sleep in a hospital bed while Danny had to negotiate the steel chair by her side.

'Are you okay?' I say, placing my palm lightly on her bump. 'The baby's okay?'

'It's all good, Becca. I honestly thought I was in labor but it was just a false alarm.' She nods towards Danny and puts a repentant look on her face. 'Let's hope it's the only false alarm.'

'Don't mind him,' I say. 'He'll have to get used to no sleep when the baby arrives.'

Danny comes back inside, takes his cell from where it is charging on the countertop and checks the screen.

'So she didn't call here?' I say.

Danny glances up.

'Who didn't call here?'

'Katie Collins. She didn't come here looking for me?'

'Of course she didn't. Why would you think she would?'

'Well, she called at Dad's.'

'She *what*?'

His face darkens with anger, like it's my fault she went to Dad's. As if I'm deliberately bringing unwanted grief down on the man.

'So Bert said. He says she called, got no answer, then asked Bert if I lived there.'

Danny walks out of the room without saying another word, leaving Joanna and myself staring after him.

'Well that's a bit weird,' I say. 'What's up with him?'

'Oh don't mind him, Becca, he's a bit crabby lately. Missing a night's sleep doesn't help either.'

-

After twenty minutes of listening to Joanna's account of her night in the hospital, I decide to leave. Danny hasn't come back. Joanna says he's probably on his computer in his man cave, but I don't know. I think I pissed him off.

The evening traffic is a nightmare, and it takes me more than an hour to get back to my apartment. I knock on Jeff's door but get no answer. Looks like I'm on my own tonight.

Standing by the window I look up at the darkening sky, wishing Jeff would call me up, ask me out to a movie or something. Anything to take my mind somewhere else for a while.

But Jeff doesn't call, Bert does. Edith has been taken into hospital.

Chapter Seventeen

Bert is holding Edith's hand. Edith is holding Bert's heart. I'm holding back the tears. I hate this part. This part of life: death. The part when everything enjoyed, or hoped to be enjoyed, loses its value. The 'what's it all about' feeling. I wonder about it, too often maybe… the power of loss.

Bert puts his lips close to Edith's ear.

'Rebecca is here, Edi. She's come to see you.' His tortured eyes turn to mine. 'I don't even know if she knows I'm here,' he says.

'She knows you're here, Bert,' I say, even though I have no idea if Edith knows Bert is here or not. It doesn't matter; lots of truths no longer matter. Edith is on her way out and Bert is going to have to hang around a bit longer in this world alone.

It's important that he thinks Edith can hear him. It matters that he gets to tell Edith a million times how much he loves her, how much he has loved her, how much of his world was built by her and how happy he is that it was.

I place my hand on Bert's shoulder and feel the bones, a carcass beneath his sweater. His face has shrunk, sucked in like all the fat has melted and only the skin remains. Bert looks sicker than Edith. That can happen to people; one big shock can literally drain the life out of them. I saw it happen to Dad when he walked out of the hospital the day Mom's diagnosis was confirmed.

I was living in a different part of the city at the time, not far from the hospital. Dad rang and asked me to meet him there. I didn't rush, presuming he was looking to kill some time while he waited on Mom to finish more tests. I didn't know he had just been told his world was about to change forever.

I remember being annoyed at getting damp in a light shower of rain as I made my way towards the sliding doors at the hospital entrance, the doors that opened and closed, opened and closed. People were going in, anxious about what they would discover today. People were leaving, some happy, others not giving anything away. Then I saw Dad standing to one side in the lobby. He was giving everything away. His whole shape had changed, it was as if he'd been squeezed by a giant hand. I rushed towards him as slowly as I could.

–

Back in Edith's room, Bert is sitting on the only chair, so I hunker down by his side.

'Can I get you anything, Bert? Some water, a cup of coffee?'

'I'm fine, Becca. And thanks for coming down. I didn't know who else to call… you can go now, if you want.'

I've only just arrived.

'I can stay a while, Bert.'

'No, I don't want to keep you here late. I just thought you might want to see Edith before… before…' He tries his best to hold back the tears but his best isn't good enough. I lean in and give him a hug. He needs more, though. He needs a miracle but I don't have any miracles. I tell him I'll say a prayer for Edith. Praying isn't something

I usually do but hospitals have a way of making people reconsider their belief in the next world.

I stay with Bert until a nurse arrives to tell him they will be moving Edith to a private room as soon as possible. Bert nods a thank you. He is humble now, humble and broken.

Bending over the bed, I kiss Edith goodbye, wipe the tears from my eyes. I squeeze Bert's hand, unable to look him in the eye, then shuffle through the curtains and out into the ER. More sick people. I am sick of looking at the sick.

Finally, I make my way to the reception area, where dozens of people sit waiting patiently to be called. Heading towards the exit, I notice everyone's eyes are fixed on the wall behind me. I glance behind to see what's going on, and I see her. Katie Collins.

Her face is full screen on the big TV bolted to the wall. There's no sound, so I don't know what is being said, but I can read the words scrolling across the bottom of the screen. The room goes into a tailspin. My body seems to be shutting down.

Katie Collins is dead.

Chapter Eighteen

'Jeff!' I yell, banging on his door, but there's no answer. Jeff must be out. He isn't answering his phone, either. Shacked up with some new date, probably. Walking back to my apartment, the empty corridor seems eerie somehow. All I want to do is scream.

Back in my own space, I flick from channel to channel. Katie Collins was discovered in Treehill Park, a public park not far from Dad's. We used to go there for picnics when I was a kid. It has a playground surrounded by forest. A big, lonely forest. Danny went missing in that forest when he was a young boy. Or so we thought. After searching for what seemed like hours, but what Danny remembers to be just minutes, he poked his head out from behind a tree saying, 'fooled ya'. Mom and Dad were happy to see him at first. I remember smiling at him from behind their backs when he got chastised for scaring them.

According to all the crime reporters, Katie's body was found by a man out walking his dog. The forensic experts are at the scene now. All the evidence points to a violent death.

Hours pass. Still no sign of Jeff. I flick from one station to the next. Katie Collins' death is the lead story on every local channel. Funneling down coffee, I stay glued to the screen. What will happen now? Will Detective Turner think I'm involved? Curled up on the sofa, my body does not feel like it's mine. I'm an alien here. *Jesus, Becca, how the hell did you get dragged into this?*

When the phone rings I nearly jump out of my seat. It's her, it has to be her. She's going to want to talk to me. I answer expecting to hear her dull voice. But it isn't Turner. It's Barry, calling from Oakridge. He has the CCTV coverage I was looking for. Do I want to look it over tonight?

Now I don't know what to do. I know what I *should* do – ring Turner and tell her I think Katie Collins visited my mom. But what if it wasn't her? What if the visitor was a different Katie Collins visiting someone else at Oakridge? Turner will go mad with me for wasting her time. She'll think I'm trying to mislead her, maybe slap me with an obstruction of justice charge. Right now there's a knot in my stomach wrapping all my fears into one hard ball. *Kick the ball, Becca, kick the ball away.*

I need to see that CCTV coverage. I want to know if Katie Collins visited my mom. If she was the one who put those crazy ideas in Mom's head.

I took you, Becca. You're not my daughter.

–

There's no need for me to knock the building down this time. Barry is waiting by the door.

'Are you okay?' he says as I slip past him, in behind the desk.

I'm shivering. Coming back here has taken a lot more courage than I ever thought I had.

I'm nervous about what I'm about to discover, but I believe I already know the truth. All I'm looking for is confirmation. It would be too big a coincidence if the visitor was some other Katie Collins.

'I think this is the one,' Barry says.

My head is ready to explode here.

'I'll just fast forward to visiting hours,' he says. His voice is soft, comforting. He even handles the computer gently, pushing buttons like they might break under any pressure.

Barry starts the footage running at two p.m. The picture is crystal clear, so it won't be difficult to spot her. A nurse opens the door to a young family arriving with a huge bunch of flowers. They are quickly followed by more visitors. Everyone looks as frustrated as I feel entering this place. They all present with worry scraped across their faces, putting on their polite smiles. I never considered the other people here. I always felt as if I was the only visitor and Mom the only sick person. I can be so selfish at times.

'Will you recognize her?' Barry says, his eyes on the screen.

'I'm pretty sure I will, yeah.'

I will, Barry, and so will you. Her face has been front and center on every TV screen for the past six hours. Shit, I never thought of that. What's Barry going to think when he realizes I'm stalking a dead woman?

After watching people entering and leaving for over an hour we have come up with nothing. No Katie Collins. I thought once or twice I saw someone that could be her, but when Barry zoomed in, they didn't fit.

'Well, that's it,' he said. 'You don't see her?'

'No.'

'And you're sure it was the 24th?'

'That was the day she signed the book,' I say. I'm feeling deflated even though I should be relieved. 'Thanks, Barry.'

'Hold on,' he says, pulling the visitor's book from below the counter. 'Let me just check something.' He flicks through the pages. When he gets to the 24th, he reads through the list of names.

'Katie Collins...'

Then he turns the page to Saturday. It's empty.

'Oh,' he says.

My heart leaps. 'What is it?'

'Saturday's page is blank.'

'What does that mean?'

'It means that either not one person came to visit on a Saturday, which is unlikely, or that the page wasn't turned over onto the 25th.'

'So she might have been here on the Saturday?'

'Could be. Let's see what we have.'

The clock in the corner of the screen is displaying 2.34p.m. when I see her, blonde hair tied back, wearing jeans and a pink sweatshirt. Katie Collins visited Oakridge on the 25th October at 2.34p.m.

I was here that day; I'm here every Saturday. Christ, I must have missed her by a few minutes. Maybe we even passed one another in the corridor.

My eyes lock onto the image. My heart races. This is her. Katie Collins. Moving closer to the screen I scan every inch of her face, her neck, her eyes. *Why did you come here, Katie? What did you want from me?* With my eyes ingesting every detail, her shape steps further into the distance. Away from the camera, closer to the danger.

Who killed you, Katie?

–

It's pink, baby pink. My heart almost jumps out of my t-shirt when I see it.

The photograph hangs alone on the wall inside the door. Moving closer, I see a child sleeping, cradled in her mother's arms, wearing a tiny knitted coat.

There's a little girl standing by their side, her face glowing with happiness, her smile showing the gap created by two missing teeth. In her hand she holds a naked doll with painted hair and one plastic eye.

The mother is also smiling for the camera, but there's a shadow across her face, proof of sadder times etched around her blue eyes. Her lips are bare, no makeup, no curls in the dark greying hair that hangs in clumps to her shoulders. Her floral dress droops loosely over her skinny body. Her feet are bare.

In the background the sky is flawless, a painted blue without a cloud in sight. The door to the trailer is open, showing the mess inside; clothes scattered across the floor, empty cupboard doors ajar. A teddy bear. A burnt out candle.

On the wooden steps leading to the open doorway a can of beer sits beside an overflowing ashtray, some of the butts dotted on the dry dusty soil below.

The baby is about three months old, a small tuft of hair jutting out from the center of her forehead. Her shiny lips are tightly closed.

But it's the coat that scares me. The pink coat with the second button missing. Putting my hand on the frame I glide my finger over the baby's face, over my face.

Chapter Nineteen

I don't think I slept at all last night. My mind was playing games, wondering if Katie Collins spoke with my mom. Did she tell her why she was looking for me? Nothing makes sense, and I still can't figure out why she looks familiar. Maybe she reminds me of someone I once knew.

I ring Jeff, but the call goes straight to his message minder. Where are you, Jeff?

In the meantime, I better go back to work, get this Stephen Black thing over with, face the music.

'You're going to have to face the music,' Mom used to say. I don't know where that saying came from, but I know what it means, having heard it a lot growing up. Like the time I broke my grandma's plate with the American constitution engraved on it. You'd swear it had been presented to her by President Lincoln – well, maybe not Lincoln, perhaps George Bush, the older one… she was a big fan of his. Anyway, uproar exploded when it broke. I ran out of the house and refused to return, until eventually I was told I had to face the music. And then there was the time I was caught stealing in school. It wasn't much, just some coins one of the teachers had left in a drawer. After refusing to return to school for a week, kicking and screaming and making myself sick, I eventually had to return and face the music.

And here I am today. Standing outside Bridgeway about to go in and see Stephen Black for the first time since he threatened me. I don't expect music.

Taking a deep breath, I push through the glass doors into the foyer. My stomach feels twisted, sweat clammy on my forehead, and the elevator seems to be taking forever. What will he do? Will he even speak to me? Eventually the elevator comes to a stop and I step out into the office, the constant office. It's as if no one else bothers to go home at night. Like the space is permanently full of these people and I am the only one who comes and goes. The only thing different about it today is that everyone is looking at me. They don't even turn away when I notice. I, for some reason, am today's gossip.

Oh shit. I hope they don't know about me and Stephen. But it's not that – it's her. Standing outside Stephen Black's office. Detective Ivy Turner and her partner the tall quiet cop. What the hell are they doing here?

Stephen has a look on his face I haven't seen before. Most likely it's his 'Why the hell are the cops looking for you?' look. I'll know soon enough because he's heading in my direction.

'What have you done *now*?' he says under his minty fresh breath.

'Nothing, honestly, it has nothing to do with me.' He asks – no, orders – me to follow him into a nearby room, one of the settlement rooms, while I continue my plea of innocence. 'The cops seem to think I know something I don't.'

'Get rid of her quick,' he says, leaving to get Turner and bring her to the room.

Turner is ferocious in her questioning, wanting to know where I was at every given moment over the last week, as if I might be Katie Collins' killer. I'm not a killer, Ivy; I'm many things but not a killer. Her hair is annoying me. The straight black fringe etching a line across her forehead as if it was painted on. It doesn't move even when she does. I don't like her jacket either, it's too casual for her important role. Her face, however, is gifted with perfect features, all sharp corners and piercing dark eyes, and her long lean body looks fit enough to catch an escapee. She won't need it today. I'm not going anywhere. I have nothing to hide.

'I cannot impress on you enough how important it is that you try to remember every little detail, anything at all that might help us find out what happened to Katie.' She says *Katie, Katie, Katie* over and over again, appealing to my tender side, making the victim human to me. But she's wasting her time. I've nothing to tell her.

'I wish I could help you, detective. I wish there was something I could say that would help. But I never met the girl.' Her eyes bore a hole in my head. I don't think she's even blinking. She makes me feel vulnerable, weak, in danger.

'What about your family?' she says. 'Did you check to see if Katie tried to get in touch with any of them?'

'I mentioned it to my brother and my father, but they know nothing about her.'

Suddenly I'm lying. I'm not telling her about Katie being at Dad's house. If she starts bothering him, Danny will blame me, and anyway, I don't even think Dad knows Katie was at his house. At least, he never mentioned it. The last thing that man needs is more crap to worry about. Mom's deterioration is enough.

'And your mother?'

'My mother is in a nursing home. She has Alzheimer's.'

'Right.'

Fuck, I'm lying again. Katie Collins was at my mother's nursing home but I don't want to tell Turner because if she calls there this whole thing will blow up and everyone will get dragged into it. People who have nothing to do with it. Or should I tell her? Maybe Katie was followed by the van that followed me. The killer could be working in the nursing home and if I say nothing, it could stop them finding him.

'I think she may have visited my mom,' I say at last.

Turner's eyes open wide. 'Why do you think that?'

My hands are sweating, trembling below the table.

'Rebecca, why do you think that?'

'Her name was in the visitor's book.'

'When?'

'I saw it the other day. I think she was there last Saturday.'

'Last Saturday.' Turner sneaks a glance at her colleague, the quiet guy, he's wearing a navy jacket and seems to stand by her side doing nothing. 'Did you see her there?' she says.

'No, I didn't see her. Why is she looking for me?' It's frustrating that she won't say why this dead woman wanted to contact me. Surely I should be told.

'Did she speak to your mother or anyone else?'

'Mom is unable to communicate, and I don't know if she spoke to anyone else.'

'What's the address of the nursing home, Rebecca?'

The bitch won't tell me why Katie Collins was looking for me.

'Why won't you tell me why she was looking for me?' I say, sounding braver than I feel.

'I can't tell you at this point in the investigation.' She opens a page in her notebook. 'The address, please.'

Then I see him, standing outside the glass-paneled door, staring in at me. His eyes are black with anger, lips pressed tightly together. For a brief moment I picture him lying on top of me, his heavy breathing in my ear, his hands squeezing as he huffs and puffs his way inside me. Stephen Black is threatening me with his piercing eyes; he's making sure I don't mention his name. My heart is beating hard and I think I'm going to get sick. I want to stand up. I want to run out of this place.

'Rebecca? The name of the nursing home. Now.'

'Oakridge nursing home, Braintree.' I say, and watch her scribble it down. 'I need to get back to work, detective.'

'Just one last thing and then you can go.'

Shifting in the chair, I straighten my back, thankful that this is almost over.

'Where were you last Saturday night?'

The shape hovering behind the glass moves closer. Stephen's eyes are wider than a teenage boy's watching a woman undress. My head is going to cave in. I don't know who I fear most. My boss or the cop. Both are frightening the life out of me.

'I was working in Mattie's.'

'Until what time?'

'About two a.m.'

'And did you go anywhere after that?'

'No, I went home.'

'Is there anybody who can vouch for you? Were you with anyone else?'

I can feel his eyes through the glass, drilling a hole in my honesty.

'No, I was alone.'

Chapter Twenty

I should not have left. Stephen Black will be pissed when he emerges from his office and discovers I've done a runner. But I couldn't stay. I'm sick of being treated like the bad person in all this, the one letting everyone down and getting everyone into trouble. This was not my doing. I did not ask for any of this.

The deli on the corner does a nice bagel. I consider going in but my stomach is not up for much. My nerves have me full. Down the street a crowd gathers, puffing on cigarettes. They seem to be happy with their fix, chatting, laughing, ignoring danger. I can't ignore danger. I'm knee-deep in it.

The watery sun blinds me so I open my bag and search for my sunglasses. They're not there. Instead I see the light flashing on my cell, which I'd turned to silent for my interview with Turner. Checking the call, I see it's Stephen Black, on my case already. Hastening my step, I kill the call and put the phone in the pocket of my jacket. He won't stop, I know that, the guy is nervous, which makes me nervous. He'll call and call and call, probably leave a few texts too. He has a lot to lose.

I walk all the way home. When I get to the corner of my street, I step right into the aroma from the coffee shop on the corner. I realize that I've never sat in that coffee shop, that I only ever got coffee to go. I decide that today

I'm going to buy a coffee and sit near a window like a normal person. I will read for a while and then survey the passers-by. People-watching, imagining their stories while I drink coffee. If I'm going to prison, this is the sort of thing I want to miss.

-

When I get back to my apartment block, Lenny is behind the reception desk reading a magazine. Ignoring the phone buzzing in my pocket, I walk over.

'Hi Lenny,' I say, resting my bag on the counter.

'Hi Becca.' He puts down the magazine. 'Everything okay?'

'I was just wondering about the keys.'

'The keys?' he says, standing up. Lenny is about six feet tall and four feet wide. His dark hair is dusted with grey and his skin is tough as car tyre rubber. He yawns constantly, no matter what time of the day it is, and when he is about to be asked a question, his face assumes a worried expression.

'Did you give anyone a key to my apartment last week?'

'Of course I didn't. I wouldn't do that without your permission.'

'Is there any way someone could get the key without you knowing?'

'No way. All the keys are kept in a safe in the basement. Why? Was someone in your apartment?'

'I don't know. I thought there was, but now I'm not sure.' Taking my bag from the counter I pull the strap over my shoulder. 'Maybe it was just my imagination,' I say, walking towards the elevator.

'Are you sure? I'll come up and have a look with you if you want.'

'No thanks, Lenny. I'm fine.'

I'm about to put the key in my apartment door when Jeff shouts down the corridor. 'Up for a coffee?'

Immediately I feel happier. I'm hoping he has found out some information on Thomas Collins.

'Sure.'

I walk towards Jeff's place, and I'm about to step inside when my cell rings again. I check the caller ID. I don't recognize the number but I guess it's him again. Stephen Black, ringing from a number I won't recognize. My hand shakes as I kill the call. I don't want to talk to him now. I don't want to talk to him ever.

Inside, Jeff is standing at the kitchen island. 'I haven't been able to locate a number for Thomas Collins, Becca, but I'll keep trying. Have you any more news for me?' he says, brewing the coffee.

'There is,' I say, pulling out one of the stools. 'The cops called to Bridgeway and King this morning. Said they'd been to my apartment but I'd already left so they went to my workplace. They were asking me for an alibi.'

'An alibi for what?'

'For Saturday night.'

'Why Saturday night?'

'They think that's when she was killed.'

'When who was killed?'

'Katie Collins.'

'She's *dead*?'

I can't believe he doesn't know this. Where has he been?

'I'm afraid so. They found her body on Sunday morning in Treehill Park. Some guy walking his dog.'

'Christ, Becca. What the fuck?'

'I know. And for some reason, the cops think I killed her.'

'What?'

'Well, why else would they want my alibi?'

'Saturday night,' he says. 'That's the night you were with the guy from work, isn't it?'

'Yes.'

'So you have an alibi,' he says, his wide eyes staring at me while he lifts his coffee.

'I guess so.'

'You *guess* so?'

When I tell him I didn't give Turner Stephen Black as an alibi because he was staring at me through the glass, he goes quiet, sipping his coffee and concentrating. My eyes are glued to him, waiting for him to speak, waiting for him to tell me how big a fool I've been, how I will have to tell the detective the truth.

'You have to tell them,' he says.

'I know. But I got nervous, and...'

'It doesn't matter. They'll understand. Ring that detective now, Becca, don't wait.'

Jeff convinces me I have no option. The wrath of Stephen Black is nothing compared to getting chewed up by the justice system. I know he's right so I take my phone from the end of my bag and dial her number. When I get no answer I leave a message telling her I need to speak to her, urgently. Then I hang up and wait.

Right now, I feel the whole world is sitting on my shoulder, its weight threatening to break me. Turner is going to think I'm lying, that I'm inventing the alibi. She's bound to believe Stephen Black over me. I would if I was in her shoes. With this nightmare scenario spinning around in my head, it feels like the room is closing in. I have to get out of here, I have to get out of everywhere.

'Are you okay? Becca?' Jeff moves around to my side of the counter. 'You've gone a funny shade of green.' He stands in front of me, but all I can see is a blur.

'Becca? *Becca*...'

–

When I come to, I'm lying on Jeff's sofa with a damp cloth on my forehead, Jeff sitting by my side.

'Jesus, Becca, I was about to call an ambulance.'

My body feels numb, so I wiggle my toes and fingers.

'I'm okay. Sorry about that, I couldn't help myself.'

'No need to apologize, it's not your fault you checked out. Are you okay now?'

'I'm fine, I think.'

'Right, stay there for a while and rest up.'

Taking the cloth from my forehead, he gets up, leaving me to close my eyes and fall into a deep sleep.

–

The music is what wakes me. Jeff is sitting on the floor with his back resting against the sofa, with his guitar, his precious friend, in his hands. I pull myself up into a sitting position and rub my eyes but Jeff continues to strum his guitar, singing, 'If you think this is bad you should hear your snoring.'

'What time is it?' I say, my eyes searching the room for my jacket. I need to check my cell. Jeff picks my phone from the floor and hands it to me.

'Did she ring?'

'Not yet.'

'What if she doesn't believe me, Jeff? What if she believes Black instead and I look like I'm making up an alibi?'

'You don't need to worry about him, Becca. He can deny it all he likes, I saw him leave the building.' Jeff says, winking.

'But what if he comes after me, calls at my apartment?'

'Well, don't be there.'

'What do you mean?'

'Stay here tonight.'

I don't know how to read this. Is Jeff suggesting I sleep with him?

'Don't worry, Becca. I'm not coming on to you.' He stands up and slips his guitar back into its case. With his back to me says, 'You're not my type.'

I'm silenced, left with my mouth open. Why am I not Jeff's type?

'You can stay in my sister's room,' he says, pushing open the door to the second bedroom.

Chapter Twenty-One

We stay up late, drinking wine and making a plan. Jeff advises me to go to Turner first thing and tell her Stephen Black is my alibi. He also suggests we go to Algiers and meet this Thomas Collins guy, find out why his wife was looking for me. This sounds a bit drastic, but I decide to keep my mouth shut for the time being and go with the flow. It's not like I have any better ideas.

Now the light is streaming into the room from a crack in the curtains, highlighting the beauty of this space: the shabby chic furniture, the gentle atmosphere created by the soft colors and paintings on the wall. Jeff's sister's bed is much more comfortable than mine with its crisp white sheets and fluffy pillows. I could stay here all day, wrapped up in someone else's comfort, wishing for someone else's life. But I can't, I've got to get to the precinct.

When I leave Jeff's apartment I close the door gently so as not to disturb him. As I turn to head for my own apartment I see him. Stephen Black. I can't see his face but I can tell by the suit and polished Prada shoes that it's him. My heart leaps as I reach to open Jeff's door again and realize I don't have a key. I don't want to knock because that will alert Stephen Black, so I slip into the alcove housing the fire extinguisher, squeezing my body up against the wall. The blood drains from my head. *Deep breaths, Becca.* The knocking continues, louder now, more aggressive. Clutching my bag to my chest, I wait, wishing for him to go away, to leave me alone.

Stephen Black must be terrified his wife will find out about our little deception. That Grace will leave him, taking their baby with her. And she'd be right to do it; the guy is a creep, a bully and a cheater. What was I thinking when I let him into my bed?

The banging has stopped. Slowly I peep out from the alcove. With a bit of luck, he got the message and retreated. But no, he is still there, running his hand through his hair before leaning to peer at the keyhole. Does he not know how they work? Then he turns this way. Quickly I pull myself back out of sight, my heart pounding, my body shaking. Is he ever going to leave? Christ, please don't let him walk this way.

I peer out again. This time he has his phone in his hand. Fuck, he's going to ring me. My head is about to burst. I pull the zip open on my bag and shove my hand inside. Pulling the cell from my bag, I flick the silent button just as the screen lights up. I think I'm going to puke so I suck in air and lean against the wall, watching Stephen Black's name flashing on my phone. That was close, very close.

I remain leaning against the wall for a few more minutes, breathing deeply, trying to normalize my body. Then I look out again, hoping, praying.

He is standing at the elevator staring at his phone. He calls me again. My cell lights up again. When he gets no answer he presses the elevator button and waits. I listen for the ping of the doors before I look out again and see him step out of sight. The door closes. He's gone.

Flopping to the floor, I drop my bag and rest my head in my hands. My body is still shaking. What was he planning to do?

Eventually I pull myself together and go back to Jeff's apartment. I listen outside for any sound that might tell me he is up, but there is only silence. I consider knocking but decide not to. Jeff stayed up half the night to comfort me. The least I can do is let him sleep in. I wait until I'm sure Stephen Black is well out of the building, then I go to my own apartment to take a shower. When I find the courage I leave and head for the elevator. My nerves are expecting Stephen Black to be standing in front of me when the elevator door opens. But he's not.

Out on the street, the morning commuters act as camouflage as I slip into the crowd. The precinct is only about fifteen minutes' walk away, so I zip up my jacket to shield myself from the cold wind that seems to have arrived overnight. Winter is coming.

Chapter Twenty-Two

Detective Turner takes me down the corridor to an interview room. I sit, nerves jangling, at the table opposite her. This room is smaller than the last one. There's no glass window, no spare chairs, just the table, the recording machine and the knife-edge atmosphere. The white walls do nothing to brighten the darkness of this place. I unbutton my jacket and take a deep breath.

'Is there something you want to tell me?' she says, putting her cell on the table.

'It's about last Saturday night. My alibi.'

'I'm listening.'

'I was with Stephen Black.'

'Stephen Black,' she says, just as her phone beeps.

'Yes. He came back to my apartment after I finished my shift in Mattie's.'

'Okay.' Her attention is still on the phone. She swipes the screen to read her new message.

'Just a minute,' she says, standing up and walking to the door.

Ten minutes later there is still no sign of her returning. Has she forgotten I'm here? I'm about to go find her when the door opens and she walks back in.

'Sorry about that,' she says, returning to her chair. 'So you've decided to change your story.' Her eyes are searching mine. I'm afraid she doesn't believe me.

'I'm telling you the truth.'

'Why didn't you tell us this yesterday?'

'Because Stephen Black was staring at me during the interview and I was afraid to give his name.'

But she's not interested in my alibi.

'Is there anything else you'd like to tell me?'

'Like what?'

'Like, say, where the note is?'

'What note?'

'The note Katie Collins left for you.'

'I already told you, I didn't get any note.'

'Someone did. Someone sent Katie Collins a text arranging to meet her in Treehill Park. They got the number from the note.' Turner stands up, walks to the rear wall and rests against it.

'Well, it wasn't me.'

'Have you any idea who did contact her?'

'How would I?' I'm confused now. I came here to tell her about my alibi and all she's worried about is the note. 'Can't you tell from the number it came from that it wasn't my phone?'

'It came from a disposable phone. Was it yours, Becca? Did you contact her from a burner phone?'

'No, I didn't. Look, I already told you I have an alibi. Stephen Black. Why don't you believe me?'

'I do believe you. We checked the club's CCTV, and saw you leave with him.'

'So why do you still think I have anything to do with her death?'

'You could still have contacted her. Maybe you changed your mind after, decided Stephen Black was better company, let her show up at Treehill Park in the middle of the night on her own.'

My head is thumping. What is Turner suggesting? That I made a date, didn't show up and someone else killed her? Or that I made a date, am deliberately using Stephen Black as an alibi and got someone else to kill her? I can't think straight. She is unnerving me, making me feel like I'm guilty of something, I just don't know what.

There's a knock at the door and some guy sticks his head in, telling her they have it. Her eyes light up.

'I'll be right out,' she says, then she comes back to the table and sits down across from me again.

'Rebecca,' she says, 'it's crucial we find that note. It was left at your address, so for now we have to conclude that you're the person who made contact.'

'It could have been stolen,' I say.

'Stolen?' she repeats.

'That's right. I had a break-in at my apartment last week. Nothing was missing so I didn't call it in, but someone was definitely there.'

Shit, I just realized what I've said. And so does she.

'Rebecca, if the note was taken from your apartment, that would mean you would have seen it. Your mailbox is in the hallway, right? You would have had to collect the note for it to end up in your apartment.' *Think, Becca, think.*

'Unless she slipped it under my door.'

'And did she… slip it under your door?'

'I didn't see any note, detective.'

'Okay.' Turner stands up. The guy who disturbed us earlier sticks his head in the room again, demanding Turner's attention. This time she relents.

'You can go now Rebecca, but I need you to keep looking for anything that might relate to Katie Collins' attempt to contact you.'

The cold air hits me in the face when I leave the precinct and walk out on to the busy street. People knock off me, rushing past as I move along at a pace too slow for them. I'm in no hurry. I have nowhere to be. I decide to visit Mom, see if I can tease any more words out of her.

Chapter Twenty-Three

Today there is a party at Oakridge. Someone has reached the big eighty, or ninety, or possibly even one hundred. It saddens me that Mom will never reach any of these milestones. She won't even make it to sixty.

Everyone is invited to take our loved ones down to the social room and join in the fun. When Mom was first incarcerated here, I used to walk her down to the room, sing songs and laugh, dance and eat cake. Not anymore. Now I push her in a wheelchair, watch her as she looks around the room wondering what's going on, and crumble bits of cake into her mouth.

People are huddled in groups in the lobby, waiting for the festivities to begin. Dad doesn't come anymore. He thinks it's a pointless exercise. Danny never came. This would be all too backward for his high-flying world.

Leaving behind the carnival atmosphere, I walk down the corridor and take the elevator to Mom's room. I don't make that wish anymore, the one where I hope she knows me. No point setting myself up for disappointment. I have lowered my standards: now I just hope she is comfortable and in no pain. Today I find her strapped into a wheelchair, a nurse tucking a blanket around her useless legs. Her hair is brushed into a shape more suited to an eighty-year-old and someone has put lipstick on her lips.

'Look, it's Rebecca,' the nurse says to Mom.

'Hi, Mom.' I kneel down beside her but she barely notices me, if at all. She is still smiling at the nurse and nodding her head.

'Do you want to go down and sing some songs, Nancy?' the nurse asks, not expecting an answer. Then she directs her query to me. 'Are you going to take her downstairs for the party? She's in good form today.' The nurse turns back to Mom. 'You're feeling good today, aren't you, Nancy?'

Christ, it's like she's talking to a dog. Good girl, good girl, Nancy.

The enthusiasm shown by Oakridge staff always amazes me. Their competence in trying to entertain the unentertainable deserves a medal. The excitement is growing as I push Mom into the social room. I will try to relax, forget what's going on in the outside world.

Balloons float in every corner. A table of sandwiches, cakes and brightly colored napkins sits in the center of the room. Smiles beam on the faces of every staff member as they help organize seats and spaces for everyone. Their ability to live in the here and now, to make this moment matter for the people in their care, is second to none. One nurse in particular looks like I do after a few too many. She is dancing from chair to wheelchair, holding the hands of each patient before moving onto the next one. A lady, introduced to us as Mae, is giving it socks on the piano, bashing the keyboard like she's the star attraction at Symphony Hall. Already some of the patients are singing along, bringing smiles and laughs to their families. My mom isn't. She sits in her wheelchair looking around like she's just landed on another planet.

Mae moves on to another song now, I think it's from a musical. Mom used to love musicals. *Chicago*. *Singin' in the Rain*. She always said *Mamma Mia!* was her favorite. After hearing a few notes, I realize I know this song. Mom used to sing it when she was cooking, she told me her mom sang it to her. 'Moon River'. I lean in, put my lips to her ear and croon the opening words to her, hoping that she can hear me through the fog her brain exists in. Then something wonderful happens. Mom turns to look at me and her eyes open wide. I think she knows me. She *does*, she knows me. It's as if someone is kissing my heart. Squeezing her hand, tears come to my eyes. Happy tears. Then I notice her dry lips parting. Holding my breath, I wait, leaning in to catch the words as she completes the lyrics, singing in a small, cracked voice. Wiping tears from my eyes, I feel a warmth travel through my body. It's like a present from an angel.

Nothing else matters in this moment. Not Stephen Black or Detective Ivy Turner or Katie Collins. Just 'Moon River' and Mom back in her own kitchen singing those words.

After a while, though, Mom tires. She becomes agitated, twisting and turning in the wheelchair, making strange squeaky noises, drooling. She looks scared, so I release the catch on the wheel and push her out of the room and down the corridor. I'm happy that I came here today, happy I had that moment with Mom.

Leaning over the back of the wheelchair I whisper, 'Like the song says, we're drifters, Mom.'

The corridor is much cooler than the overwhelming heat in the family room so I decide to push the wheelchair around for a bit to cool myself down. When I find myself outside Dr. Reilly's office, I see a notice stuck to her door.

> Clinical Trial. Information meeting in progress.

What's that about? Shit, I'm probably supposed to be there. I must have missed the email, or maybe it went into my spam. Though I don't see how, I have been extra careful to read everything since Detective Turner ordered me to monitor my social media. I think I better go in and see what's going on, explain that I didn't get the notification. I don't want her to think I just didn't bother to show up.

By now Mom has fallen asleep, her head tilted to one side, her breath slow and shallow. The blanket has slipped slightly, so I tuck it in below her legs and straighten her head. Then I move the chair against the wall and press the lock on the wheel.

–

Tapping on the door doesn't elicit an answer so I knock a bit louder. Still no answer. I open the door and stick my head through the gap. The room is in darkness and everyone is staring at the screen on the wall.

Dr. Reilly is sitting sideways on her desk. There are four other people in the room, all facing the screen. No one turns around at first, but when I open the door a bit wider, Reilly slips down off the desk and walks towards me. She instructs the four women, all of whom are about my age, except for one who looks a good bit older, to continue watching. I step back and wait for her to come out.

'Rebecca,' she says looking confused. 'What are you doing here?'

'I didn't get any notification about this,' I say, pointing at the sign.

'That's because I didn't send you any.'

'Oh.' Now I feel like an idiot. But then I think, why? Why *didn't* I get any notification?

'Is this not the clinical trial I signed up for?'

Reilly seems nervous, like she doesn't know what to say. She assumes a forced smile.

'I wanted to talk to you about the trial in person, Rebecca, but I didn't get a chance.'

'Well, here's your chance. Talk to me in person now.'

Folding her arms, she says, 'Rebecca, we won't be needing you to take part in the trial.'

'Why not?'

'We have enough participants, who are better suited for this particular trial.'

'I thought you said you needed as many participants as possible.'

'I'm afraid I can't talk about this right now, Rebecca. Can you call me, and we can schedule a meeting for later this week?'

'Is it my blood results? Was there something wrong with them?'

'It's nothing like that, Rebecca. Please, call me and we'll meet during the week.'

Then she's goes back inside. It's infuriating – why can't she just tell me the truth? All this *see you next week, nothing is wrong, too many participants* – it all reeks of deception.

'What is going on, Mom?' I whisper as I push her back towards her room. The nurse is waiting to settle Mom back into bed when we get there. When she leaves the room, I sit down and pull in close to Mom. Holding her hand, I look into her glossy eyes.

'What did you mean, Mom? Why did you say you took me?'

She's smiling now. Her teeth look too big for her mouth.

'Please, tell me.' I lean in closer, brush my fingers down the side of her face. Mom looks at me but I can tell she does not know who I am or what I'm doing here.

'Mom,' I whisper. 'I know you're in there, Mom… come back to me… What am I to do, Mom? My world is falling apart ever since you said you took me… I slept with my boss, I robbed a bottle of gin from Mattie's, I haven't been to work in days. All these things that are so not me. Who am I, Mom?'

But my words just float above her head like the rest of her world. Out of reach. Taking her hand, I kiss her cheek. 'I have to go now, Mom. We're drifters, the two of us,' I say, echoing the words of 'Moon River'.

Chapter Twenty-Four

Stale air refreshes me as I walk the dimly lit corridor of Mattie's. I'm looking forward to working, staying at home doing nothing allows my mind travel into some very dark places.

Behind the bar, Brian is making a job out of wiping the countertop, rubbing it vigorously with a dirty grey cloth. It's like he is trying to remove bloodstains from a crime scene before the forensics team arrive.

'How are things, Brian?'

'Good, Becca, good,' he says, not bothering to look at me. That's not like him. Brian always stops to say hello. *Is something wrong? Please don't tell me Detective Turner is here again. Everyone gets so obedient when she's about the place.*

'Is everything alright, Brian?' I say, glancing around to see if I can spot Turner. Apart from the usual early birds drinking beer and ignoring one another at the bar, I can't see anyone who shouldn't be here.

'Yes.' He's still not making eye contact.

'Brian, what's going on?'

Before he has a chance to answer, I hear Mattie's wheelchair behind me.

'Rebecca.'

'Yes?'

Mattie looks serious. 'Can I have a word?'

'Sure,' I say, glancing over at Brian, but by now he has turned his back.

Mattie doesn't say anything on the way to his office. His silence is unnerving. Inside, he rolls in behind the desk near the back wall and tucks himself in close. Should I take a seat or stay standing? Mattie is giving no instructions. Why is he being so quiet?

'Rebecca,' he finally says, in a low deep tone that leads me to believe this is not a prelude to good news. Leaning back into the chair, he taps the top of the table. 'We have a problem.'

'A problem?'

'Some bottles have gone missing from the cellar.'

My thoughts freeze. I feel like I'm going to puke. My eyes are locked on his as I pray for someone to beam me up out of here, for the ground to open and swallow me, for the building to blow up.

'Do you know anything about that?'

What will I do? *Lie, Becca, lie. Don't lie, Becca, don't lie.*

'No,' I lie.

'Are you sure?' he says.

The room seems to be shrinking. I don't know what I should do. What if someone saw me? But no one saw me, they couldn't have. Mattie is probably questioning everyone. I guess that's why Brian practically ignored me, he was probably questioned too. If I admit to this, I'm out of here. I'll have to take my chances.

'Yes, I'm sure, Mattie. I wouldn't dream of taking them. Maybe they were broken or misplaced or something?'

I sound stupid. Which is how I always sound when I'm trying to deny something I've done, rambling on with a big guilty sign flashing across my forehead. *Shut up, Becca.*

Mattie turns his attention to the Mac on his desk.

'It seems the CCTV says different,' he says, clicking open a file on the screen. Blood rushes to my head. I try to stay standing but I'm drowning here, drowning in my own thoughtless actions.

'Mattie, I'm sorry, so sorry. I don't know what I was doing. I thought maybe they were left over and going to be thrown out. I was going to tell you to take the money from my wages but I forgot and…'

There is no point adding a verse to this crazy song. I'm fucked.

'Please don't sack me, Mattie. I need this job. I swear I will never take anything again.'

Tears roll down my face. If I had a gun, I'd shoot myself. How could I be so careless, stealing from the only place that was keeping my life in any sort of order? I am now officially a bad person.

Mattie sacks me. He says he won't report the theft, but he never wants to see me near the club again. It turns out he only checked the CCTV because Turner asked him to. She called in and wanted to see everything recorded from Saturday night, which is how she knew I left with Stephen Black. Shit, now she knows I stole the liquor as well. She won't believe anything I tell her.

Brian is nowhere to be seen when I drag myself back out to the bar. And even Al, who I'm sure has some unsavory background stories of his own, isn't there to see me off. Out in the parking lot I wave goodbye to the big old building and cry. *What now, Becca Wall? What now?*

Jeff is going to hate me, Danny is going to judge me, Dad is going to worry. Mom… well, at least Mom, stuck in her prison of bad genes and good medicine, won't know a thing about it.

Chapter Twenty-Five

'Not going out tonight?' Ms. Cannister says, stepping out of the elevator, her red coat buttoned tightly around a velvet scarf. An explosion of perfume assaults my nose, forcing me to hold my breath for a few seconds while she moves past.

'Later,' I say, not wanting to admit that I have nowhere to go and no one to go with. She probably wants me to ask her where she is going, but I don't want to discover that even the oldest woman in the building has a better social life than I do. Pressing the elevator button, I watch her walk towards the exit, her head held high, a lightness in her step.

Ignoring the door to my apartment, I go straight to Jeff's. The sound of my knocking echoes through the corridor, begging. But I get no answer. Everything is still. It's like the world has been put on pause and I'm walking through it, searching for my space. For where I'm supposed to be.

Back in my apartment I finally confront what losing my job at Mattie's means. Not only will I miss the friendships and the laughs, but also the money. How the hell will I pay my rent now? How to pay for that big glass wall that allows me spy on the world? I place my hand on the pane and look out at the darkening night. Shadows paint the buildings as couples walk hand in hand on the street below. In the distance I see the red coat chaperoned by a grey suit. Ms. Cannister and her date walk to the end of the street, then turn down Holden Street, which houses all the restaurants and bars, dreams and possibilities.

The silence is broken by the rumble the refrigerator makes every now and then. It's beckoning to me from the corner of the kitchen but I know it's just teasing, there is nothing inside. The only thing I ate today was a chunk of chocolate cake I couldn't get into Mom's mouth. Her eyes welcomed it but she'd forgotten how to open her lips.

In the cupboard I find a half eaten bag of Lay's chips and sit on the sofa feeding myself, hoping to hear Jeff's footsteps passing my door. I scrape the crumbs from the end of the bag then toss it in the trash before looking around the room that eight months earlier promised me a new life. A new beginning. It was supposed to be great; the new job at Bridgeway and King, the part-time job at Mattie's, dreams of a love life. One by one it has all turned to shit, starting the day Katie Collins came to town.

Switching on the TV, I flick through the stations, but nothing holds my attention. Nothing is more engaging than my own disastrous life. So I turn it off and go to bed.

The following morning, I wake up, surprised that I have managed to complete a full night's sleep. I remember it's Sunday, 'let's play happy families' day. Pulling the duvet around me, I close my eyes. I don't want to be awake, don't want to face the music.

After sleeping for another few hours I pull myself out of the bed and take a shower. I have to be at Dad's in an hour.

–

Bert's front door is open when I arrive outside Dad's so I walk over and tap on the door.

'You in here, Bert?' I say.

Bert sticks his head out from a door halfway down the hall.

'Becca,' he says. 'Come in.'

Before entering I glance across the street. Danny and Joanna haven't arrived yet and Dad's house looks empty. Hoping I haven't come all the way out here for nothing, I check my phone to make sure I haven't missed a message from them. I haven't.

Bert is in Edith's room, the room where she sat out her last few months in her own home by the fire. Her chair sits in the same spot, empty. As empty as empty can be. I know that empty; it's the same kind of empty that kicks me in the head when I'm at Dad's house. When I look at where Mom used to sit, where Mom used to stand, or where Mom used to sing while she baked. *Two drifters.* That same implosive empty, like the whole world lived in that one spot and now that whole world has disappeared.

'Is there anything I can do for you, Bert?' I say, knowing there is absolutely nothing I can do for Bert. It is his turn to be tormented by loss; there is no sharing the agony.

'No, Becca,' he says, lifting clothes out of a bag. 'I have everything I need.'

I stand there looking at him, wondering what to say. How can I take that broken soul look from his face? But I don't get the chance. As he zips closed the bag, Bert says, 'I see that young girl who was looking for you is dead.'

So much for the sadness. It hasn't diluted his curiosity.

'I know. Dreadful, isn't it?'

'What did the police have to say about it?'

How does Bert know the cops were talking to me? I didn't tell him. And how is he so sure it's the same girl who was looking for me?

'What?'

'The police, I saw them at the Wall's a couple of days ago.'

'The cops?'

'Yes, when I arrived back from the hospital they were walking out of the yard.'

'Was Dad there?'

'I don't know. They were leaving at the time, so I don't know if they got an answer. Did your father not mention it?'

What will I say? My heart is beating like a late night party and Bert is looking at me for an answer.

'No, I haven't spoken to him yet, maybe he wasn't there when they called.'

'Oh. Well, his van was outside.'

I'm ready to explode. Surely Dad would ring me and tell me if the cops called asking about me? He would, I know he would. He must have been down in the shed at the end of the yard and never heard their knock.

'He was probably out back,' I say, wanting Bert to stop talking about it.

'I guess so,' Bert replies, placing the bag on the floor. I hope he didn't talk to the cops, that he didn't tell them Katie Collins was at my dad's house.

'Did you talk to them?'

'Who?'

'The cops?'

'God no, Becca, none of my business,' he says.

'I think I better go, Bert. Dad is waiting for me. I'll call into the hospital tomorrow or the next day and check up on you. And you have my number if anything happens.'

'Thanks Becca, it was nice to see a friendly face,' he says, walking me to the door.

'I'm sure the nurses are friendly, Bert.'

'Oh they are, they are. Just not the kind of friendly you want.'

Stepping out onto the porch, my thoughts are twisted. Did the cops say something to Dad? Maybe they didn't get to speak to him; it's possible he doesn't even know they called. His van would have been there if he'd gone to the bar. I want to ask Bert what time he saw the cops, but I don't want to bring up the subject up again. But Bert will not let up.

'Did you ever find out why the young lady was looking for you?' he says.

'I never did,' I say, turning to walk away.

'Oh,' he says. 'I thought you might have got some idea from the note she left you.'

–

I'm glad my back is to Bert because my face has probably turned grey. That's it: the note. Katie Collins did not deliver the note to my apartment, she delivered it to my Dad's house. Wherever she got her information from, it was not updated with my move to the city.

Chapter Twenty-Six

Dad's van stands in the usual place at the side of the yard but when I get inside, the house is empty. I call out his name but there's no reply, so I go upstairs to see if he is still in bed. If he's not, this is my opportunity to search for the note.

The door to the bedroom is closed. With my hand on the handle I slowly open it and peep inside.

'Dad, are you here?'

The room is empty, a cool breeze drifting through the open window. A tall freestanding wardrobe sits in the center of the wall. At the front of the wardrobe a dark suit hangs against the door with a tie hung over the right shoulder. A black tie. A pair of newly polished black shoes sit on the floor below. My heart shudders, sending a shiver through my body. I cross over and take a sleeve of the suit in my hand. I see him. Walking behind the coffin up the aisle of the church, standing by the grave tossing a rose into the ground. One last rose, one last goodbye.

Is Mom going to die soon? I'm scared, worried. Why is Dad getting ready? In the early days, before Mom took sick, Dad was always ready and waiting for whatever was going on. No last minute rushes there, not like me. Mom said it was the army that had him like that. She would laugh at his efficiency, at how he spent so much time standing, waiting for the rest of us. But that all changed. Now there are days when he doesn't even shave.

If the note is anywhere it's probably in the kitchen, amongst the piles of papers that seem to sprout from every counter. I hope Joanna hasn't done one of her mighty clean-ups this week. If she has, the note is probably playing its part in a recycling center by now. My big secret, beginning a new career as toilet paper. Pushing myself through the gap between the bed and the wall, I stretch to close the window. My foot bumps something under the bed. I reach down to see what it is and pull a pile of newspapers from under the bed.

My heart skips a chorus when I see Katie Collins staring back, her blue eyes focused, her blonde hair with its center parting. It's one of those high school yearbook photos, I think, but what a coincidence that the newspaper is folded open on the page covering her story. Even from the other side the woman seems determined to find me.

Only it's not a coincidence. Taking the pile of papers from the floor I toss them on to the bed. Each newspaper is folded open on the page covering the Katie Collins story. What is Dad doing? Fear threatens to pull me to the ground. Does he know? Does Dad know I'm a suspect?

I've been doing my best to keep this drama away from his door, but somehow it arrived, knocked, and got an answer. Oh poor Dad, he certainly does not need any more worries. Maybe he's just intrigued by a local murder story. Most people are; it can inject a bit of excitement into an otherwise bored community. But I don't think Dad's like that.

I shove the newspapers back under the bed, praying Dad doesn't know Katie Collins came looking for me.

Then it occurs to me – the note. Did he find the note and recognize her name at the end of it? Did that send him into a panic, send him rushing out to buy newspapers? Or did Turner actually get to talk to him? Oh God, I don't know what to think. Surely if she did speak to him he would have told me, or at least Danny. Yes, he would definitely have told Danny, and Danny would have called me by now.

The kitchen is a mess, mugs and plates piled up in the sink. A half eaten block of cheese stands on the counter uncovered. There are bite marks in it, where Dad didn't even bother slicing it up before he ate. The floor and table around his chair are covered in crumbs and bits of wrappers and there's a loaf of bread going hard on the countertop. Things have definitely changed around here.

At least that means there's a chance the note is still here somewhere. I check the drawers in the dresser and the units. No sign. Though I'm not really sure what it is I'm looking for. A piece of paper? Was it written on a card? I should have asked Bert what he saw but I'm not going back there now.

After exhausting the kitchen, I'm about to turn my attention to the hallway when I see a piece of paper sticking out from under a half dead plant sitting on a little shelf by the kitchen door. Pulling a chair from under the table, I step up and slip the piece of paper from under the pot. My mouth is dry, stomach turning. I turn it over and read *Remember to take your memory tablets*.

Mom's handwriting. This note hung on the refrigerator door when she was first diagnosed and able to medicate herself. Taking a deep breath, I start my still heart beating again. As I get down from the chair I hear a key in the front door, so I push the chair back into place by the table and sit on it.

Dad startles when he sees me.

'Jesus, Becca, you frightened the life out of me.'

'Didn't you see my car outside?'

'No, I didn't. I wasn't expecting you.'

'But it's Sunday, Dad. Where's Danny and Joanna?'

'They're not coming today. Didn't Danny text you? He was supposed to text you.'

Dad crosses to the refrigerator and stocks it with the beers he takes from the brown bag in his hand.

'Dad?'

'Yeah?' he says, twisting the cap off a bottle of beer and lifting it to his lips.

'I'm looking for a note that was left here for me. Have you seen it?'

'A note?'

'A friend of mine left it here with her number for me to call her.'

'I didn't see any note,' he says. 'When was that?'

'Last week.'

'How do you know someone left you a note if you didn't get a note?' he says, turning to face me.

'Bert saw her leave it in the mailbox.'

'Bert.' He swigs some more beer. 'That old man is half blind. How would he know what he saw?'

'She spoke to him.'

With the bottle to his lips he stops drinking and gazes at the wall for what seems like an age.

'I didn't see any note, Becca,' he says eventually. 'Hey, do you want to go to Benny's for lunch?'

'Did the cops call here?'

'What?' Dad splutters, almost choking on his drink. 'Cops? Here? What are you talking about?'

'Bert said they called here the other day, what did they call for?'

'No cops called here Becca, not to my knowledge. Sounds like that Bert fella is losing it, Becca. Seeing things. There were no cops here.'

'Are you sure?'

Dad puts his beer down and turns his head to look directly at me. 'What is going on, Becca?' His pale face scrunches up, looking worried.

'Nothing, it's just Bert said…'

'Stay away from that mad man, Becca. I don't trust him, never did.'

'So you didn't speak to the cops… and you didn't see a note?'

'No Becca, I didn't, now do you want to come to Benny's or not?'

But before I have time to refuse his offer my cell rings. It's Bert. Edith is dead.

Chapter Twenty-Seven

Pulling the duvet over my head, I close my eyes, hoping to get a couple more hours sleep. I was with Bert until late last night, pouring him whiskey and listening to his pain until eventually he nodded off on the sofa.

I hear knocking. At first I think I imagined it but then it comes again. Someone banging on my door. I check the time: 8.45am. It's a bit early for Jeff but who else could it be? Turner, maybe? I hope not. Hoping whoever it is will leave, I tuck the duvet tightly around my neck. If it is Turner she will probably leave, presuming I've already left for work.

When the banging stops I creep out of bed and tiptoe out to the living room. But when I'm crossing to the kitchen to put the kettle on, the knocking starts again. This time I decide to answer it; no point in prolonging the pain. If Turner wants to speak to me she will get to me somehow.

Checking the peephole, I can only see the warped picture of an empty corridor. Whoever it was is gone. Pulling my bathrobe tight, I unlock the door to glance outside and make sure. The moment I pull on the handle the door swings into my face, knocking me to the ground.

'You bitch,' he snarls, his face distorted by anger. Red eyes, burning skin, teeth displayed like a pouncing wolf, he storms into the room. 'I told you what would happen,' he says. 'I warned you.'

Stephen Black is scaring the life out of me. I try to stand up but he walks over, plants a Prada shoe on my hip and pushes me down again.

'Did you think you'd get away with it?'

He turns away, giving me the chance to lurch upright. That's when I realize my bathrobe is wide open and I'm naked underneath. Tugging it tightly around me, I search for the belt that's swinging somewhere at the back. I can't find it, so I hold the robe closed and slip in behind the couch to protect myself.

'You're going to have to take it back,' he growls, his eyes popping in their sockets. I have never seen anyone so angry. He looks possessed, like he could sprout horns and a tail at any moment.

My body is shaking, teeth chattering. Blood rushes to my head. I don't want to anger him any more but I don't want to be a victim of his bullying either.

'I can't take it back,' I say, in a voice I can barely hear myself.

'What? What are you saying?' he snarls through expensive porcelain teeth as he walks behind the sofa. Clenching his fists, he pushes his face up close to mine. 'What did you say?'

'I can't take it back,' I say, louder this time.

'You *will* take it back, because I'm going to deny it, say you made it up, that you have a crush on me.' His eyes are wild, almost on fire, spit flecking his lips. 'And who do you think the cop will believe, me or you?' He looks away, down to the shaking hands holding my bathrobe closed. 'Me, the successful lawyer with an impeccable reputation?' Reaching for my hands, he grabs them and pulls the gown open. His eyes travel up and down my naked body. 'Or you, Rebecca Wall, the little slut?'

I open my mouth to cry for help but the words are stuck somewhere; all that comes out is a squeaky whining noise. I try again but I still can't talk. I'm dying here, I feel like my soul is being crushed. I want to puke, to run, but I can't move. Sucking air into my lungs, I know I must keep breathing. *No, please, no.* I feel the heat of his hands travel down my arms, taking my robe with them. *No. No, please don't.* I can hear myself pleading on the inside but for some reason the words won't come out of my mouth. *Please don't rape me.*

I fall back against the wall, as if I'm going to collapse, but it doesn't stop him. My robe is now crumpled at my feet. Closing my eyes, the noise of his belt opening screeches in my ears. Something inside me dies.

'Get the fuck off her!'

I'm frozen, unable to open my eyes, unable to move from the wall. But I know it's Jeff.

Now he is threatening Black, but for some reason Stephen isn't fighting back. As I allow my eyes to open, a blurred picture unfolds. Jeff, gripping the collar of Stephen's jacket and pushing him out of the room. Jeff, with something in his hand.

I think it's a gun.

When the door slams, I slide down the wall, pulling my robe over me. My body has never shaken like this before. I can see it – my hands, legs, feet – but I can't feel it. Every part of me is numb. I don't cry, there's no point, tears can't express how I feel now. I'm not sad. I'm broken.

Jeff slides down the wall and rests his body beside me. He places his hand on mine but doesn't speak, just sits by my side, squeezing my hand every now and then, letting me know he is there. Gradually the fear holding my body hostage starts to evaporate. Heat is the first sensation I get back. It travels into my hand from Jeff's grip.

Chapter Twenty-Eight

The smell of garlic is making me sick. Clouds of steam surround Jeff as he stirs something on the hob, making him look like he has appeared as the result of a magic trick.

I have to eat. It's Jeff's answer to everything.

I'm trying not to think about what would have happened if Jeff hadn't been going past my apartment. If he hadn't rushed back to his own apartment and grabbed the guitar tuner, which held in a certain way resembles a gun.

'Spaghetti or linguini?' he says, opening one of the cupboards.

'Is there a difference?'

'Of course there's a difference,'

'Well…' I'm not about to ask what the difference is because Jeff can go on for hours about food and wine and tastes and textures. 'Whatever you think,'

He looks up to the heavens. Maybe he's right, maybe I'm not his type.

–

Letting the room darken around us, we sit and eat the spaghetti – or linguini, I'm not sure. It's been two days since Stephen Black assaulted me and I haven't been outside the door. No one has called, no one has missed me. Everyone is caught up in their own shit. I thought Turner might call, that she might have found out something, but no, nothing.

'Do you think everyone has forgotten I exist, Jeff?'

'What?' Jeff laughs. 'Why do you say that?'

'Well, no one has bothered ringing me to ask me how I am.'

'Did you tell anyone what happened?'

'No, but…'

'Becca,' he says, turning to face me. He has that expression, the one he seldom calls on. The one he wears when he's about to say something serious. 'Becca,' he says again, placing his hand on my leg. 'It's time.'

'Time for what?'

'Time to get your act together. You've been wallowing in self-pity for two days now and, well, it doesn't suit you.'

It doesn't *suit* me? Has he any idea what I've been through?

'Get up, get dressed and get focused,' he says. He gets up from the sofa, walks to the fridge and pulls out a big bag of greens. Bill and Hillary, Jeff's sister's rabbits, bounce to the front of the cage when they see him coming. 'Do you still want to find out why Katie Collins was looking for you?'

'What? Yes, of course.'

'Right. Well, let's do that then. Let's see what Thomas Collins has to say.'

–

Back in my apartment, Jeff waits while I shower, change my clothes and put on some makeup. I feel better now, not so much a victim. But I'm still nervous.

It won't take me long to empty out this place when I leave, which I will have to do as soon as the landlord realizes I haven't paid my rent last month, and won't be paying it this month either. Everything is spiraling out of control. I need to find out why Katie Collins was looking for me. Maybe if I get some answers then I can start to rebuild my life.

Jeff is suggesting I leave my apartment now, and take his sister's room until she gets back, whenever that is. He doesn't know. I'm not going to make any decisions at the moment because everything is so fucked up. 'Let's wait and see what happens,' I tell him.

'You're very quiet,' Jeff says when we get back to his apartment.

'I'm worried, Jeff. Like, *everything* is wrong. What Mom said, Katie Collins, Stephen Black...' My phone buzzes, it's Bert.

–

Edith's funeral is to take place at St. Brendan's Church, tomorrow at ten a.m. Bert sounds shy as he asks if I'll be there.

'Of course I'll be there, Bert. Do you need me to do anything for you?'

Turns out Edith's sister Agnes arrived and took over. A whirlwind of organization. Bert said he didn't care too much so long as it's what Edith would have wanted. Flowers, lots of flowers, and a few psalms, her favorites, the ones she loved to sing along to.

He sounds defeated. I hope he's okay.

When I finally hang up, I see Jeff is flicking through websites on his laptop.

'What about Friday?' he says. 'We could go for the weekend.'

'Go where?'

'New Orleans.'

'New Orleans?'

'Algiers?' he says.

'Algiers?'

'Where Katie Collins' husband lives. Remember?'

How could I have forgotten? Of course I have to go to New Orleans, it's my best chance, my only hope to get an answer. Turner is not letting up. She won't tell me anything, just question after question. Well, now it's my turn to ask the questions. Let's hope Thomas Collins has the answers.

I'm wondering why Jeff is so interested in all of this. Maybe he just wants a trip to New Orleans, but with me? *Really, Jeff, the woman who's 'not your type'?*

'You don't have to come to New Orleans, Jeff. I can go on my own.'

'I want to go, I've been meaning to go for a while now, catch up with Winters.'

'Who's Winters?'

'A buddy of mine… Friday suit?'

'Fuck, I have that stupid baby shower thing for Joanna.'

'Well, when *would* suit you?'

I think about this for a while then suddenly remember I haven't got any money. I don't even have a spare dollar to buy Danny and Joanna a gift for the baby shower, never mind a trip to New Orleans.

'Sorry, Jeff, I don't have any money.'

I empty my bag out on the couch – lipsticks, ticket stubs, keys, a few coins, a few dollars. 'That's it, that all I got,' I say, glancing quickly at Jeff before turning back to grab the stuff from the sofa and stuffing it back into my bag.

'Who said anything about money? I don't have much cash lying around either, but what I do have is this.'

'What's that?'

Jeff is waving a plastic card at me.

'Air miles,' he says. 'My sister said I could use them as I please. In fact, she said they'd go out of date if I didn't use them.'

First thing next week I'm going to New Orleans after funerals, baby showers and whatever else God decides to throw my way. If I'm going down, I want to know why. Jeff also got us a place to stay, with some friend of his who left college the same time he did, after the first semester. Hank Winters. He went to New Orleans, sang a few songs, and wound up buying a couple of dingy hotels in the French Quarter. Jeff was going to go in with Hank but discovered that babysitting his sister's rabbits and playing the odd gig in the venues he liked to play suited him better. 'One or two nights should do it,' Jeff says, before ending his call to Hank. 'If we're going to be lucky, we're going to be lucky.'

Chapter Twenty-Nine

The tall building looms in front of me, its spiral going all the way up to what looks like Rapunzel's tower. Rapunzel, Rapunzel, forgive me my sins. I don't like churches, not since the day the priest roared from the altar. He was bragging about some sort of miracle or prophecy when someone a few benches behind start laughing. The joy became contagious, infecting everyone around, until half the sinners were choking into their sleeves in an attempt to feign despair. The priest didn't like it. He lifted his eyes and his voice, frightening all the younger members of his flock, including me.

I remember that day as if it was yesterday, Mom tightening her grip on my hand, trying her best not to laugh. It was a poor attempt on her behalf because tears rolled down her face into the lovely new pink lace gloves she'd been given for her birthday a couple of weeks earlier. Nervously I stood there, lips tightened, waiting for everyone who was laughing to disappear into thin air, banished by the Lord onto the devil's radar. You fear like that when you're only five years old.

'Stop laughing Mom,' I whispered. I didn't think she heard me because she kept giggling, her shoulders shaking as she hid her face in her gloves. Standing up on the wooden pew, I leaned in close to her ear.

'Stop laughing, Mom, or he'll send you to hell.'

There's no reason to laugh today. Edith is going home. Her coffin is moving up the aisle to the pleas of 'Nearer, my God, to Thee.' Bert walks behind, head bent, tears leaking from his frozen stare. Edith's sister walks alongside, accompanied by an old man in an old suit and two younger guys. They must be Edith's nephews.

A few neighbors are gathered in the pews, standing while the procession proceeds. In the distance, the priest stands waiting at the altar.

I glance around to see if Dad has shown up. I thought he might – the woman lived across the road from him since the beginning of time. Maybe he can't face it, the preview, not able to stand here knowing his turn to walk up that aisle will arrive only too soon. Danny just flat out dismissed any possibility he might attend.

'I'm too busy with work,' he said.

Which left Joanna to appease me.

'If I'm feeling okay I will pop down.'

I wanted them all to come, for as many people as possible to be here for Bert. But it looks like I'm the only Wall in the hall.

No I'm not, here she comes, well done, Joanna. Do not let that giant baby bump stop you praying for the happy repose of Edith's soul. Joanna sees me and nods, letting the cortège pass by before slipping into the bench beside me. Her hair is tied back from her face, her makeup only lightly applied. Joanna's smile is her best feature. She can beam as if a light comes on inside her head. And she's always in control. If you need anything done, Joanna is the woman to call, even now, even pregnant.

Resting her hand on the back of the bench she lowers herself into the seat then leans in close to whisper, 'the cops were at the house this morning.'

'What? Why?'

'They wanted to speak to Danny.'

'Danny? Why Danny?' The toast in my stomach changes direction. What brought the cops to Danny's house?

'I'll fill you in later.'

Joanna lifts her head to pay attention to the ceremony. I can't concentrate, not now. I tried to keep the saga away from the family but Turner is not letting up. Why is she dragging them into it? It's nothing to do with them.

'What did they say?' I ask, unable to wait for the ceremony to end before I ask.

'Shush,' Joanna hisses, making it clear that she is not going to have this conversation now. I'm going to have to sit here, listening to the priest tell us that this is how it was meant to be, that Edith has returned to God.

The ceremony feels like it has gone on for hours and yet when I look at my watch I have only been here twenty minutes. Hurry up, Father. Eventually the coffin is carried out of the church and into the fresh air. Bert looks even older and more wizened than before.

'Everything was lovely, Bert. Edith would be happy.'

'I hope so, Becca. I still can't believe she's gone.'

I give him a hug and drift away to the side of the churchyard, where Joanna is waiting.

'Tell me,' I say, edgy with nerves.

'They called to the house just as Danny was about to leave. I was upstairs and looked over the bannisters. I saw Danny lead them into the kitchen. I don't know what was said, but when they left Danny was in a weird mood, and the cops were carrying a bag they didn't have when they came in. They must have taken something of his away with them. I asked him what they wanted and he said they were just doing some house calls in the area, asking if anyone saw anything suspicious the night that girl Katie Collins was murdered. He ignored me when I asked what was in the bag.'

I say nothing, but I know Joanna doesn't believe him.

'I don't know, though,' she says. 'I looked out the window when they were leaving and I didn't see them call at any other house. And they didn't ask to see me, either. Doesn't seem right if they were calling house to house.'

Danny is going to go crazy at me, blame me for dragging these people into his life. But I need to talk to him, find out why they were looking for him, what they wanted to know.

'I asked him what it was all about,' Joanna says, 'but he told me not to worry, it was nothing. And then he left.'

'Where did he go?'

'Work, I guess.'

Bert struggles to get into the hearse. I'm really not in the mood for going to the graveyard but I will have to, because Bert will notice if I'm not there. When the crowd disperses, Joanna heads home, asking me to let her know if I get any info out of Danny.

I say I will, but I know I won't.

The sky is dull with grey clouds as the cortège moves out of the churchyard and on to the cemetery. I should be sad, thinking of Edith, but my mind is consumed with worrying about what the cops were doing at Danny's. Were they asking him about me? Does he know I might be a suspect in the case? Or were they questioning Danny about his whereabouts on that Saturday night? I wonder what they took away in the bag.

In the car, the old lady I offered a lift to is wiping tears from her eyes. I put my hand on her shoulder and tell her Edith is in a better place, that she's gone past her pain now. But these words mean nothing. I know that. Loss is loss, grief is grief. Knowing someone is in a better place does not stop you wanting them back.

Bert walks over when the ceremony ends, dark rings circling his eyes.

'Thanks for coming, Becca. I know you're busy, so it's nice you took the time. Edith is grateful.'

'I couldn't have missed it, Bert. How are you?'

'Okay, I guess. I'll be better when this gang go home and leave me alone.' Bert nods in the direction of Edith's family, making me laugh. 'I have to suffer them a while longer, they're all coming back to the house.'

'It'll be all over soon, Bert. I'm sure they won't stay long.'

'I hope not,' he says, turning to accept an old man's condolences.

–

The world carries on as it did before; the sky blue, the trees green, the traffic a nightmare. Turning out of the graveyard I find myself stuck in a jam, cars beeping like they have the code to break the gridlock. Thinking about Danny and the cops' visit is torturing me, making me fear all sorts of stuff. With one eye on the car in front, I take out my phone and dial his number. No answer. I dial again; again, no answer.

Where are you, Danny? Why won't you talk to me?

Chapter Thirty

All the way home I tried to call Danny, but with no success. He'll probably pretend he was in an important meeting and couldn't be disturbed while he fixed some issue the world was having. But I know that's not the case. We have a pact: phone calls must be answered no matter what, in case it's about Mom. With no other option, I decide I'll call to the house, later, when he's home.

I spend the afternoon clearing out my apartment and moving my stuff into Jeff's. It's only temporary until I can get another job, then I'll find another place, somewhere Stephen Black can't find me. Thinking back on that morning, I cringe. I want to throw up. Jeff thinks I should tell Turner what happened, but I don't want any more hassle at the moment. Turner thinks I'm crazy as it is. Which reminds me, I haven't heard from her in a while. She's obviously been too busy calling on my dad, and now Danny.

Closing Jeff's door behind me, I walk down the corridor and pass my old apartment. Should I be sad? I'm not. If anything, I'm relieved I don't have to go back in there, back to all those broken promises.

The screechy elevator takes me down to the lobby, where Lenny is snoozing behind the desk. He scrambles to his feet when I call his name.

'Everything okay?' he says.

'Yes, everything is fine.'

'Did you find out who was in your apartment?'

'No, but I won't be staying there anymore.'

The keys crash onto the counter when I let them drop. Lenny looks at me, mouth open like he's expecting food.

'But…' He picks up the keys. 'I'm not sure that's how it works, Becca. I think you have to contact the leasing company.'

'The leasing company didn't care when I was broken into, Lenny,' I lie, implying I notified them. 'So they can do what they have to, but I'm out of there.'

Switching the keys from one hand to the other, Lenny looks at me, then back to the keys. I walk away, hoping he'll buy it, that he'll tell them I'm leaving because of the break-in. That way they might not hound me for the rent.

'Where will you go?' he says.

'Not far.'

Lenny probably thinks I'm cool but my heart is thumping as I walk away. Out on the street I see Jeff, cradling brown bags in each arm. I'm nervous, wondering if I did the right thing. Will Jeff regret his act of kindness, want me out after a week? *I* might want out after a week. It makes no odds really, because no matter how much I question my decision I keep coming up with the same answer. No money, no choice.

Before Jeff sees me, I turn the opposite way. The next person I need to talk to is Danny. The wait is crucifying me. Red lines imprint my hand where I've gripped the phone all day waiting for the buzz that never came. I'm surprised, really. I thought he'd gloat over my latest disaster, take pleasure out of chastising me, counseling me. Shrinking my soul. I know he cares for me, a lot, he always has, but he can also make me feel like a piece of shit when he's doing it.

Danny's house is halfway down Ash Street, close to the local college with a Boston Donuts shop on the corner. Which is a waste; Danny never puts sugar in his mouth. If you look out the bedroom window at the back of his house, there's a clear view of Treehill Park. Although not the spot where Katie Collins body was found, that was hidden in the forest, by the redundant bridge.

Knocking on Danny's door I realize that that might be the reason why the cops called here. Maybe they called at all the houses that have a clear view of the park. But when Danny answers the door and I see the stress in his face, I reconsider.

'Becca,' he says, turning away without a smile or an invitation to come in. In fact, I think he sighs.

'How are things?' I say, following him into the back room where Joanna is sitting with her feet up on the sofa watching TV.

'Becca,' she says, smiling. 'Did you go back to Bert's house after the funeral?'

'Yes, just for a short while,' I say, watching as Danny attempts to leave the room. 'Danny, I want to talk to you,' I say, but he puts his phone to his ear, pretending he's taking a call. Joanna pulls a face, warning me he's not in a good mood, but I don't care. I didn't come all this way for nothing. So I follow him into the little office he built for himself off the hallway.

'Danny,' I say.

He turns around, too casually.

'Danny, why were the cops looking for you?'

'What cops?'

'The cops who called this morning. Joanna told me.'

'Oh, those guys.' He picks up a sheet of paper off the desk, making out it's entertaining him more than I am. 'They were just doing house calls, wanting to know if anyone saw anything the night that young woman was killed.' He puts the page down. 'Anything else?' he says. 'How are you doing? All set for the baby shower, I hope.'

I'm not buying that. He's brushing me off, trying to change the subject.

'And did you see anything?'

'Did I see anything where?'

'In Treehill, in the park, the night the—'

'Becca, stop. I saw nothing and told them so.'

Danny should be asking me why I'm so interested, why I came all the way out here to find out what the cops wanted.

'Did they ask about me? And what did they take in the bag?'

'What bag?'

'Joanna said they took something away with them, was it something belonging to you?'

'Why would they ask about you, Becca?'

The sound from the TV in the other room can no longer be heard. Joanna must have her ear to the wall. I'm anxious now. Danny is staring at me.

'Why would they ask about you?' he repeats, hands clenched, leaning on the desk, ignoring the question about what was in the bag.

Should I say I'm a suspect? I don't know.

'No reason,' I say. 'I was just wondering.' Looking down at my feet, I can feel his eyes drilling holes in my head.

'Becca.'

'Yes?' Lifting my head to look at him I sense fear – not mine, his. It's like he doesn't know whether to say what he's about to say.

'Becca,' he says, moving out from behind the desk. He puts a hand on my shoulder. 'Stay away from it, Becca.'

'Stay away from what?' I say, unable to decode his warning.

'Katie Collins. Stay away from anything to do with her.'

Danny is pleading with me, telling me to leave it alone, to walk away. But why?

'Why?'

Without answering, he walks out of the office. After a few minutes I realize he's not coming back, so I follow.

Joanna comes into the hall and tries to defuse the atmosphere, expressing mixed feelings about the upcoming baby shower, telling me what she's worried about, hoping she's still here for it. Apparently the doctors told her she could go early. I see her lips move, her words fall on me, bursting into nothing when they land. What is Danny hiding?

Chapter Thirty-One

I wasn't expecting to find myself knocking on Bert's door. But the thought of driving all the way back into the city with my head filled with fear, holding my concentration at gunpoint, is not a good idea. I'll take a break, call in on Bert and have a coffee, see if that calms me down a bit.

Bert is delighted to see me. His one-sided smile creeps across his pale face as he holds the door open for me to come inside.

'Has everybody gone?' I say, looking around the empty room that was filled with mourners a few hours earlier.

'They have.'

'Well, that wasn't too bad.'

'They had to go. I told them to get out.'

'And who cleaned up?' I say, noting the tidiness of the place.

'I don't know, I waited upstairs 'til they were gone.'

I laugh, then Bert laughs. He gets some leftover food from the fridge and places it on the table. I'm starving. I haven't eaten since Jeff's egg wraps this morning.

'This is delicious,' I say, spooning meat pie into my mouth.

'It is, isn't it? I think Agnes made it, the witch.'

He laughs again. I keep eating. At the back of my mind I feel the tension swelling up, waiting to burst. Should I tell Bert what's going on? I better not. He cuts a slice of apple pie for me, hands me the plate, suggesting I put some cream on it. Everything takes longer now, slower steps, slower hand movements, slower smiles.

When we've both had our fill from the witches' cauldron, I help Bert put the stuff away and tell him I have to go. I'm feeling a bit stronger now, ready to take on the journey without crashing into someone on the way. Bert asks me when I'll be back and I tell him as soon as I'm able.

'It won't be Saturday, though. I have to go to a baby shower.'

'A baby shower?'

'Joanna's baby shower.'

'Oh, right. Hang on a minute.'

Bert walks into a little side room off the kitchen, more like a closet than a room. He reaches up to a shelf that hangs over a work bench and takes down a gift bag. I think Bert has got me gift, but it's not for me.

'For Danny,' he says. 'For the baby.'

–

Grief must be having a strange effect on Bert. Never before has he expressed any kindness towards Danny. In fact, for as long as I can remember both men have harbored an indiscreet dislike for each other, Danny taking every opportunity to give out about Bert and Bert throwing his eyes up to heaven whenever I mention my brother. So this is quite a turn up for the books.

I take the gift and thank him. Tell him how grateful Danny and Joanna are going to be.

Walking to the car I look over at Dad's house. There's no sign of life, just the shadowed loneliness of a broken house, a broken home. Dad must be in the pub with his mates.

Struggling to open the dodgy lock on the trunk of my car, I twist and turn the key until eventually it gives way. I place Bert's gift inside, even though I'm tempted to look in the bag. But I can't, Bert still has his eye on me through the window; I'll have to wait until I get home. Driving away, I think about what Danny's warning about Katie Collins. I wonder if he knows I'm a suspect, that Katie Collins visited Mom in the home. Maybe he's just playing the big brother, looking out for me. But I don't think so, not this time.

This time is different. Danny is hiding something.

Chapter Thirty-Two

Danny won't be at home today, it's ladies only and boy, do I mean ladies. A gaggle of them are sitting in the kitchen when I arrive, all primped to perfection in pinks, yellow and blues. I'm in black. My hair is tied back into a plait because it's still wet. Unlike all the other contestants, who must have been sitting in an adjustable chair first thing this morning, I didn't have time to dry it.

There's nothing new in the feeling that I don't belong here. I get it every time I'm forced to attend one of Joanna's get-togethers. All her shiny friends, with their shiny degrees and even shinier husbands. I never did get it. Joanna seems so much nicer than this lot.

'Edel from college', which is how she is routinely introduced by Joanna, is doing an awesome job of everything. There are glasses of bubbly lining the counter with strawberries drowning in each glass, reminding everyone how far they've come. The table is covered in trays of tiny little sandwiches and other nibbles. A tower of cupcakes – more pinks, yellows and blues – stands center-stage. Why, I don't know; none of these bony creatures eat cupcakes. Joanna sits like a ball of wool amongst a stack of needles. But not for long. If I know Joanna, she'll be back in the gym before the baby has its first nappy change.

I don't plan on staying long. I'll wait for the gifts to be opened, then I'm out of here. I've too much to do, too much to think about, and I want to finish unpacking the stuff I brought over to Jeff's.

'I can't wait for this baby to be born,' Joanna says, struggling to stand when I hand her my gift. It's not actually my gift, I didn't find the opportunity or the money to get one yet, so I'm giving her Bert's for today. I'll explain all when I get the real one. The small gift bag looks a bit miserable beside the mountain of impressively wrapped gifts in the corner of the room.

Joanna kisses me on the cheek. 'Thanks, Becca.'

Shit. Now I feel guilty. Maybe I should tell her it's from Bert; that I forgot to get one. But I'm afraid of being judged by her friends: 'Imagine that, her sister-in-law never got her a gift.' I can almost hear their acquired accents.

Standing on my own with a half eaten cupcake in my hand, I think about what Danny said about staying away from anything to do with Katie Collins. I'll have to tell him it's a bit late for that. Inform him that his sister is a frigging suspect. I wonder how he'll react. I hope he'll help me.

The judgment of a young solicitor is being delivered close by. The woman has managed to drop her current profession into the conversation at least twice so far, while discussing how poor Lisa Evans' husband has left her for Mila. Her audience stand aghast, except for one brave girl who says she's not surprised. No more bubbly for her.

Another topic of interest seems to be the sudden growth of Janet Jones; apparently she has put on at least two stone since the solicitor last saw her, 'the poor thing.'

I'm glad she's not aware of my production. Wanted for murder. That would keep them all here long enough to dip into the tiny sandwiches.

I'm considering making an early exit, faking an urgent phone call or something, when Edel calls for order, clinking a spoon on one of the bubbly glasses. The unwrapping of the gifts is about to commence.

The smell of expensive perfumes crash into one another in the rush to get a seat near Joanna. The resulting concoction would upset even the nose blind. I stand as far away as possible without giving the impression of being disinterested. I didn't realize these things were so serious, that there's a protocol to follow.

Please don't open my gift first, I pray, leaning close to the gap in the open patio door. She doesn't; Joanna goes straight for the one on top. She rests it on her bump, unwrapping it as if the paper is on loan and has to be returned in perfect condition. When I get a gift, I like to tear at the wrapping paper – it's half the fun. And Mom knew I loved it, she wrapped all my Christmas gifts separately, no matter how many there were. After ten minutes the room would look like a storm had blown in from Walmart. I loved it.

Three gifts have been unwrapped already to a chorus of oohs and aahs. With my nerves on edge I watch Joanna lifting my gift – Bert's gift.

'And this is from…?' Edel's eyes search the room like she's waiting for a final bid at Sotheby's.

That's my cue to put my hand in the air, so I do, and everyone turns to look, then nod at me and acknowledge my presence. It's the most attention I've had since I was down the precinct and I find myself equally as uneasy.

Joanna pulls on the ribbon of the small rainbow colored bag and takes out something wrapped in tissue paper. When she removes the tissue paper she's holding a Ziploc bag with something pink inside. Fuck, I should have told

Bert it was a boy. Joanna opens the Ziploc and takes out a small pink coat that looks like it was bought at a jumble sale. It's old and dirty, with a button missing. She tries to hide her embarrassment as she quickly picks up the next gift. But it doesn't work, doesn't take their judging eyes off me. I'm going to die here. What the fuck, Bert?

Chapter Thirty-Three

Naturally there were no oohs and aahs for my gift, just a load of gasps and stares.

I can't stay, fearing they might surround me, tie me to a tree and burn me. This is really bad. Joanna thinks I gave her a dirty old knitted baby coat. Oh God… Danny.

I'll have to get to Joanna before she tells him, explain to her that the present was from the old man across the road, probably some family heirloom. But I'm not attempting to fight my way through this angry mob. I'll ring her later. Right now I need to get out of here.

Without saying anything to Joanna I slip out the patio door. What the hell was Bert thinking in giving them that gift? Is it some old heirloom he's resurrected and wants to pass on now that everyone is dying? He better have some frigging excuse when I ask him because I've never been so embarrassed in my life. Poor Joanna, I feel so bad for her. Her only sister-in-law, letting her down in front of all her flawless friends. Will she ever forgive me?

Driving away, I decide to call in to Bert and ask about the coat. I will make out there were more questions of interest than disgusted faces. Regardless of its history, Bert should at least have washed the coat before he passed it on. But I won't say that, not to an old man who has just buried his wife.

There's no answer at Bert's house. I hope he's okay. Walking back to the car I resolve to invent some heirloom story on his behalf. It's not like they're going to check.

–

Jeff is out when I get back to the apartment. I vaguely remember him telling me about some gig he was playing tonight. I wish I knew where it was, I could go along, take my mind off my latest fuck-up. On the counter stands a plate of risotto covered in film, with a note, *Heat for 3 mins*. Jeff is determined to fatten me up.

The first few bites satisfy what little appetite I have, so I dump the rest in the trash and reach for the wine. It's going to be a long night without Jeff here. Just me, the wine, the fears, the plans. Ringing Joanna's phone brought no success, each time the same response. 'I can't answer right now, please leave a message.' I hope she's not ghosting me.

Hours pass, hours spent searching the web, hoping for some small piece of new information about Katie Collins. Anything. My eyes are stinging and there's still no sign of Jeff. I decide to go to bed. To try to sleep even for a few hours. Putting my phone on silent, just in case Danny rings to moan about the horrible present, I wish I could do the same with my mind. Put it on silent mode, stop hassling me mode, or just switch off.

The next thing I know the sun is creeping in between the crack in the curtains. I'm happy I slept all night, and without the help of any medication. The phone is flashing on the duvet. Shit, someone is calling me. It's Danny.

'Danny?'

'What the hell, Becca? I've been ringing you all night. Is that phone ever on?'

'Sorry, I had it on silent. What's up?'

'It's Joanna. She went into labor when I got back to the house after the baby shower.'

'Is everything okay?'

'Great, everything is great… *Auntie* Becca. You have a beautiful nephew, seven pounds, one ounce.'

'Oh, that's fantastic news. How is Joanna?'

'Tired. She's sleeping now, so I'm heading home to grab a couple of hours myself.'

'Can I visit later?'

'Yes, of course. Liam is dying to meet you.'

Phew. He doesn't know. Maybe I can keep it like that if I get to Joanna before she tells him. Before she shows him.

I wonder if Edith knitted that coat, hoping to put it on her own daughter some day. Maybe over the years she took it out, hugged it, hoped, until time extinguished the dream. Or it could be an heirloom she wished to pass on. Wherever it came from, I don't understand why Bert gave it to Danny. Surely he knew the condition it was in?

Chapter Thirty-Four

My father is coming down the stairs when I open the door.

'Congrats, Grandpa.'

The smile on his face brings back memories.

'Great news, isn't it?' he says, running a comb through his wet hair.

'The best, Dad, the best, and I like the name Liam.'

Dad's eyes are so bright, it's like someone switched his power back on. I haven't seen him this animated since before Mom went to Oakridge.

'I'm on my way to tell your mom,' he says. 'Do you want to come with me?' Then, before I have a chance to answer, he stops in his tracks. 'Are you in Mattie's tonight?'

Now is not the time to spill paint on Dad's picture by telling him I can't go back there. Instead I tell him I have worked up hours; that I called in earlier to claim them so I could go and see the baby.

'So are you coming then?' he says, whistling as he takes his jacket from the back of a chair.

I decide to go, even though I hate visiting Mom when Dad's there. Watching his face change to match the wretchedness of her situation is pure agony, no one in their right mind would willingly put themselves through it. His eyebrows descend, as if trying to stop his eyes from seeing her. His lips clench, his face turns grey. He transforms into some sort of misery machine. It eases after a while, after he has said his first hellos and holds her hand. But it's not pretty to watch. Today might be better, with the news of the new arrival. I'm praying it is, that he manages to inject his reaction with some joy.

He doesn't. My father is turning to stone in front of me; in fact, it's the worst I have ever seen him. We manage to get as far as Mom's room when he stops abruptly.

'I can't go in,' he says, turning his face away. I don't know what to do. What do I say? He's going to cry, *please don't fucking cry.*

'Don't cry, Dad,' I say taking his hand in mine. 'Please don't cry.' But before I know it, I'm crying too.

'I'm sorry, Becca.'

He's a blubbering mess, both of us are, standing here outside Mom's door.

'I thought… I thought I'd be able, Becca… but…'

'It's okay Dad, I'll go in. I'll tell her.'

'It's just I always imagined this day would be different. Our first grandchild… We often spoke about it.'

'It's okay, Dad.'

'Actually,' he says, finding a smile amongst the sniffles, 'we thought it would be you.'

'Me?'

'Yes. We were waiting for it ever since you turned sixteen, if I'm being truthful.'

'Well, thanks a lot,' I say, forcing a chuckle. I don't blame them. I was a bit wild in my early days. 'Dad, do you want to go down to the coffee shop first? Relax a bit before we go in?'

He smiles. 'You're a good girl, Becca. I don't know what I'd do without you.'

'Thanks, Dad. I love you.'

'Okay, let's do this,' he says, taking my hand. 'Let's go in and tell your Mom she's a grandmother.'

–

It didn't get any worse. My dad settled, and even got excited when Mom smiled. She smiled when he told her the name, but it was just a coincidence. At least, I think it was. It's hard to know anything anymore.

The smell of mass-produced powder soup wafts through the building, announcing mealtime. Dad stands to leave. 'Goodbye, grandma,' he says.

Mom stares ahead like she's looking into a field, searching for a particular blade of grass that isn't there. I wish she knew what was happening; she would have been so happy to interfere with how Joanna was raising Liam.

My father's demeanor changes the moment we step out through the doors.

'Time to meet Liam,' he says, inhaling the fresh air.

I feel like Florence Nightingale, but Dad's insisting we go to meet Liam straight away. His sad visit is over, his joyful one is ahead. I don't agree; facing Joanna is going to be a bit weird for me. I'm hoping the pain of birth and arrival of her new baby may have erased her memory of yesterday.

Lovely little Liam doesn't look like anyone in particular but I am aware it's my duty as a visitor to point out some similarities, so I fake a few, all the time avoiding looking directly at Joanna. Dad's happiness seeps out through every breath he takes, swooning at Liam until the nurse tells us visiting time has ended.

As we're leaving, I walk down the corridor with Dad, then pretend I've left my phone behind. Joanna is lifting Liam in her arms when I walk back into the ward.

'I'm so sorry about yesterday, Joanna. I didn't know that was going to happen.'

Joanna doesn't seem to give a goddamn shit about yesterday. She has moved on, got herself a baby.

But I continue, telling her about the gift, the dirty pink coat, explaining that it had been given to me by Bert and how I had forgotten my own present. I'm still rambling on about how Bert had it in his family for years and wanted to pass it on to someone, that he was probably confused with grief, when she turns and smiles at me.

'It's okay, Becca. And don't worry, I won't tell Danny.'

Chapter Thirty-Five

Liam smells like chocolate. Not the actual cocoa, but the comfort. There's a tuft of dark hair at the top of his head, his skin is the pink of strawberry marshmallows. His eyes are closed. Joanna is trusting me to hold her baby while she makes the supper. I offered to make it. Joanna should be resting. But no, Joanna insisted she make the supper. Nothing will make her relinquish control. Not even giving birth to a baby.

Feeling his warmth, I think about what it must feel like to have a baby, bring a life into the world. I wonder what Mom thought, cooing at little Becca while I slept in her arms. What were her wishes for me? I bet she didn't wish for me to get sacked, or wind up embroiled in a murder case. Or develop Alzheimer's before I even get married. I wonder if Josie Reilly got the results of that blood test? Just because she dropped me from the clinical trial, with no real explanation, doesn't mean she didn't get the results. Maybe I should pay Dr. Josie Reilly a visit.

Liam's eyes open, blue pools of innocence flickering with interest. He gurgles wet bubbles onto his lips. Watching the bubbles burst, I think about what it would be like to have a baby of my own, a little peach like Liam. But not yet.

Joanna didn't complain much about the birth, took it all in her stride. Unlike Danny, who waffled on like she was the first woman ever to have a baby. But it was great to hear the delight and excitement in his voice, he has been so edgy lately. It must be something to do with the cops. He's expected home any minute now from the office that can't survive without him. The smell of whatever is happening in the pot is making me hungry. I should be hungry, all I ate was a couple of cookies this morning.

'How's life with you?' Joanna asks, stirring the contents of the pot.

'Fine.'

'How was your mom yesterday? I heard you called in to tell her the good news with your dad.'

'Yeah, she seemed happy, she smiled when Dad told her Liam's name.'

As he wriggles in my arms, I sense Liam's discomfort. 'I think he might need to be changed,' I say.

The pot is pushed to the back ring. Joanna, rushes to her duty.

'I'll do it,' I say.

'No, thanks,' she says, smiling at Liam as she takes him out of my arms.

I'm in the bathroom when I hear Danny's car pull up outside. The king of the castle is home and I'm nervous. I haven't been in the same room as him since he warned me off asking about Katie Collins. I'm going to have to tell him what's been going on, that Katie Collins came to Boston looking for me, that Turner is questioning me like I've something to do with her death. I wonder, should I tell him now, while he's in good form, or should I let him enjoy this moment?

'Hi Becca,' Danny says, pushing past me into the kitchen with a lightness to his step. New dad syndrome. His voice sings Liam's name when he sees the crib. Devoted, standing there all coos and aahs, Danny cradles Liam close to his chest. Liam's eyes are blinking at his daddy. I haven't seen Danny this happy in a long time. I don't want to ruin it.

But I ruin it. We're all sitting down at the table slurping Joanna's bolognese when Danny walks over to the pile of gifts stacked in the corner of the room. He's picking something out of his teeth with a toothpick when he says, 'Some amount of gifts.'

Instantly I look to Joanna. *Did you hide it, Joanna? Please say you did.* I nod my head at her, my face red from the blood I can feel rushing to my head.

I mouth my question. *Is it still there?* But I know by Joanna's nervous expression that it is. She didn't get rid of it yet. Closing my eyes and crossing my fingers I pray that he doesn't see the pink coat.

God must be busy. After checking out two other presents, he sees the Ziploc bag. Joanna's eyes flash at me, teeth clenched, hoping like me that he doesn't investigate it.

No such luck.

At first Danny says nothing, staring at the jacket with a strange expression on his face. His skin burns red. His eyes seem frozen open, unable to believe what he is looking at. Then he turns to Joanna, his lips moving but no sound, like he's miming at her. Eventually he shouts, 'Where did you get this?'

Joanna rushes over to where Liam is lying in the crib, saying, 'Danny, take it easy, the baby.'

'Where did you get this?' he repeats, gripping the old baby coat tightly in his hand.

Joanna looks at me, then back to Danny. She doesn't know how to explain it.

'Bert sent it,' I say. Danny is speechless again, eyes wide with madness. Why is he so upset? It's only a baby coat. Why is it freaking Danny out so much?

'He didn't mean for it to upset anyone,' I say. 'It's old, it belonged to someone in his family. He thought he'd pass it on.'

Danny is looking through me now. Jesus, it's only a coat.

'He told you that, did he?'

'Yes. I thought you'd all laugh at it, see the funny side. It's no big deal, Danny…'

Danny clearly doesn't agree with me. With the wretched coat still in his grip, he walks over to Liam, who is now fast asleep, his soft baby breath the only comfort left in the room. Looking down at Liam, Danny wipes his eyes. Is he crying? Fuck, what's going on? What is with that stupid smelly coat?

There's something more to this baby coat, something Danny knows about. That's the only explanation for his completely irrational reaction. I know he doesn't like Bert but the poor man was only trying to be nice… Or was he? Maybe he did it on purpose, to upset Danny, to undermine the occasion. Maybe they dislike one another more than I know.

-

I leave Joanna with a big hug and apologize that I had ever brought the stupid thing to her baby shower… into her life. Joanna being Joanna, says not to worry, that it will blow over, that Danny was wrong and will eventually see the funny side of it.

I'm not so sure she's right.

Chapter Thirty-Six

New Orleans is a great place for lunatics. Bourbon Street is fantastic, music blaring from every bar, the street busy with tourists, performers, drinkers. Jeff looks like he's on a day trip to heaven. His friend's hotel is fine – high ceilings and dodgy balconies, but it will do the job. I'm glad to get away from home, especially after last night – Danny seeing the coat and then Turner showing up like that, standing outside Jeff's apartment when I arrived back. Lenny had told her where to find me when she didn't get an answer at my apartment. More questions, no answers. The woman is convinced I know more than I'm saying. I don't. Not yet. Hopefully after this trip I will.

I told Jeff I can only stay one night. If I go missing for two it might set alarm bells ringing and I'm in enough trouble with Danny as it is. And Turner. God only knows what she'll do if she finds out I've come looking for Katie's husband.

The plan is to get a ferry to Algiers in the morning, sniff around, see what we can find out. Hopefully we will get to speak to Thomas Collins. Until then we will savor the atmosphere of this amazing city. Dance the dance.

I'm nervous about tomorrow, about how I'll approach Thomas Collins. I might be the reason his wife is dead. Thomas Collins might think I'm the enemy.

'What are you having to drink?' Jeff shouts over the riffs of blues guitar, breaking in on my worries and forcing me to enjoy myself.

'I don't know,' I say, scanning the selection of bottles on display. I don't think Jeff appreciates my indecisiveness; he's shaking his head, tapping his fingers. 'Whatever you're having.'

Which leaves me drinking some sort of bourbon with lime, and boy, is it potent.

'What do you think?' he says, slipping up onto the stool beside me.

'It's strong.'

'It's supposed to be strong.'

Jeff turns to watch the band. The heat of the bourbon snakes through my body, making me relax, feel good. I'll take it easy though, maybe have just the one or two, because I need my wits about me for tomorrow.

–

The following morning, I wake feeling like a baby being pulled with forceps from the womb. Ouch. My head is caving in. Oh, the pain.

Dragging myself into a sitting position, I glance around the room. Jeff is sprawled out, fully dressed, his leather jacket keeping him warm on the bed opposite. Well, that's something; at least I didn't hook up with him. I hope. My memories of last night are keeping Mom's memories company, floating out there somewhere in the solar system. We moved from bar to bar, from drink to drink. Most of it bourbon. Some of it poison. I think I fell at one point. Or was that Jeff? One of us fell, I know that. Someone must have been watching over us to get us back safely into the convivial beds of the Blues Bay Inn. That's one blessing used up.

Where's my phone? Shit, I hope I didn't lose it. Jumping out of bed, I pat my jacket and jeans, but there's no sign of it. I search under the bed, still no phone. In the bathroom – a small dark room with a cistern that requires the pulling of a rope, its mismatched wallpaper peeling off the walls – I see it. It's on the floor by the toilet. Sighing with relief I bend down to pick it up when my nose is assaulted by the putrid smell of vomit. I'm afraid to look, I know what's in there. I must have puked for liberty last night. Grabbing the rope, I pull, expecting the toilet to flush, but no, it's not that easy. There were instructions handed out when we got the room but I didn't bother listening. Christ, how will I flush it before Jeff sees? I grab the rope again, this time pulling on it quicker. Still no flush. Out in the bedroom I hear Jeff waking up.

'Oh Christ,' he groans.

I stay silent, wondering what to do.

'Are you there, Becca? That was some session.'

I pull on the rope again but only a gurgle of water drops into the bowl.

'Don't forget to release the silver catch at the top of the rope,' Jeff shouts from the bedroom.

'It's after twelve, Jeff. We're late,' I say, coming out of the bathroom, relieved I buried the evidence.

'Okay, give me a minute,' Jeff goes to the bathroom arriving back after a few minutes. If he knows what went on in that room last night, he's choosing not to mention it.

'This is not going to be easy,' he says. 'I can't remember the last time I felt so bad.'

'Take these,' I say, handing him two Advil.

Twenty minutes later we are on our way to Algiers, ready to bulldoze through the mission. There's a cool breeze on my face, making me feel a bit more normal than I did earlier. Standing at the ferry's rail I watch the Mississippi flow by. Jeff brought two coffees on board, which we sip quietly, and I pray, pray it stays down, that I don't throw up all over the deck in front of all the sensible people who are not pickled in bourbon.

–

Algiers is quaint. The fresh air blowing in from the Mississippi keeps it alive, awake. Walking down a small hill that brings us to the edge of the town, I hear music. More music, like we didn't have enough last night. A festival of some sort is taking place in a field by the river. People are gathered, watching, dancing, as the band playing on the back of a truck blasts out 'Sweet Home Alabama'. Burgers, ribs, po'boys and all kinds of food stalls send their authentic scents into the air, making my stomach turn. *Jesus, Becca, don't puke now.*

'Do you want something to eat?' Jeff says, heading straight for one of the stalls.

'No, thanks.'

'Well I'm going to try something.'

Jeff gets himself a po'boy, which is basically a bread roll loaded with stuff. I can't even look at it.

The crowd continues to celebrate. I find myself looking at their faces, looking for Thomas Collins. There's a fat guy in the baseball jersey slurping a beer by the burger tent? A skinny, freckled guy slotting baby doughnuts into his mouth one by one? A tired looking guy pushing a buggy? No one resembles the Thomas Collins I seen in the photo.

Jeff puts his wrapper in the trashcan and wipes his face with his hand.

'That's just what the doc ordered,' he says, his eyes focused on the guitar. I'm beginning to feel my nerves twanging. All these people, strangers; why did I come here?

'Where should we go?' I say. Jeff seems more interested in the fender on the truck than our mission.

'What?'

'What do we do now?'

'Oh yeah,' Jeff turns to me. 'We'll go to a bar,' he says, looking up the street opposite.

'What?'

'Yeah, it's the best place to start.'

I'm not sure I agree with his plan but with none of my own, I go along with it.

'People expect to be asked questions in bars,' he says, walking away from the fair. 'They talk more freely with the booze on board.'

'But it's only two o'clock. There'll hardly be anyone in the bar.'

'We'll see.' We walk past a big old red building with a sign proclaiming it to be the local courthouse, and on towards a bar a few streets away.

'It's festival day, Becca. There will be people in the bar.'

–

The grey door of the Goose Inn creaks when Jeff pulls it open. A crowd of people, swallowing beer like it's the Fourth of July 1776, turn to stare at the new arrivals. The smell of yesterday's beer lingers amidst the musty scent of age. It reminds me of Mattie's, only with daylight. The furniture looks like it was picked up at a bring-and-buy sale; nothing matches or looks like it started out life here. Even the customers have a haphazard look about them. They're odd.

We move to the empty bar stools by the counter and sit down. Everyone is still looking at us.

'They mustn't get many outsiders around here,' Jeff says, looking over the counter, pretending to be interested in what beers are for sale. At least, I hope he's pretending; I couldn't go through another night like last night. Eventually a woman comes down to us from the far end of the bar, chewing something, looking like she just got out of bed. She wipes the counter with a cloth she keeps tucked into the top of her jeans.

'You looking for something?' she says.

Jeff stalls a bit, inspecting the shelves.

'Two large beers.'

When the woman moves away to the taps, Jeff notices the fear on my face.

'Trust me,' he whispers.

'You're not from around here,' the woman says, putting down the two beers.

'No, just visiting,' Jeff says.

'Anyone in particular?'

'Not really. Just checking out this beautiful place.'

The beer is cool and refreshing and bound to make me vomit shortly. The woman walks back to a guy at the far end of the bar.

'What are we going to do?' I say, leaning in close, noticing Jeff's bloodshot eyes, smelling last night's poison ooze from his breath.

'Well, first thing we'll do is sit here and drink our beers.' He nods in the direction of a middle-aged woman who looks half shot, sitting alone near the door, a pack of cigarettes on the table. 'Then, when that lady goes out for a cigarette, you're going to join her.'

'But I don't smoke.'

'That doesn't matter. Just take your drink outside, she won't notice.'

Soon the woman's craving re-appear so I follow her outside like Jeff suggested and sit at the table beside her. I can see Jeff winking at me through the window. Struggling to get her lighter to work, the woman looks at me as if I might offer to help. *Move, Becca, move.*

'Are you looking for a light?' I say in a posh sounding voice, *don't know where that came from*.

'You got one?' she says, watching as I rummage in my jeans pocket.

'Hang on, I must have left it inside.' Walking back into the bar, I rush over to Jeff.

'Have you got a lighter?'

He does. I hurry back outside and hand it to the woman.

'Thanks,' she says.

Speak, Becca, speak. Ask her something, anything.

'Are you from around here?' I say.

She puffs on the cigarette a few times before taking it out of her mouth.

'Why do you wanna know?'

'I was just wondering about the place, it seems a nice place to live.'

'It's a shithole.'

'Oh.' What can I say to that?

'Spent thirty-five years of my life serving beer to beggars in this shithole.'

I move my chair closer to her table.

'So you must know everyone who lives here,' I say, taking a sip from my glass.

'I know most folk, all beggars and liars.' Wow, this woman does not like her neighbors. Something hard has bitten her soul. 'I have twelve guns,' she adds, wriggling her shoulders, real proud.

'Wow.'

'Yep, twelve guns. Plan to use them all before I die.'

'Oh,' I say, craning my head to see if Jeff is watching. 'Hope you're not planning to use one on me,' I chuckle, but she just glances at me and goes back to her cigarette.

'Did you know the girl who died?' I say.

'Which girl?' she says. 'Everybody dies.'

'The girl who died in Boston. The colonel's wife, Katie Collins.'

'The murdered girl.' Clearing her throat of phlegm, she struggles to catch her next breath and says, 'Not everyone gets murdered.'

I'm remembering her twelve guns and her plans to alter the statistics.

'I knew her,' she says.

'You did?' My heart jumps, my stomach joins it. I'm completely focused.

'Sweet girl, I spoke to her once.'

'Where did she live?'

'Someplace down at Houston Street, I think. Lived with a bastard. I might use one of my guns on him.'

'And where is Houston Street?'

'Why're you so concerned about this kid? She a friend of yours?'

'No, I just…'

'You the media?'

'No, I'm not the media, I… I'm just interested.'

'I hate the media, bastards. Tells the lies they do, tell the lies.' She stands up from her chair to leave. I stand too.

'Well, I can assure you I'm not from the papers or anything, I'm just—' but before I can finish, she walks back through the door into the bar, muttering, 'Tells the lies, tells the lies,'

Well, at least I got the name of a street. Smiling my way back to where Jeff is sitting, I tell him the good news. 'That woman is one bitter woman, she must have had her heart broken by a nation, but at least I got an address. Well, the name of a street anyway.'

'Great, where did she say she lived?'

'Some place called Houston Street.'

'Houston Street.' Jeff repeats the name, then calls for the barwoman's attention and asks her for directions.

'Houston Street or Houston Boulevard?' she says. Jeff looks at me.

'I'm not sure. I think she said street.'

'Think who said street?' the woman asks.

'That lady there.' I nod towards the mad woman. I think she is still muttering, 'tells the lies.' The barwoman laughs.

'You don't wanna believe the time out of her mouth. Carries on like God ain't looking, that one… Who are you searching for?' With one hand wiping the counter, her eyes stay focused on me.

'I was hoping to find out where Katie Collins lived.'

'Katie Collins?'

'Yes, the girl who was murdered in Boston.'

'You the papers?'

'No, I'm her cousin.'

The woman looks away, concentrating on the cloth in her hand for a moment before looking back at me.

'And you're asking me because…?'

'We didn't get on, there was a family feud and…'

Raising her hand, she says, 'No need to say anymore. You look like her, those dopey eyes, so I'll tell you.'

What? I *look* like her? I look like Katie Collins?

Chapter Thirty-Seven

The house is fronted by a small yard like every other house on the street. There's no sign of the trauma its inhabitants have endured. Unlike me, every bone I have is shaking. A few steps away from the front of the house I stop, staring at the green wooden gate. If I push it open, I cannot go back. So much has happened in the past few weeks I feel I'm being sucked into the center of a tornado. *Don't drop me.*

'I can't do this Jeff, I can't go in.'

Jeff turns, puts his hand on my shoulder. Dark rings circle his eyes. Last night has taken a lot out of him.

'You can do it, Becca. This is what we came here for; this is where you will find the answers.'

I know he's right but it doesn't feel like that. It's like I'm volunteering to walk into a blazing fire. I want to back out, walk away like I always do when the going gets tough. My mother always told me I needed to see things through to the end. 'Don't give up,' she would say when all I wanted to do was give up. But more often than not, I did give up. I gave up swimming when the lessons got too hard, gave up the guitar at the first sign of sore fingers and gave up college, twice.

In front of me I see a simple white door with a flyscreen attached. The flyscreen is open.

Jeff is hovering, his eyes still on me, his arm outstretched to show me the way.

'Come on Becca, what do you have to lose?'

I don't know, Jeff. How do I know what I might lose when I don't know what I'm going to hear? I don't know why this woman was killed looking for me. Closing my eyes, I take a deep breath. Before pushing the gate open, I pause. There's no turning back now. 'Okay, here goes.'

The path is only about twenty steps but it feels miles long. Every journey starts with a single step and all that crap. I'm walking slowly so I don't get there, yet. Jeff walks ahead and rings the doorbell. Eventually I'm standing beside him. There is no answer. Great.

'No one here, we'll have to come back later.'

Just as I turn to leave, the door opens. A small dark woman, hair tied back showing her youth, a small tattoo of a butterfly on her neck, stands in front of us. She looks at us cautiously. Words elude me so I look to Jeff.

'Is this Thomas Collins's house?' he asks.

'Who's asking?' she says, in an accent that isn't local.

'Well, my name is Jeff and this is Rebecca Wall. We were hoping to speak to Thomas.'

'Thomas is not home, he's at the base.' She is about to close the door on me, on my hopes, when I hear a voice calling out from a room behind her. 'Wait!'

A tall handsome guy, his face molded by sadness, arrives behind the woman and pulls the door open. His dark, lifeless eyes seem far too old for his face, in total contrast to the photo I've seen of him on the internet where he stands tall in his army suit. Honor carved on his happy expression.

I'm trembling, blood rushing to my head, legs weakening. This is him, it's Thomas Collins. The man whose wife lost her life while looking for me is standing right in front of me. The man who can tell me why Katie Collins was looking for me is within my reach. *Don't give up, Becca.*

'What did you say your name was?'

'Becca. Rebecca Wall.'

Thomas Collins stares for what feels like a day before speaking again.

'I'll take this,' he says to the woman, who walks away towards a room at the back of the house.

'Rebecca Wall,' he says.

'That's right.'

'Why are you here?'

'I... I...' I don't know what to say, I never prepared a pitch. What do I say? Jeff notices me buckling.

'Rebecca came here to find out why Katie was looking for her,' he says, loud and clear, like he is reciting from the bible. No nerves Jeff. I nod in agreement.

'You don't know then,' Thomas says. 'I guess you better come in.'

The house is small but quaint and well maintained. He leads us down the hallway to the room where the woman went. There is a kitchen at one end a couch and TV with computer games stacked beneath it at the other end.

My eyes are drawn to the baby crib in the corner. I want to go over and have a peek at the child who is motherless because of me. But I don't, I can barely move. Jeff's shadow is my map, I'm taking every step he takes as we walk to the center of the room. I don't think I'd have got this far without him.

Thomas nods at the woman and then to the baby, giving some sort of telepathic order. She lifts the baby from the crib. The little girl's head sticks out of the top of the blanket. She has pale pink skin with a dusting of fair hair at the sides. I think of Liam, his tiny head. What would happen to Liam if Joanna was killed? I don't want to think about it.

'What's her name?' I say.

The woman looks at Thomas, like I've asked an off-limits question. She doesn't answer and continues to walk out of the room with her head nestled into the baby's bundle, leaving me feeling like I've just been punished.

'Louise,' Thomas says. 'Her name is Louise.'

'That's a nice name.'

'After Katie's sister, Louise Johnson,' he adds. 'The sister who was abducted when Katie was three years old.'

My body shuts down. I can't feel myself; where have I gone? I hear my mother's words loud and clear crashing against the wall of my soul.

'*I took you, Becca.*'

Stumbling a few feet to the nearest seat, I collapse. Is this really happening or am I dreaming? I pinch myself to make sure I'm here. I'm here. This is happening.

Jeff follows. Kneeling down in front of me, he says, 'Are you okay, Becca? What's wrong?'

Thomas rushes to the faucet and fills a glass with water.

'Are you okay?'

I can hear him, but I can't answer him; can't think, can't move. Stuck in this thing, this fear. Jeff hands me the glass which I attempt to sip from.

'What are you thinking, Becca?'

I lift my face to look at him. My thoughts must be etched onto it because Jeff says, 'It's not you, Becca. Don't think like that. You are not Katie's abducted sister.' Jeff is trying to reassure me, but what does he know? Nothing.

There's no face now, just a blur. Someone is speaking but I do not understand the words.

Eventually the world becomes familiar again, the room, the noise, the smell. In the distance a baby cries. In front of me is Thomas Collins. He looms above me, a tornado approaching. It doesn't make sense, none of this makes sense. I'm panicking, creating something that doesn't exist. I'm *not* the abducted girl. I can't be. I have a birth certificate, photos of Mom pregnant with me, and I know it's me because Danny is there too. Then there's the photo of me two hours old, in hospital, in my Dad's arms. Well I always thought it was me, was told it was me. But what if it wasn't me? What if that baby was somebody else?

Relax, Becca. Stop building a world that doesn't exist.

'I'm sorry,' I say. 'It must be the heat.'

'Can I get you something else?' Thomas says.

'No, I'm okay now.'

I need to ask him the question. That's why I'm here.

'Thomas,' I say. 'Did you know I'm the person your wife was looking for?'

'One of them,' he says.

'One of them?'

'Yes, it was ongoing. Every year there was someone new. "It has to be her, she's my sister… or maybe this one," she'd say, showing me a picture from some magazine or the laptop.'

A warm gush of hope sweeps through me. This is not just about me, there are others.

'I can show you her room if you want,' he says.

I want, of course I want.

'If it's not too much trouble,' I say.

Thomas takes us upstairs. He continues to talk, telling us Katie had become obsessed with finding her sister ever since they got married. Apparently Boston wasn't the only cross-country trip she'd taken. She'd been to New York, Senora Virginia, chasing down girls she thought were her sister. The strain the search put on both of them became unbearable, almost ending their marriage. Then it stopped; after a lot of therapy and tablets, Katie stopped the search. Two years later Louise was born and it all started up again.

I should not be happy to find out that this woman was on the edge, but I am. The realization that I was not her only target makes me feel a lot better. I'm breathing normally now.

Then he opens the door.

Chapter Thirty-Eight

I can't believe my eyes. The walls are covered in charts, dates, pictures of women. All types of women – young girls, women my age, some with dark hair, blonde hair, one with no hair. It's like walking into one of those horror movies where the psycho has thousands of photos of their victims pinned to their bedroom walls.

Some of the photos have a large x marked across them. A desk against the far wall is deep in scattered papers, except for an empty square where I guess the computer stood before the cops took it away. The room reeks of desperation. It seeps from the floor and the walls, the curtains opened on the large window to the left. The light has no effect. This room is *dark*.

Through the window the Mississippi flows by, a prospect for the strong, temptation for the weak. Large barges creep up on the city, crawling through the constant waters, laden with produce. Along the riverside two boys cycle their bikes, stopping to wave at a barge, maybe it's their daddy, maybe it's a stranger.

'Wow,' Jeff says, leaning in close to my ear. 'Nut job.'

Thomas is standing by the door. I'm tapping Jeff on the arm, telling him to hush, when I see myself.

The page has been pulled from a magazine and is pinned right above the desk. The photo is mainly of the band taken at Mattie's club, but I'm there at the bar, in the background. Excited and terrified, I move closer. The cameraman did not catch me at my best; in fact, I look fat, the uniform shirt is far too big on me. It's hard to see the expression on my face from the distance, which I'm glad about; I doubt it's flattering. I haven't seen this picture before. But Katie Collins has managed to track it down and she has drawn a big red circle around me.

I beckon Jeff, show him the picture.

'Not your finest hour,' he says.

I want to thump him, say something smart, but I'm aware the bereaved Thomas Collins is standing in the room with us.

'How long has she had this?' I say.

'I don't know. I lost interest in her quest a long time ago.' Pushing his hand through his hair, he moves over to the desk and lifts a few of the papers in his hand, throwing them back down before adding, 'Katie was challenged by reality. It wasn't her fault, she had a rough start.'

'Where did she grow up?'

'In a hellhole at the edge of Maine. They lived in a trailer for the first few years. When I say they, I mean her mother, her sister and herself. She didn't know her father, and when her sister was abducted the mother lost all capacity to carry on and drank herself to death. That left Katie with a foster couple, who apparently she was very fond of. She stayed with them until she moved to New York at eighteen. I met her when she was twenty-one. She was working in childcare at the time. She seemed normal to me and I loved her, still love her. It was when we married that the cracks began to appear.'

Thomas is becoming weary talking to us but I have to keep going.

'Was there more?'

'More what?'

'Well, any more pictures of me. Stuff like that.'

Making for the door, he says, 'Not that I know of. Like I told you, I paid no heed to what she was at over the past few years. Maybe I should have been more helpful.'

I feel under pressure to leave this man alone, to stop stirring his pain. Walking towards the door, I see every picture and note covering the room and wonder, did Katie Collins put those thoughts into Mom's head the day she visited Oakridge?

'I suppose her computer would have more information but the cops have that now,' Thomas says, moving into the hallway. Jeff and I follow. Closing the door behind us, he leads us back downstairs to the hallway.

'I don't know what more I can tell you,' he says, making his way towards the hall door. The baby's cry echoes down the hallway; the whole atmosphere is surreal and creepy. Pulling the strap of my bag across my shoulder I thank Thomas for his time. I ask him to get in touch if he thinks of anything else he might want me to know and then I give him my number. I also wish him the best of luck in finding out who killed his wife; probably not the best language to use, 'Good luck finding out who killed your wife.'

But what do you say in situations like this? I'm a novice. He doesn't seem to register my inappropriateness and I don't think finding the killer is going to bring any peace. The woman is dead. Her life has come to an end without her finding her sister and that's a pity, a big pity, especially when there's a new Louise starting out in life without her mommy.

The child must be asleep now, the crying has ceased. Moving towards the door, Jeff looks at me and says, 'All done here?'

I feel like I came all this distance for nothing. Even though I now know why Katie Collins was looking for me, I'm a bit disappointed. I don't understand why I feel like this. Did I *want* to be the sister she was looking for? But I was just another photo, another prospect, another failure in her quest for an answer that she never got.

Zipping up my jacket I nod at Jeff. *It's over, we can go home now. I'll put all this behind me.*

I'm about to step through the door when I turn and look at a picture on the wall. At first it doesn't register with me; it's just a family picture. Two young girls with their mother. The woman is holding a baby in her arms. The older child is standing by her side near the open door of a trailer.

My heart shrinks. The baby is wearing a pink coat. With a button missing.

Chapter Thirty-Nine

'Come on, Becca. There must have been thousands of pink baby coats.'

Jeff is trying to calm me as I sit on a wall down the street from Thomas Collins' house. I'm so weak I can't stand up.

'Surely every little girl has a pink coat,' he continues, but his words hold no comfort. I know that coat, I have seen that coat, I have held that coat. Bert Ryan gave that coat to Danny for a reason. Bert Ryan knows something.

I can't reply to Jeff, can't seem to be able to digest this finding. It's like a fishbone stuck in the back of my throat preventing me from concentrating on anything else. What am I to do? How do I find out?

The first thing I need to do is call into Bert and ask him where he got the coat and why he gave it to Danny. That is the first thing I will do. Lifting my head, I look at Jeff's concerned face. He's as confused as I am.

Who is the baby in the pink coat? The missing Louise? And why is that pink coat in Danny's house right now? Is the baby in the pink coat me? Did Katie Collins find her sister? From where I'm standing it's looking that way.

'I need to get home, Jeff,' I say, unable to move. My body feels lifeless, like I've no blood left. My questionable blood. I know I will keel over if I stand up. Lifting my head towards the white clouds moving without worry across the blue sky, I inhale deeply. Once, twice, three times. *Stand up, Becca.*

'I need to get home.'

–

The journey is a silent one. Jeff attempts conversation but to me he is speaking in a different language. Nothing feels right and I'm about two watts of willpower away from screaming my head off. But I won't, I don't think JetBlue would appreciate the drama. I'll hold it together until we land at Logan. Then I will scream my head off.

To my surprise the three hour flight seems shorter than it did coming out. Having refused the alcoholic support Jeff was promoting, I feel calmer. I need to take control.

We get outside the airport, hop in a cab and travel back to the apartment. Jeff rushes in to make sure Bill and Hillary have not passed away from a day without greens. They haven't. The two fluffy heads look as uninterested as ever and this makes Jeff happy. Dropping my bag onto the couch, I walk over and gaze out the window at the starry night. I have always found solace looking up when I feel down. The vastness of the unknown tends to put my small issues into a bigger world and shrink their value. But it's not working tonight. I feel the burden of finding out the truth pushing down harder on me.

'What now?' Jeff says, placing a load of green leaves into the rabbit's cage. I look over at him, his cool lean body kneeling down in front of the open cage door, and I wonder what I would do without this guy. I would never have gone to Algiers, that's for sure. I would have said I'd go, I would have pottered around making plans, but without Jeff pushing the venture it would never have happened. I have a lot to thank him for, or blame him for, I haven't quite decided yet.

'I'm going to call on Bert.'

'Now?'

'Yes, now.'

Jeff stands up and stretches his arms above his head.

'You could wait until tomorrow,' he says. 'It's a bit late to go knocking on an old man's door.'

'I can't wait until tomorrow, Jeff. I've got to go now.'

I know Bert will still be up. He is one of those night birds, he told me himself.

'There is just one problem,' I say, looking away. 'I can't take my car, Dad might see it and wonder I'm doing there at this hour,'

Jeff shakes his head, disappointed, I know, that he has to go out again. Jeff would prefer to be boiling pasta, sipping wine and plucking strings.

'Okay, we'll take my sister's car.'

–

The radio is playing some song about leaving the past behind. I'm not familiar with the artist but his lyrics hold my attention, talking to me as I struggle to understand what is going on. What has happened in my past? What is it that I must leave behind? The moon hovers bright in the clear sky; everything's calm except me. The pink coat holds the answer. I know it does. I have to find out why it ended up in Danny's house, how Bert came to have it in the first place. And why did he wait until now to bring it out? Jeff has stopped trying to convince me it's just a pink coat, that it might be a coincidence. The missing button put a stop to that. Could all this mean that Mom's words weren't some random moment of imagination falling from her lips? That she was telling the truth? Or is there some other explanation for all this?

Jeff parks the car down the street from Bert's house. I feel sick, my stomach doing a dance inside. Jeff consoles me, tells me to turn back, wait until tomorrow. But I can't, I have to go in now or I might not make it to tomorrow. He moves to get out of the car with me.

'No, Jeff, you stay,' I say, resting my hand on his leg, nodding a smile at him. Bert wouldn't like to see a stranger at his door at this hour of night, even if that stranger is accompanied by a deluded neighbor.

This is mine, I must do this alone.

The street is quiet as a graveyard when I step out of the car. Nothing moves; the large oak trees seem painted into place, a backdrop on the stage of my drama.

'Wish me luck.' I bend down to say before closing the door.

You're on your own now. Becca Wall. Except I'm not. In the distance the dark shape of a man walks out of Bert's yard. It's definitely not Bert. The step is too quick, the frame too thin. Moving out of the streetlight, I pull open the car door and jump back inside, lowering my head so I'm peering over the dashboard.

'What's going on?' Jeff says.

'Sshh.' I wait for the man's face to come into view, for him to look this way. And then, stepping out on to the road, he turns his head, checking both ways.

Danny?

What the hell is Danny doing coming from Bert's house at this hour of the night?

Chapter Forty

'Maybe he was just checking up on him,' Jeff says, trying to calm me down while I sit in the car, shocked and confused.

'But Danny doesn't like Bert. Doesn't even speak to him. Why would he check up on him?' It's then I realize he must have called to confront him over the coat.

The SUV's lights brighten up the whole street when Danny drives off.

Bert's house is in complete darkness. With a trembling finger I press the doorbell. No answer. I try again, holding the button down for longer; still no answer. Then I bang, not so loud as to wake the neighbors but loud enough that Bert should hear. Still no answer. Stepping back, I look up at the house to see if a light is coming on, but no, there's no sign of life here. Maybe Bert's not at home. Placing my ear up against the door I listen for any signs of him moving around inside the house. Nothing. A wasted journey. Jeff won't be happy I dragged him all the way out here for nothing.

To my right is a wooden fence at the side of the house. It's tall, not one I could climb easily. The gate in the middle is always locked so that's a no-no. Bert is a fanatic about security. Locks, chains, alarms. Edith used to get bawled out if she overlooked any of his security measures. I remember hearing him once. I was about fourteen at the time and he was going on about the ruthless people, the robbers, how they would take anything. Edith stood with her back to him, listening, pulling faces, trying to make me laugh. I did laugh.

Moving closer to the fence I get a shiver down my spine. Where's Bert? I push the gate, not expecting it to open, but it does. Swings at my touch. This scares me even more. Something isn't right. Feeling like a criminal, I look up at the rear of the house, but there's no light on here either. 'Bert? *Bert*,' I call in a hoarse whisper. He's not going to hear me, I know, but it's just something I do. I need answers; I need to talk to this man.

Scattered leaves crunch beneath my feet. That's not like Bert either. He's usually standing at the trunk of the tree with his yard brush waiting for the leaves to fall so he can gather them all into the recycling bin he's so proud of. Maybe Bert is sick, lying in bed on his own, unable to move, unable to reach the phone.

A small wooden decking stands between me and the back door, so I step across it and reach for the handle. If the door opens, Bert is in trouble. Pushing down on the handle, my heart beats louder. Part of me wants it to open, to know what's going on; the other part is shaking. The lock stays firm, no movement, a barrier to the story on the other side. Slowly I realize I'm not going to find out anything about the pink coat tonight.

Walking away from Bert's house, I look across the street at my own family home. Did something happen in that house? The old wooden door stands worn, beaten, tired. Mom always kept it open when I played in the front yard or on the porch, calling out every so often to make sure I was still there. Looking back now she seemed a lot more vigilant than my friends' moms, who would let them play out on the street for hours before checking on them.

Maybe she was nervous of something, expecting someone to come along and take me.

To take me *back*.

Jeff's eyes are closed, headphones in, when I open the car door. He jerks forward, pulling the buds from his ears.

'Well, has all been revealed?' he says.

'I didn't get an answer.'

Jeff has the foresight not to say *I told you so*. Checking his mirror, he turns the engine on and drives away.

'You can call again tomorrow, Becca.'

Taking my cell out, I dial Danny's number.

'Who are you calling at this hour?'

'Danny.'

'Danny?'

'Yes. I want to know what he was doing at Bert's.'

Jeff clenches his lips. He knows when to let me be. The phone rings out. I try again. It rings out again.

'He might have it on silent, with the new baby and all that, Becs,' Jeff said.

'He never has it on silent. He's avoiding me. Drive to his house.'

'What? Now?'

'Yes, now,' I say, my tone not inviting any argument.

I direct Jeff to Danny's house, but the driveway is empty. No Danny. He has not come home yet. I make Jeff wait for a while but realize I'm pushing our friendship a little too far. I'll contact him tomorrow. I want some answers about what he was doing at Bert's.

Chapter Forty-One

As soon as Jeff finishes dipping bread into egg and grilling it, I head back to Bert's. I couldn't sleep last night thinking about the pink coat. How did it end up in Bert's hands? What is he going to tell me? The car in front crawls along like it has no place to be in a hurry so it takes me quite a while to get there.

The street is blocked by groups of people standing around chatting. When I park the car and push my way through, I can't believe what I'm looking at. An ambulance, with a body on a stretcher being slid into the back by two paramedics. Something has happened to Bert.

'What's going on?' I ask the paramedic who is stepping back out of the vehicle, closing the door.

'Who am I speaking to?' he says, not bothering to look at me.

'I'm Rebecca Wall. Bert's friend.'

'You're not family then?'

'No, but I'm his best friend.' I hear the words and suddenly realize they are true. I *am* Bert's best friend, ever since Edith left.

'I'm sorry, but this man has passed away.'

'What?' I can't believe what I'm hearing. Bert's dead? He's being taken to the coroner's office for a post-mortem. Freda, the girl who cleans his house once a week, found him in bed this morning. Freda is standing in the front yard with tears in her eyes, telling me what happened. When she arrived, she knew something was wrong because Bert is always already up and waiting to give her orders. Bert never mentioned Freda to me before. I wonder what else he never told me. She went to his room thinking he was asleep but when he didn't answer she knew he was dead. Suspected heart attack.

'How long has he been dead for?' I asked but she didn't have the answer. I realize Bert could have been dead for days. Apart from the weekly visit from Freda, no one else except me ever calls at the house, and I haven't been here since he gave me the pink coat last week. That's why I got no answer last night: while I was prowling around outside hoping to talk to him, he was lying dead inside. Oh sweet Jesus, why didn't I call the cops when I got no answer? And Danny – what the hell was he doing at Bert's?

I look around to see if my dad is amongst the crowd of neighbors gathered in packs to discuss the terrible news. He isn't. He's standing in his doorway on the other side of the street, looking straight at me. A shiver runs down my spine.

–

The smell in here belongs to hell. Rolling my tongue around my mouth, I suck up some saliva, anything to quench the thirst.

The coins have rolled under the seat in front, grabbing the attention of a young man, his face the perfect ad for addiction. Pale, decorated with marks, his skin sucked in so I can make out exactly how he'll look in his coffin. His bottom lip drops open, his eyes watching my every move. He wouldn't have the balls to rob me, not in here, but stray coins… I bet he could do with them.

Bending down I gather the cards scattered around my feet. Lots of cards.

Holding the purse open, I slip the first card back into its pocket.

She shouldn't have told him. That was mine to tell.

Then the second.

Why did he tell her anything in the first place?

Then the third card.

Will he still want me now?

The fourth card doesn't slip in as easy as the other three so I pull out the blockage. Notepaper. White. Folded over two times. If this is it, everyone is wrong. Including me.

I hear screaming, crying. It's not far away, a few feet maybe, but I don't look up. I'm unraveling the truth with trembling fingers, reading the words that were meant for me.

Chapter Forty-Two

I want to go to the coroner's office and see what happened to Bert. Freda said the ambulance guy is pretty sure it was a heart attack. I also want to go over to Danny's and find out why he visited Bert last night. Though I know, deep down, that he went to confront him over the coat.

Poor Bert, he didn't last long after Edith. I didn't think he would but this is very soon. Edith will only be settling in up there when he knocks on the door; what a nice surprise for her.

I realize now that I may never know the history of the coat, and maybe it doesn't matter, maybe this all happened for a reason. Mom always said things happened for a reason. Like the many times I didn't get called back after the dancing auditions I went to. Or the time Luke Brennan canceled bringing me to the prom in order to ask some new girl who joined the school. There were many occasions when Mom got to unload these words of wisdom. I wonder what she thinks of them now. I wonder how they fit into her diagnosis. Things happen for a reason.

The ambulance drives away leaving the curious in its wake. My head is heavy with sadness as I cross the road and enter Dad's kitchen.

'So Bert has gone,' I say.

'So I see.' My father turns, a strange look on his face. 'What happened?'

'They're not sure, a heart attack maybe.'

'May he rest in peace.'

I doubt my father cares if Bert rests in peace; he didn't care if he lived in peace. His dislike for Bert was there for as long as I can remember. But he never stopped me going over to visit him. He tried at first, but Mom said it was okay. Even though she didn't talk to him either. Maybe she liked Edith.

I'm not going to bring up the subject of Dad coming to Bert's funeral with me because I know the answer. He won't go, no one will go; in fact, I may be the only one there. Hopefully some of Edith's family will show up. I doubt Bert cares, though. He didn't care when he was alive so he is not going to care now that he is dead. God, I can't believe he's gone. Everything I care about is slipping out of my world one thing at a time. My phone rings, interrupting my thoughts. It's Jeff.

'Hi Becca, just calling to see how you are? How did you get on with Bert?'

I can't answer him.

'What's wrong, Becca?'

'He's dead, Jeff,' I say, my voice cracking.

'What?' Jeff can't believe it, struggling to digest that we were outside Bert's house when he might have been taking his last breath. He tells me to come straight back and not to bother visiting Mom today, but I tell him that I'm okay, I need to see her and I'll be back later.

Chapter Forty-Three

Now I'll never find out about the pink coat. Bert was my only hope and now he's dead, gone to Edith. But it has to mean something; someone must know why that coat started off in a trailer park in Maine and ended up in Danny's kitchen.

Having spent the rest of the day in Dad's house trying to contact Danny. I finally get through to him on the phone.

'Danny, why were you at Bert's house last night?' There's silence for a moment.

'I wanted to ask him about the coat.'

'But why would you want to hassle an old man, Danny? Could you not leave it?'

Danny is clearly as interested in the coat as I am. He doesn't believe the heirloom story. I knew his reaction when he saw it in the kitchen was out of proportion.

'Well I didn't get an answer, Becca, so don't worry about it... how did you know I called at Bert's house anyway?'

'I saw you leave... I... I was leaving Dad's and I saw you...'

Quick, change the subject. Don't mention New Orleans, Becca, or he'll think you've gone mad.

'Bert is dead.'

'What?'

'Yes, he had a heart attack.'

'Holy fuck.'

I listen carefully to his tone of voice, try to hear any traces of secrecy, before asking the question. 'Why are you interested in the coat, Danny?'

'Becca, I have to go, Joanna is calling me.' Before I have time to say anything else, he hangs up on me.

–

Oakridge is closed, but as luck would have it, Barry the security guy is on duty when I arrive.

'Back again?' he says, pulling the door open. 'Mom not doing too good?' Barry leads me to the reception desk to sign in.

'No, she didn't have a good day and I was in work earlier so I thought…'

'No worries, Rebecca. Glad to be of help, go ahead,' he says, pointing to the elevators. He doesn't mention the mystery visitor, the tapes or the fact that Katie Collins is dead. He just plods along, minding his own business. There should be more Barrys in this world.

Snores in all keys and tones vibrate through the hallway. In the distance I see that Mom's door is open and light is flooding out into the hallway. Why is it open? Who's in there? Rushing down the corridor, I arrive at the door with my heart pounding. Lucy the night nurse is holding Mom's hand, talking to her, and there's a doctor, one of those on call amateurs, fiddling with something in her stomach, pushing in a tube or a needle.

'What's happening?' I cry, rushing over to Lucy's side. 'What's wrong?'

'It's okay, Becca,' she says.

Taking Mom's hand from Lucy's, I kneel down by the bed and look into her eyes. They're red; Mom has been crying, her face is wet. Something washes over me, scares me, weakens me.

'What happened?' My voice is barely recognizable, the words snowflakes in a blizzard.

Lucy puts her hand on my shoulder.

'Everything is okay now.'

'What do you mean *now*?' I want to scream, pull the bedclothes off, push the nurse away, drive the doctor away. What are these people doing to Mom? Why did she cry?

'Becca, Nancy pulled out the feeding tube in her stomach earlier and, well, she tore the skin. We've given her painkillers, she's not in pain anymore.'

The doctor ignores me, concentrating on what he has to do. I squeeze Mom's hand, telling her everything is going to be okay. Who am I kidding? It's only been two days since the tube was inserted and already there's a problem. Nothing will ever be okay again. This is just another battle in the war, another shadow in the room, another flame in the crematorium.

Mom's eyes look back at me, helpless and confused. The world is a stranger now, pain is just pain. I kiss her cheek. Her salty tears coat my lips and I lick them. I swallow them.

Mom has fallen asleep with her hand still cradled in mine.

-

When the doctor leaves, I lay my head on the side of Mom's bed. Lucy tidies things up, then tells me to press the red button if Mom shows any signs of being agitated.

With the room empty of strangers I straighten up and pull the chair in closer to the bed. I look at Mom's eyelids flickering in her sleep. I want to see her secrets, see behind the fading windows into her soul.

'Tell me, Mom. What did you mean? What do you know?'

Her breathing sounds like the second hand printing machine Dad bought when I was a kid – puff-puff, chukka-chukka, puff-puff-pow. Mom went crazy when he assembled it in the back room of the house. Said it was like living at the *Boston Globe*. It lasted for less than a week, then Dad had to sell it, at a loss. He moaned for a while but Mom said he would have experienced a much bigger loss if he'd kept it.

With my head resting on the bed I close my eyes and fall asleep until a trolley passes by the door, the noise from the squeaky wheels waking me up. Jolting into an upright position, I look out the window to see shades of tomorrow piercing the darkness. I check my phone and see Jeff has sent two text messages, asking where I am, if I'm okay. I'd forgotten about Jeff, that there was someone out there who cared. I look to the parking lot below, where a nurse is getting out of a car, cup of coffee in hand, blue uniform freshly ironed. It's not even six a.m. yet.

Then I think of Dr. Reilly, and wonder what time she gets to her office. I doubt it's this early. The idea hits me like a baseball bat to my unprotected head.

Dr. Josie Reilly's office is empty now.

Chapter Forty-Four

Passing Barry wasn't an issue, I told him I was going for a stroll to stretch my legs. He asked if everything was okay with Mom and I told him what happened. He sighed, shook his head, and made some comment about being in the hands of our Maker.

Dr. Reilly's office is the third door down. Standing outside, the keypad glows like temptation. I know this could get me into a lot of trouble, but I need to find out what's in that report, what led to me being dropped from the trial. A loud crash echoes from the lobby. I freeze, keeping my eye on the door at the end of the corridor, but no one comes through it.

One-nine-nine-one, the year I was born. How could I forget? Click, the door unlocks. Hands shaking, breath quickening, legs ready to give up, I step inside the dark room. If I switch on the light it might alert someone to my being here. My phone's flashlight maps out a route to Reilly's desk, creating an eerie atmosphere. To the left stands a filing cabinet, which also has a keypad. Doubt creeps in. This is not going to work. On her desk is a computer, so I sit down and switch it on. The silence is blasted by the musical introduction coming from the computer. It sounds like a live band doing a sound-check in the room. Banging on a few keys, I try to stop it, but I'm not familiar with this computer so I'm not sure what I should be hitting. Eventually it plays out and I slump back into the chair, staring at the door. Nothing happens, no one heard. Back to my mission.

It's worthless, the password is keeping me out, so I hold the phone up and shine it around the room, hoping something will speak to me. But nothing jumps out, nothing except the filing cabinet with the keypad. What if…?

Well, who would have thought a qualified doctor with fancy shoes and gleaming teeth would use the same keypad code twice? Not me, but I was wrong. The click is loud and clear: the filing cabinet opens.

Footsteps interrupt my progress, distant but getting closer. The slow trot makes me think it's Barry. Probably wondering where I am. I switch off the phone and the room is plunged back into darkness. On my knees behind the desk I listen as the steps pass the door. Holding my breath, sweat prickling on my forehead, I wait.

A minute or so later I hear him pass back down the corridor again. On with the phone flashlight. The first cabinet drawer holds a bunch of folders. None of it means anything to me. It's mostly brochures, information booklets, courses Reilly must have to attend. The second drawer opens with a slight squeak and I find myself telling it to hush. Medical things – syringes, swabs, scissors, all sorts of intrusive apparatus. Nothing of interest. The third drawer doesn't open at first. Jammed. I give it a hard tug, and it flies open, landing me on the ground. Crawling over to the treasure inside, I see a load of files, brown manila files, just like the ones Josie Reilly had on her desk on that first day. The day she blackmailed my conscience into taking part in her charade.

The OCD order of things speeds my search. 'W' is right where it should be at the back of the pile.

One by one I lift them out: Wakai, Webster, Williams, Wall. Taking it out of the cabinet, the folder shakes in my trembling hands. I rest it on the ground reminding myself to breathe, to calm down. *Stay focused, Becca. It might be nothing.*

It's not nothing: it's me, Rebecca Wall, all my details, the forms I filled in, details about Mom. Then a small slip of paper slides out onto my lap. Blood results. My eyes peel the information from the page.

> Conclusion: not the daughter of eFAD patient Nancy Wall.

There's a bomb in my head, tick-tock tick-tock, thumping inside my skull, blurring my sight. Grabbing the bin by my side I throw up until I'm empty. Then I drag myself to the water cooler in the corner and drink. And then puke again.

My body is numb from head to toe, my soul too. What does this mean? Am I not me? Who am I?

Her words arrive like a swarm of bees attacking.

'*I took you, Becca. You're not my daughter.*'

My mouth won't close. I'm sitting on the floor trying to get my body to move. Down the corridor activity is growing. More footsteps, more secrets. I have to get out of here, leave it as I found it, but it's taking all my energy just to breathe. Closing my eyes, I pray, *please God, help me.*

–

The lobby has come to life in my absence. The change of shift. Barry is still behind the counter. He stands to speak as I pass, but I lift my hand to stop him. I can't think straight. Squeezing the piece of paper in my pocket, I press the elevator button and wait.

A thousand questions whirl through my mind. Is it true? Could there be a mistake? Am I adopted? *I took you, Becca.* The elevator crawls to the second floor. Who else knows? The Walls? Bert? *She came here looking for you*. The door opens to the sound of another day starting. Another day of keeping the dead alive. Down the hallway I smell the decaying lies, the secrets, the past. Mom's door is open when I get there, her head still, eyes wide and staring at the ceiling. Are they the eyes of a liar? Is this the shape of a liar? I sit down beside her. *Breathe, Becca, breathe.* Nurse Lucy walks in just as I'm about to speak, and I order her back out the door.

'But I have to change—'

'Get *out*,' I shout this time, louder, more guts, more hate.

–

Mom jolts in the bed when she hears my shout, eyes scared, fluttering. I take her hand in mine, her bony hand. The hand that held me, fed me, soothed me, guided me. The hand that squeezed mine on that first day of school. The hand that wiped the tears when Scott McCarthy broke my heart. This is the hand.

'Mom, Mom,' I say, squeezing her hand softly hoping to make contact with her other side. 'Mom.' Tears slide down my numb face, an iceberg surrendering to the sun. 'Who am I, Mom? Did you take me, Mom? Am I adopted?'

There's no reaction, no confession. Unraveling the piece of paper burning a hole in my hand, I lay it on the bed and read it.

'Nothing makes sense, Mom. You have to help me. Does Dad know, does Danny know?'

Her eyes move slightly, her lips part. My heart is going to explode. Leaning forward, I hold my ear close to her lips.

'Tell me, Mom. Tell me.'

'Woof-woof.'

Chapter Forty-Five

'It must be completely gone now.'

'What's gone?' Jeff says, handing me a mug of coffee.

'Her memory. She barked at me, for fuck's sake. The woman thinks she's a dog.'

Jeff sits facing me from the opposite side of the kitchen island. The piece of paper I took from Dr. Reilly's office sits on the counter between us. Jeff thinks it's self-explanatory. Mom is not the woman who gave birth to me, according to these results. Unless, he says, there's been a massive mistake.

I'm holding out for the mistake. Hoping that maybe the blood samples got mixed up or something. I don't care if I get into trouble for breaking into Reilly's office. I'll make up some shit. Actually, I'll tell the truth.

'You'll have to face your dad, Becca,' Jeff says, swiveling on the stool. The coffee is doing very little to invigorate me. Missing a complete night's sleep has dulled my ambitious plans. I need to sleep, to put the night between yesterday and today.

-

The rain crashes against the window like it's trying to break in. For a split second I forget where I am. This room, the beautiful decor, the crisp white sheets – this is not my home. Blood, blood results. My body slumps into the pillow, heart racing, palpitations putting a beat to my fear. It all comes flooding back: Oakridge, the office, the results, Mom, not Mom.

'Jeff!' I fly into a panic, jumping out of the bed and running into the living room. Jeff is sitting with his back to me on the couch, strumming his guitar, headphones on.

'Jeff,' I say, lifting the earpiece of his headphone. He hears my fear, pulls the headphones from his ears, wraps his arms around my trembling body.

'It's okay, Becca. It's going to be okay.'

Nothing is going to be okay. I don't know who I am. Taking comfort from Jeff's embrace, I try to calm myself, taking deep breaths. Pulling away from his hug, I wipe my eyes and notice the big moon lamp switched on in the corner of the room.

'What time is it?' I say.

'It's after six. You slept for hours.'

'I have to go.'

'Do you want me to go with you?'

'No, Jeff. Thanks but no. I have to do this by myself.'

–

After changing my clothes and taking a quick shower I head to my dad's. Is he my dad? I think about what I'm going to say to him. 'Dad, am I adopted? Dad, did Mom abduct me?' What if she did abduct me; what if Dad doesn't know? What if it happened when he was away in the army? What if she lied to him too?

But the photos, my birth, the happy smiles, Mom, Dad, me, all huddled together on that hospital bed. Nothing is making sense.

The rain slows me down, making it twice the usual time to drive to Dad's. Sitting at traffic lights I consider going back to Jeff's. This is probably all a big mistake – it happens all the time in hospitals, I've seen it on TV, things get mixed up in the labs. People get diagnosed with diseases they don't have or given the all clear when they're practically dead. I should have waited, asked Dr. Reilly about it, asked her to do the test again.

Dad's truck isn't in the driveway when I pull up at the house. He's probably down in Sam's bar. Across the street Bert's house lies empty. Pulling my hood over my head I get out of the car and rush to the front porch, my slippery hand struggling to get the key into the lock, like I'm not welcome. Like the house does not want me to enter, does not want me to discover its secrets.

When I get inside I take my jacket off, shake like a dog and go to the kitchen where Mom is standing by the stove singing 'Mad About the Boy'. Dad is sitting at the table, screwdriver in hand, replacing the back cover of a Sony Walkman. Danny has his schoolbooks spread all over the floor in the corner and is kneeling down reading. I'm not here, I can't see me. Opening the window to let the steam escape, Mom smiles. She is still singing when she goes to the cupboard, takes out some plates and calls Danny to the table. Dad shoves his tools to the side, making space. One, two, three – three places, three plates, three glasses. No Becca.

The room is empty when I switch on the light. No steam. Sitting at the table with my head lowered, I let the magnitude of my loss eat away at me. Time passes. I go to the window and watch the rain grease the darkness. Pools of water shimmer in shadows. The sky is barely visible when I look up. Armies of clouds charge past. No stars. The pipe below the sink gurgles like a scared animal. As I lean against the counter with my back turned to the threatening night, my cell phone beeps. Danny.

I look at it, his name, Danny Wall, flashing in my hand. There's nothing he can say that could make this day any worse but I'm not going to take the chance. I cut the call, let him wait.

–

I've been here for over an hour and there's still no sign of Dad. One part of me is glad, the nervous part that doesn't want to have this conversation. The other part is anxious, hoping he'll arrive soon. The first thing I'm going to ask is if I'm adopted. Which I know I can't be, because Mom has photos of me taken the day I was born. Which also means she couldn't have abducted me. Maybe, after all, the blood tests are wrong. Maybe I'll go home, talk to Dr. Reilly before I add any more fuel to this blazing fire.

Taking my drenched coat from the back of the chair I decide to leave. Dad might not be home for hours and he isn't answering his cell. Resolving to do a bit more investigating before blowing up his world, I walk to the window to pull the blinds. Lightning cracks through the air, flashing onto the white cross at the bottom of the yard. Shivers travel up and down my spine, Mom's words shout inside my head.

'*Put Rover in the ground, Danny. Rover's gone to heaven.*'

My legs seem to buckle so I grab the chair for support. The room is spinning. I see the glass circling around in front of me, full of water, but I can't seem to put my hand on it.

Her eyes were fixed on mine; she was trying to tell me something.

Woof-woof.

Chapter Forty-Six

My body weakens with every breath. The giant hand squeezes tighter. My thoughts fly off the grid. What was Mom trying to tell me? Sinking onto the chair, I rest my head on the table, trying to calm myself. I go back to that day, the day she said she took me. Her eyes were staring into mine, not floating around the room smiling at nothing, she was definitely focused on me. And she gripped my hand. Something she hadn't done since she'd entered that place. I should have paid more attention. Should not have dismissed her so easily. I remember her need to talk, the words flying out of her mouth, her eyes alive, familiar even.

'*I took you, Becca. You're not my daughter.*'

I clench my hands together and look towards the sky. God, God, God, help me here. Dragging my body from the chair, I go back to the window and look out at the yard. Lightning cracks again, illuminating the white cross at the end of the yard like a super trooper highlighting the star performer. I flinch.

'*Put Rover in the ground, Danny. Rover's gone to heaven.*'

Mom was trying to tell me something about the dog. Directing me to where the dog is buried. *Woof-woof.* There's only one way to find out.

Pulling up the hood of my jacket, I walk into the storm. The wind howls, rain crashing like gun pellets into my face. Pulling my jacket tighter, I make my way to the end of the yard. The storm whirls around, pure energy flying in all directions, touching everything in its path. Just like the dangerous storm inside me.

Strength comes from somewhere, dragging me to the cross at the bottom of the yard. Kneeling down, my knees sink into the softened soil. My heart too. Grabbing at the soil around the cross, hands, nails, caked in muck, I make my first hole. It quickly fills with water, so I reach for a plant pot close by and use it as a bucket. Digging, emptying, digging, emptying. The rain has drenched my whole body, seeping in through any open gap it can find. But I don't care, I need to dig this hole, need to find out what lies beneath.

A loud crash echoes through the air, closely followed by a flash of light. Near the center of the hole something glistens in the light. It's a wet plastic bag. It's dark now, a black dark that brightens slightly when the clouds shift from blocking the moon. The bag is difficult to uproot, so I move into a sitting position, my legs spread out, feet each side of the hole. The rain is falling into my open mouth as I pull and tug. Eventually it moves slightly. Pushing my body forward, I feel the soil shift under my feet. The bag is almost free. I look up at the tormented sky and pray. *Help me, God, help me.* One more tug and it's free. I place the torn bundle onto the ground beside me. What is it? What am I going to find here?

The plastic comes away in pieces. A pile of bones lie on the ground. There's a skull, a dog's collar with a rusty disk attached. Holding the disk to wash in the downpour the letters slowly appear. R.O.V.E.R. My shoulders slump. *Put Rover in the ground, Danny*. What did she mean?

Wiping mud from my face, I stare at the hole. The storm continues unabated, the rain filling the hole. In the distance I hear a siren howl with the winds. Annoyed at myself for thinking stupid things, imagining crazy scenarios, I stand and kick the water from the hole. *What did you expect to find, Becca?*

My foot slips, sending me sprawling on the ground. But I felt something hard below my shoe; something moved when I slipped. Crawling on my knees, I move my hands around in the mud. Something else is in there.

Another crash, another flash. More pulling and tugging. Then I feel it. Something hard. A box of some sort. Scraping the soil from the edges, I tug at it. Slowly, it begins to shift. With a sucking sound it comes away from the hole. It's made of tin, an old storage box. I place it on the ground beside the dog's remains and pull at the lid until it opens. Something leaves me, flies out from my body into the angry night. Placing my hand on the bag inside, I feel the bones beneath my touch.

And then I can only sit here, unable to unwrap the bundle by my side. I place it in my lap. This is what she wanted me to find. This is where my story starts.

What happened here? How did this baby end up in the dog's grave? Did Mom kill the baby? Is it the other Rebecca Sarah Wall, who was on born 13th March 1991? With my hand resting on the corpse, my world spins before me. If this is true, then everything I have known up to now is a lie. My family. My name. Me. Am I that girl in the picture? The little one with the tuft of hair sticking up? The pink coat – is it mine? Did Mom abduct me?

I took you, Becca. You're not my daughter.

Unable to move out of this freshly dug grave, I cry.

With little energy left, I pull the bundle closer. There are a lot of answers in that bundle, wrapped in plastic, waiting to be freed. But where do I start? Mom won't be able to tell me anything. Does Dad even know what went on? He was away that year, the first year of my life. Did Mom do this without him?

The rain has stopped. Everything is calm now, the clouds drifting slowly in the brightening sky. I'm getting to my feet when I sense someone standing behind me.

Chapter Forty-Seven

Danny's face is whiter than the moon. His eyes are wide with fear. He says nothing as he reaches down to me, offering to help me stand. But I don't want his help. Pushing his hand away, I scramble to my feet.

'Is that me?' I say, pointing at the bundle by my feet. 'Is that me?' I shout again, moving my face closer to his.

Danny isn't answering. He knows. I punch him on the arm, then the other arm, kick his shins. 'Tell me, is it me?' I cry, thumping my hands into his chest. He pulls me close to him, gripping my arms, disabling the attack. Danny is shaking, I can feel his body against mine. His arms hold me tight, too tight.

'Let me go,' I shout, wriggling out of his grip. Then I look him straight in the eye. 'Did you know?' I say.

He answers with a slow nod. My legs buckle, I'm going to collapse. I feel like someone is pushing down on my head, trying to squeeze me down into the soil. I'm going to puke. My mouth fills, my head jerks, and I remember the bundle lying by my feet. I turn my head to avoid it and throw up all over Danny's shoes.

The next few minutes pass in a blur. Danny is holding me again, running his hand though my mud-caked hair. I still haven't heard him speak. Pulling back, I wipe my runny nose on the sleeve of my jacket. Danny holds out his hand, wanting me to take it. But how can I? I don't know who he is. Suddenly I feel afraid; am I going to die too? He obviously knows what went on, there's no surprise for him in my revelation. I need to get out of here. *Run, Becca, run.* I turn and run for the gate at the side of the house. Danny follows, calling out my name.

'Becca, wait, come back.'

The gate won't open. I'm pulling on the handle but it's locked. Danny reaches me before I have time to bolt for the open kitchen door. So I jump and grab the top of the gate, pulling my legs up behind me. Danny grabs me, pulls me back down, but I kick and kick.

'Leave me alone,' I scream. 'Get away, get away.'

Danny doesn't let go. He draws me down into his grip again, where I stand shaking, fearing for my life.

'What are you going to do?' I cry. My body feels under siege in his arms. 'Don't kill me, Danny.' I have unearthed a dark secret, one that could destroy Danny's perfect world. I am now a threat to him.

'What?' he says, pulling back so I can see his face. 'Kill you? Becca, I love you, I would never do anything to harm you.' Tears flow down his face. I can see he is shocked by what I said. But what does he expect? I'm living a nightmare, anything is possible. But I believe he isn't going to hurt me.

The tension evaporates, leaving me feeling weak. Danny takes my hand and walks me up the backyard, into the kitchen.

'Does Dad know?' I say, wiping my face with the paper towels by the sink. The mud covers the paper, sheet by sheet, as I clean what I can from my face and hands. Danny doesn't answer me.

'Sit down, Becca,' he says, pulling out a chair. Giving me orders again.

'No. I want to stand.' I don't actually want to stand.

'Okay,' he says, sitting down himself.

The kitchen feels different, not like my family home. Everything is in the same place but it's like the walls have shifted slightly. They haven't, of course, but it's how I feel. Like I'm standing on the set in a theatre. Everything in its place to fool the audience into believing that this world is real.

Parched, I reach for the glass on the table in front of Danny, empty its contents and fill it with fresh water. At least the tap works. Then I stand against the sink, glass in hand, and stare at Danny.

'Becca, we need to talk.' Danny is struggling to hold his head up. My eyes are fixed on his, waiting for him to tell me something, anything, to make sense of this crazy world I find myself in.

'Are you sure you don't want to sit down?' he says. This time I do. I pull out a chair and plonk myself at the far side of the table. 'Rebecca, something awful happened.'

Danny's voice sounds like it's coming from somewhere miles away, echoing in my head. He lets out a long deep sigh, runs his hands through his wet hair, then keels forward, resting his arms on the table. His eyes are crying without tears. I can see the pain etched across his face, pulling and dragging at the Danny I know. The Danny I thought I knew. The silence after he speaks is choking. Invisible hands, squeezing my throat, pulling at the collar of my shirt. I look upwards and take breath after breath after breath.

'Are you okay?' he says, but I don't answer. I don't have to answer him anymore. When I feel calm enough to continue, I let my gaze meet his again.

'Becca,' he says, moving his hand across the table as if waiting for me to hold it. He can wait. 'It was me.' My heart stops, my eyes freeze on his.

'It was you what?' I say, not wanting to hear the answer.

'I killed the baby, Becca.'

–

I want to ask him how he killed the baby, why he killed the baby, but I can't speak. Danny is banging his forehead on the kitchen table.

'I wanted you to know,' he cries, still banging. 'I wanted to tell you years ago but everything was so… so…' Words fail him. He is looking at me, waiting for some sort of response. I lick my lips.

I don't know how long we've been sitting here, truth festering in the air between us. Eventually I find the will to speak but all I can say is, 'Why?'

Danny stares at the wall as if the answer is written there. Then he moves his demented stare to me. His eyes are full of fear.

'It was an accident, Becca. I was only three years old.'

His words fall like acid onto my soul.

'I didn't know what I was doing, you have to remember that. I was three years old when it happened.' Danny keeps reminding me of his age, it must be his excuse, his reason for surviving the ordeal. He was so young.

'Rover died, we came downstairs one morning and found him lying on his back on the floor, motionless. Dad was away with the army, so we dug a grave, Mom and I, at the end of the yard, under the tree. It was evening time, still bright but getting shadowy.'

His voice cracks, he's finding it hard to release the truth. Turning his head away from me he looks towards the window, staring into space.

Am I going to be able to handle this? Will I survive the truth? Should I ask him to stop? But I need to know what happened.

'I remember feeling sad,' he says. 'That Rover was gone… but I also remember enjoying digging that hole with Mom. Well, she dug, I helped with my toy shovel. Then she wrapped Rover in a bag and placed him in the hole and said prayers over him. I felt really important, like an adult. It was my first taste of responsibility, digging that grave.'

What the fuck is he talking about?

'Remember Becca, I was only a child…'

My head is thumping. Reaching into my bag, I search for some Advil but find none. Rubbing my temples, I close my eyes and pray for some relief. Danny continues.

'The following day Mom asked me to watch you while she took a bath… It feels wrong saying *you*, it wasn't you, you're still here… Mom asked me to watch over the baby. She was asleep in the crib and I guess Mom expected her to stay asleep. And she did, but when I looked into the crib I saw a motionless baby lying there, and thought…'

He puts his hands in his hair, tearing at it in clumps, howling in pain. 'I'm so sorry, Becca. I thought she was dead too, she was lying just like the dog on her side, I couldn't see her breathe.'

My head spins. I'm going to be sick again. Jumping up from the chair I rush to the bathroom and close the door behind me. Wiping my hands and face, I stare in the mirror.

'Hello, Louise.'

When I get back to Danny, his head is resting on the table between his praying hands. I resume my position on the other side of the table. He looks up as I sit down.

'So what happened?' I say.

Danny looks around the room, but there's no escape.

'I decided to bury her, before Mom came back down the stairs. So I dug up Rover's grave, the clay was still soft, moved easily with my toy shovel. Then I put the baby into the hole and covered her with the clay.'

Jesus Christ, Danny buried the baby alive, *he buried the fucking baby alive.* The room shifts slightly, forcing me to focus my eyes on the empty cup in the middle of the table to maintain my balance. There isn't enough air in here. Danny is holding his head in his hands, eyes closed. This is unbelievable.

'What did Mom do?' I say.

'She screamed and screamed, dug her up, begged God to let her be okay, promising Him everything if he kept Rebecca alive. But it was too late.' Danny's face is barely recognizable as he speaks.

'I was standing behind her, bawling. At this stage I knew I had done wrong, that the baby had only been asleep... I can still see her.' Dropping his head back he looks upwards. 'Mom, blowing into her mouth, pressing on her tiny chest... Then lifting her, squeezing her tightly to her chest, kissing her head, kissing her legs, kissing her eyes. She held her for what seemed like forever. Until we were disturbed by a noise at the side gate. When I turned around Bert Ryan was standing there. He walked away when he saw me looking.'

'Did Bert do anything?' I ask.

'Nothing, not until he gave me that pink coat.'

'Why was he there? Did he often call to the house?'

'All the time when Dad was away, usually at night after I was sent to bed. He and Mom would talk for hours.'

My mind is racing here. Why did Bert used to call so often? Were he and Mom... *no, don't go there Becca. No, do go there Becca.*

'Why was Bert always in the house, Danny? Were they having an affair?'

By the expression on his face, Danny has only just thought of that.

'I doubt it, Becca. Bert is an old man.'

'He wasn't old then, he was twenty-five years younger.'

Danny's gaze falls to the table. Rubbing his hair, he lifts his eyes. 'Jesus, maybe that's what Mom had on him. Maybe he...' He stands, then walks over to the sink. His mouth is open but he's lost for words.

'Why else would Bert say nothing?' I say. 'Mom must have threatened to tell Edith.'

Shaking his head, he turns around. I can tell he is digesting my words.

'We know she had no problem lying, Danny. She lied to me forever, every day, holding me, kissing me, pretending I was hers.'

'This is a fucking mess,' he says, moving back to the table. 'He must have taken the coat out of the trash the night we came back with you. It was late, I remember the house being in darkness and Mom saying not to switch the lights on. She bathed you by candlelight, then put you in Becca's clothes, throwing your clothes into the trash.'

'Came back from where?' I say.

'The trip,' Danny says. 'The one we took to get you.'

Chapter Forty-Eight

Danny switches on the light, chasing away the darkness.

'It was early the following morning when she came into my room and told me we were going away for a while,' he says. 'She never said how long, but as I watched her pack all my clothes and toys I began to think we were not coming back. I sat on the bed crying… she told me everything would be okay, that I would love where she was taking me. But I could tell she was lying. I remember the pajamas I was wearing, the green army ones. I asked her would Dad know where to find us when he came back but she didn't answer, just continued to shove everything into the case that she'd opened at the bottom of the bed. "Everything is going to be okay" she kept repeating but I could tell she didn't believe it. Her nerves were obvious in the speed at which she was moving. Hurrying to get away. Like she was trying to escape. I told her I didn't want to go but she just kept packing. "It won't be forever," she said, but I didn't believe her.

'When she had everything in the car we left. Mom drove for what felt like hours and hours. Saying very little, her eyes wide as she focused on the road ahead of her. Stopping only to take money out of bank machines. Eventually it got dark and she booked us into a motel for the night.

'The following morning we got back into the car and traveled for most of the day, pulling into another motel that evening. The sun was still strong when she took me for a walk. I can still remember how it burnt into my skin as we passed through, what looked to me, like a real scary place. I was nervous but afraid to say anything. I could sense she was worried, gripping my hand tightly, pulling me along the pathway.

'We came to a road that had all different kinds of homes, mostly trailers, some small wooden houses. The place was dirty, trash everywhere, bits of furniture and old cars strewn around yards blocked off by fences. I asked her if we could go home and she said, "Just as soon as we find a new one." This made me even more scared – why were we looking for a new house? Why couldn't we go back to our own? Who would let Dad know where we were? Dragging my feet, the sun burning my skin, I was hungry, thirsty, but most of all scared. While passing by one of the yards a large black dog lunged against a steel fence, barking mad. Then two, three or maybe more dogs followed, sending me into Mom's arms. She ran with me.

'Eventually we stopped and Mom put me back down. A little girl was standing behind her, smiling at me, so I waved. Mom turned to see who I was waving at. In the yard the little girl stood, red-faced from the sun, a small, stained white dress, covering her skinny body. Behind her there was a pram. I couldn't see inside it, but I presumed it held a baby. Mom spoke to the girl but I can't remember exactly what she said, something about her mother. The little girl said her mom was asleep inside. Then I heard the baby crying and before I knew it Mom was beside the pram pulling the shade over the baby. She stuck her head into the open door of the trailer before taking my hand and walking me back to the motel.

'That night as I lay clutching the pillow I heard her crying in the bed beside me. I wanted to turn around and kiss her but I knew this was all my fault so I just lay there, haunted by her sobbing.

'We stayed in the motel the following day until evening, when Mom packed our bags. I thought we were leaving but she told me she had an errand to run and to wait in the room until she got back.

'I think I held my breath the whole time she was away. I'd never been on my own before. Then, after what seemed like forever, she pushed through the door, grabbed our bags and told me to get in the car. I did. I sat in the back seat, looked to my right and there you were. Lying on a blanket, wearing a little pink coat.

'Mom drove out of the parking lot and down the road. The baby just lay there, her tiny legs kicking the air. I could hear Mom gasping for air as she drove along. I said nothing, then fell asleep.

'The next thing I knew we were outside our house. Mom had driven through the night. It was still dark when she opened the car door and lifted you in her arms. I was completely confused and asked her who you were.

'She didn't answer until we were back in the house. She was bathing you by candlelight in the sink. I was eating cereal at the table. "We have a new Rebecca now," she said. I just kept shoveling the cereal into my mouth. But I could sense the madness. After dressing you in some of Rebecca's clothes, she put you in the crib. Then she gathered your clothes and threw them in the trash. Bert must have been watching, must have seen her do this, and took the coat out.

'It was later that day when I went over to see you in the crib. Your tiny face, arms, legs. I reached for your fingers and twiddled them. Mom was standing over me when I said, "Her nose isn't twitching. Old Rebecca's nose twitched when I played with her fingers." Mom pulled a blanket over the baby, then took me in her arms before sitting me on her lap on the couch.

'"Danny," she said, her tired eyes staring into mine. "We can't tell anyone what happened. You are never to say anything about this or the police will come and find out what you did." I was only three years old. Shaking on her lap.

'As the days passed I began to forget about it, played with you, laughed at you. You were so cute and you made Mom happy, which was the best thing of all. It seemed like everything was back to normal. Mom was singing in the kitchen again, baking, we went to the park and the beach and everything was great. Then one night I heard her having a big row with Bert, it went on for ages. I sat in my room with my pillow over my head trying not to hear them, until eventually Bert left.'

I'm finding it hard to take all this in, staring wide-eyed at Danny, who is shivering in front of me. I've never seen him this broken before. How did he hold this in for all those years? Carrying on like nothing had happened? She must have scared him good when she mentioned the cops. What a fucking mean thing to do to a three-year-old.

I pour myself a glass of water. 'What about Dad?' I say, before gulping down the water.

Danny sighs, his face slipping back into the comfort of his hands. 'He never knew.'

'What do you mean, he never knew? Couldn't he tell?'

Danny leans back in the chair.

'It was another eight months before Dad came home. You were one by then, and he hadn't seen you since you were a couple of weeks old, so...'

'So he didn't notice?'

'Seems not.'

I'm listening to Danny telling me Dad knew nothing; that he thought I was the same baby he left behind when he went off to Iraq. But the newspapers under his bed have me wondering if maybe he hadn't figured it out.

'Did you ever talk to Mom about it again?'

'No, never. I was just a kid Becca, I guess I just moved on, didn't know any different.'

–

The room is quiet again, both of us exhausted by the truth. Morning light begins to creep into the room. We have been here all night. My head feels like it's going to explode.

'We have to tell him.'

'I know,' Danny says.

'And we have to tell him now.'

'It's going to kill him.'

'I don't care. I can't pretend this never happened, that I'm Rebecca Wall, that I'm his real daughter.'

'But you are, Becca. You *are* his daughter.'

The sound of glass shattering fills the room as I smash it into the sink. 'I'm *not* his fucking daughter, Danny. I'm not your sister, either. Mom took me. She *took* me. I'm not me.'

Danny pushes up out of his seat, comes around the table and holds me tight.

'I'm sorry, Becca. I'm so sorry. I should have told you... I wanted to, but then Mom got sick, and, well...'

'Take your hands off me, Danny. You should have told me.'

Shoving my way out of his grip, I pick up my coat. 'That's why you didn't want me to get tested for the gene, isn't it? You knew the results would reveal I wasn't her daughter.'

I'm shouting this when I hear his cell ringing. Surely he's not going to answer it? He lifts the phone, checks the ID on the incoming call.

'It's Dad,' he says, swiping the answer button.

Lifting the cell to his ear he says, 'Dad.' Then, like the last bomb just dropped onto his shattered world, he turns to me.

'It's Mom. She's dying.'

Chapter Forty-Nine

Nothing is said on the way to Oakridge. Danny, eyes locked on the road, is driving as fast as the car will allow. Sitting by his side, I feel strange, like I shouldn't be here. This is not my Mom; my Mom isn't dying. The bundle of bones taunts me. Rebecca Wall, buried at the bottom of the yard. All I can think about is who I am and where I fit in. Am I really the baby in the pink coat with the button missing, the one Katie Collins came looking for?

Danny's in shock, driving through tears, his mind eaten by loss. Shifting in my seat, feeling I don't belong here, I open the window and let the fresh air cool my face.

The car screeches to a halt outside Oakridge and Danny jumps out of the car. My instinct tells me to stay put. *Don't go inside Becca, don't say goodbye.* But Danny has other plans. Opening the passenger door, he asks me to hurry, then sees the reluctance on my face. Kneeling down, he takes my hand.

'Becca. You have to do this. Hold it together. Please, come inside.'

But why? I want to shout. *She took me Danny, she robbed me of the world I belong to. Why should I go to her?* But his eyes are pleading with me, begging me to go in and play my part in this, the final act.

Slowly I get out of the car, into Danny's embrace. Holding me close, his tears sliding down the side of my neck, he says, 'It will be all over soon. Do it for Dad.'

'Dad,' I say, pulling back out of his arms.

'Dad doesn't know. Remember?'

'Are you sure? How do you know that, Danny?'

'He doesn't, Becca, believe me. Just hold it together for now.' Putting his hand on my back, he urges me to walk inside.

'But what about the newspapers under his bed, Danny?' I say.

Danny doesn't answer, too busy hurrying me along. 'Newspapers about Katie Collins,' I say.

'He was concerned about your safety after the body was found in Treehill Park. He said it could have been you. That's probably what sparked his interest in the story, Becca. Concern for you.'

'And why did you tell me to stay away from Katie Collins? You knew, didn't you? You knew from the start. Did you take the note, Danny?'

'What note?'

'Did you kill her, Danny?'

He stops. Steps in front of me.

'No, Becca. I did *not* kill Katie Collins. And I know nothing about a note.'

He puts his hand on my arm to lead me into the hospital. I flinch beneath his touch and pull away.

'How can you be so sure Dad doesn't know?'

'He doesn't Becca, believe me.'

'Believe you?' I don't know what to believe anymore. Maybe Dad does know, and Danny is lying in the hope I'll keep the peace for the next few mournful days. What's another lie?

Sister, my sister. Katie Collins is my sister. Memories flash through my mind like scenes from a movie trailer. The woman in the bar: *You look like her.* Turner's eyes fixed on my face the first time she saw me. The blood results, the coat. Bert. I've been tossed into the middle of an emotional tornado, thoughts swirling around destroying every memory in its path. I need to get out of here.

Danny is doing his best to keep me calm. He must be afraid I'll run away. I want to, I want to get out of here. This is not my mom; this is the woman who abducted me. For some reason my body follows Danny as far as the door. The door I passed through so many times, my heart broken, my happiness on hold. Then I bolt. Run away from Danny as fast as I can. I don't even know where I'm going.

When I get out onto the street it's empty. Which way to go? Streetlights make shadows dance through the oak trees lining the walkway. My heart is racing. What do I do now? Where do I go? I've no car, no money. Jeff, I'll ring Jeff.

He answers straight away.

'Can you come and get me?' I say, struggling to make the words audible.

'Where are you, Becca? What's going on?'

'I'm at the nursing home. Oakridge, out near Braintree.'

Jeff says he's on his way.

Leaning against a wall, I put my phone back in my pocket and rest my head in my hands. Everything is becoming clearer and more muddled at the same time.

–

I hear footsteps coming towards me. When I look up, Danny is standing there.

'I'm not going inside,' I say. 'I don't want to see her.'

Danny puts his hand around my shoulders.

'What will I tell Dad?' he says.

'You can tell him whatever you want and you can stop calling him Dad. He's not my father.'

'But Becca, his heart is broken.'

'*My* heart is broken, Danny. My heart.'

'I know, I know.' He squeezes me tightly and both of us stand in the embrace for a few moments, saying nothing. Then I pull away.

'I'm not going in there, Danny. Jeff is coming to pick me up. You go, you be with him.'

-

Danny wants to wait with me until Jeff arrives but I tell him to go back inside, that I don't need him to. Reluctantly he steps away.

'Are you sure?'

'I'm sure.'

'Well, I'll give you a call if anything happens.'

It haunts me; my sister is dead, someone killed her.

'Danny,' I say as he walks away. 'What were the cops doing at your house?'

'Not now, Becca, I'm…'

'What was in the bag, Danny? What did they take from the house?'

With his hand brushing back his hair, he takes a deep breath, Danny is as drained as I am.

'They took a jacket, Becs, suspicious of what they thought was a blood stain on it. But it wasn't. I hadn't worn that jacket in a long time, guess they were covering all their tracks.'

–

Unable to think straight, I wait by a wall at the end of the road. Burnt by the truth. I don't feel like I'm not me, that I'm any different to the girl I was last week, and yet I know I am. Everything that has gone before is nothing now, all lies. Did she love me? I know she did. I felt it every day. Saw it in her smile, in the care she gave me, the advice she gave me when I got older. How was she able to do that? Knowing I was someone else's kid. Knowing she'd stolen me. Was she able to blank out the truth? Put it in some box at the back of her mind that she never opened? She must have, because she didn't seem to worry about it. Not that I noticed, anyway. She never slipped up. Not once. I see her now, her smile, her bright eyes, her shiny dark hair falling around her shoulders. I feel her kissing my cheek. *Good morning, baby*.

Maybe I should have gone inside, said my goodbyes, but as I deliberate, Jeff pulls up alongside, distracting me from my weakening resolve. I get in, put on the seatbelt and say nothing. He glances from the road ahead, to me, and back again.

'What's going on, Becca?'

I feel drained, unable to answer. All I want to do is sleep and yet I know, deep in my heart, that I'll never sleep soundly again.

Chapter Fifty

By the time we get back to the apartment I've told Jeff the whole story. His face, one of true concern, is unfamiliar to me. He suggests I lie down on the bed for a few minutes to rest my head. The minutes turn into hours. When I eventually wake up the room is dark. I stumble out to where Jeff is waiting with a bottle of wine, he beckons me to sit with him at the coffee table.

'It's true Jeff, all fucking true.' After emptying my glass in one gulp I grab the bottle and fill it again, all the way to the top.

'What the hell?' he says.

'What the hell is right.'

'So now there's two bodies.'

'What?' Pulling my feet onto the sofa, a cold wave shivers down my spine. It's not the wine, it's the past. Katie Collins' killer is still out there. We let that elephant sit between us on the couch for a while until eventually Jeff says, 'Do you think it was Danny?'

'Danny?'

'If everything he told you is true, then he's the only one with anything to hide, the only one Katie Collins posed a threat to.'

I'm thinking the same.

'Your mom couldn't have done it,' Jeff says, 'so…'

The wine swimming through my head begins to muddle my thought process.

'So you think Danny is Katie Collins' killer?'

'Well… I'm just pointing out the obvious,' Jeff gets up from the couch. 'Looking at the facts, Becca.'

'But he could be?' I say, my words sounding slurred.

'I could be, you could be,' Jeff says.

After hours of drinking the alcohol has diluted my fear. The magnitude of my identity crisis has reduced to a simmer in my head. I can't think straight. This is far too much shit for one person to shovel.

'Jeff, what should I do?'

He sits beside me on the arm of the couch. 'You're tired, Becca. Maybe you should sleep, we can talk about this in the morning.'

Talk about it in the morning? Does the guy think I want to discuss what we'll have for dinner tomorrow? I know he thinks I've drunk too much wine, I saw him lift the bottle a few minutes ago and check what was left, but I can't switch off, not like that. My world has been—fuck, my cell is ringing.

'Can you get that for me? It's in my jacket.'

'You're not gonna like this, Becca,' he says, holding out my cell.

Taking the cell, I look at the name flashing on the screen. It's blurred at first, forcing me to squint and focus. The ring seems to be getting louder and louder but I'm not answering it. The last person I need in my head now is Detective Turner.

'You're going to have to speak to her at some point,' Jeff says.

'I know, I know, but I'm not talking to her now.'

'Maybe you should go to the precinct first thing tomorrow and tell her what you know.'

My head is spinning. I can't *do* that; if I do, I implicate Danny. But what if he did kill Katie Collins? Jeff has a point: if Dad doesn't know about the abduction, Danny is the only one who had something to lose, everything to lose. And what about Bert?

'Bert had something to lose too, he covered the whole thing up as well. He knew about the abduction.' Bert's strange relationship with me becomes more understandable now. The man knew all along I had been abducted and had tried in his own way to make it up to me. Spoiling me, soothing his guilt.

'I doubt it was Bert, Becca.'

He's right, it's highly unlikely an old man made his way to Treehill Park late on Saturday night to kill someone, especially with Edith dying by his side. No, it couldn't have been Bert.

'But what do I tell Turner? I can't tell her Danny knew about this.'

'You don't have to.'

'What do you mean?'

'You can tell her you figured it out yourself, from the blood tests and seeing the coat in the photo in Algiers. What your Mom said. Stuff like that.'

'But…'

'Becca, you'd be better off sleeping now and we'll talk about this in the morning.'

'But I can't sleep. I won't even be able to close my eyes with all this shit flying around in my head and I already slept for hours this afternoon.'

'Hold on a minute.'

Jeff leaves and goes to the bathroom. When I try to stand the rooms spins in front of me, forcing me to sit back down again. I remember that I haven't told Jeff about the newspapers under Dad's bed, that I suspect he might have been aware I was abducted too. And if he did know? That would make him a suspect too.

Jeff returns with a pill, handing it to me.

'Take this,' he says.

'What's that?'

'It's a sleeping pill. My sister's. Apparently the perfect life can keep you awake as well.'

Chapter Fifty-One

Jesus, my head is thumping. Lifting it off the pillow has taken all my energy. Then I hear it, the loud crash in my head. Yesterday's nightmare. It slams into me, sending me into total hysteria. Jumping out of the bed, I run to the bathroom. I'm going to be sick. Sitting by the toilet bowl, I curl up into a ball. What am I going to do?

Outside I hear Jeff clattering dishes. The smell of cooking wafts in, sending my stomach summersaulting. I'm nervous, helpless, each memory from the day before queuing up to unnerve me, weakening me more. I pull myself into a standing position and look in the mirror. I don't look like me anymore. Dark rings below red eyes dominate my shrinking face. My hair sticks like rat's tails to my neck. Splashing water on my face, I try to feel its coolness against my skin, but I'm numb. Am I dead? I *am* dead. Becca Wall is dead. The person I'm looking at is Louise Johnson.

I hear Jeff at the door, asking if I'm okay, but words won't leave my mouth when I open it. I reach for the door handle and press. Jeff is standing there, his face as pale as my own.

'Are you okay?' he says. Still I don't answer, walking past him out into the small hallway that leads to the main room.

I push the door open and drag myself to one of the stools by the kitchen island. I feel heavier, like someone has injected lead into my body while I slept. I grab a glass of orange juice from the counter, sipping it to refresh my mouth. Slowly I feel my body beginning to respond.

'I'm okay,' I say.

'I've made some frittata,' Jeff says and I sit there wondering what the hell frittata is. Have I forgotten? Did I ever know? Does Louise know? I force a miserable smile.

'Thanks, Jeff.'

The room feels like it's closing in. It's clear neither of us wants to start the conversation. So we sit there, me breaking pieces off the frittata slice, pushing it around the plate, Jeff managing to eat half of his.

After about ten minutes Jeff pushes his plate away and leans on the counter.

'Becca,' he says, eyes heavy, the shadow of a beard wrapped around his chin, his hair a mess. 'I think you should go straight to the cops. Call Turner and tell her you want to speak to her. She needs to know you're a victim here; that you're only finding out the truth, that you knew nothing about Katie Collins being your sister before now.'

For some reason it all seems futile; I don't have the same interest anymore. Everything is wrong. I'm living in a world full of deception, a world where everyone I cared about has lied to me. Why should I bother?

'You need to move on this, Becca, get to her before she gets to you. As things stand, the only thing between you being a victim or a suspect is the alibi from that guy in the office, and that only covers you for half of Saturday night. They will try to prove that you still had time to get to Treehill Park.'

His words are like tissue paper floating on the ocean, they are having no impact on me. He doesn't realize I don't care anymore.

'Are you listening to me? This is your life. As bad as it seems now, it will get a lot worse if you're arrested for murder. You need to pull yourself together. This is not the time to check out. It's time to take action.'

Reality slowly seeps through my body, wakening me up to the facts. Jeff is doing his best to convince me I need to do something before something is done to me.

'You're the one who was wronged here, Becca. Do something about it.'

My eyes meet his. He's right, I need to take action.

I need to talk to Turner.

The room tightens around me, squeezing my soul. It's harder than I could have imagined, this living with the truth. A lot harder than living a lie.

Sipping strong coffee, I feel it travel through my veins. My honest veins. I realize the truth has been in me all along. I've always been Louise Johnson. No matter what I was called, no matter who pretended to be my mom, my dad or my brother.

I was always her. Louise, Katie's sister. The girl in the pink coat.

Slipping off the stool, I turn to Jeff.

'I'm going to take a shower.'

Jeff nods, lifting the dishes off the counter, readying for action. He must not know what to think. He didn't expect this drama when he said hello to me the first day we met in the elevator. Giving me his big flirty smile, winning me over straight away. But he's been in my life, in one shape or form, ever since. I wonder, is he regretting that 'Hi' now?

Water washes over my body, refreshing me, and I find myself wondering what Louise is like. Will she be strong? Becca wasn't. Will she survive this? I hope so. I also hope Danny doesn't get into trouble, what with little Liam and lovely Joanna. But what if he did kill Katie Collins? What then? Even the idea seems completely bizarre: Danny, a killer. But something inside me argues back. Is it really so unrealistic? Did he not do it before? He said it was an accident, that he was only a little kid himself at the time, he thought he was helping Mom, thought the baby was dead. But what if that's a lie? What if he didn't want the new baby there? What if Danny was jealous of Becca, of having to share his adoring mom with this new baby? What if he decided to bury her knowing she was alive? What then?

Chapter Fifty-Two

Jeff holds my hand as we walk in through the sliding doors of the precinct. My nerves are tingling, making me shake all over. But I have to be strong. I have to do this. The cop at the desk tells us to wait while he gets Detective Turner.

Around me people come and go, reporting their life's dramas, looking for answers, for help. A young man shoves past, eyes wild, anger bubbling in his blood as he rushes outside. I feel strange; this institute of trouble is not where I belong.

I check my cell to see if Danny has called. He texted twice during the night when I was out cold on Jeff's magic pill.

Her breath is labored

Her breathing is slowing down

What does Danny want from me? Does he expect me to stand by his side and mourn the woman who abducted me? I haven't thought yet about the funeral, or whether I'll go. If Dad doesn't know Mom took me, it makes the decision harder. Maybe I should go for his sake.

After a few minutes of tossing thoughts around in my mind, Detective Turner comes through.

'Rebecca?' she says. 'This way.'

I turn for one last confidence boost from Jeff. He nods.

'You'll be okay,' he says. 'Just tell her the truth. I'll be waiting here.'

–

Inside the interrogation room Turner fiddles with the usual buttons while notifying me of my rights. Her eyes are frightening. She looks as if she can read my mind, like she knows everything and I'm just an innocent fool. Her confidence is almost edible.

'Rebecca,' she says. 'I called your cell last night but I didn't get an answer.'

I shrug, unwilling to tell her I saw the call but ignored it. 'Sorry, I didn't hear it.'

'I need to tell you something, something that might upset you.'

It's a bit late for that; there is nothing she can tell me that can top yesterday.

'Detective, I came here to tell *you* something.' My voice sounds okay to me. Strong. Turner sits back, an inquisitive expression on her face.

Taking a deep breath, I say, 'I am Katie Collins' sister.'

That's it, I've said it.

Turner doesn't move, just holds her stare, says nothing.

'I found out yesterday for sure,' I say, 'but I've suspected it over the last few days. I wasn't aware of this when Katie Collins was killed.'

Glad now that I rehearsed my words with Jeff on the way over in the car, I tell her how I came to the conclusion, how the blood results proved I wasn't Nancy Wall's daughter. I tell her about the pink coat that turned up, which I then saw in the photo of the missing child, and the words, Mom's words, that cracked my identity.

She listens without interruption until I finish. I'm waiting for her to react but she takes her time, carefully filing my story in her head. Eventually she says, 'Rebecca.'

'I'm not Rebecca. I'm Louise.'

She looks down at the file in front of her, her fingers circling the cover.

'I called you last night because I wanted to meet with you. I know who you are, I'd suspected it all along, but I had to wait until the DNA results came through. The investigation needed some stimulation, so I made the decision to let you know, to see what came of it.'

'I didn't kill Katie Collins.'

'Rebecca – I hope you don't mind me calling you that for now. Katie Collins came here looking for you. She knew you were her sister. How? I don't know. She'd been through the process with plenty of girls in the past but this time she was willing to leave her new baby daughter and travel here to find you.'

'I know all about Katie Collins,' I say. 'I've been to Algiers, spoken to her husband, seen the walls of the spare room.'

Turner looks surprised by this, but she moves on to the coat.

'How did the coat show up?'

'Bert, my neighbor. He gave it to me last week, a few days before he died.'

'How did he die?'

'He had a heart attack.'

'Did he tell you how he came to have the coat?'

'No, but maybe he saw her arrive home with the baby, took it out of the trash after she threw it out. Maybe he even abducted me with her... I don't know. He's dead now, and she's dying as we speak.'

'She's dying, the woman who abducted you?'

'Yes, they're all by her bedside now. She got pneumonia a few days ago and has been going downhill ever since.' I can feel tears at the back of my eyes when I say this, thinking of Mom taking her last breaths. 'So there's no one else to ask.'

Turner thinks about this for a minute, staring at the table in front of her.

'Your father, did he know?'

'Dad was away with the army at the time. I don't think he knows anything about it.'

'Why? Were you supposed to have been born while he was away?'

If I say yes, this could all go away. There would be no need to mention the real Rebecca Wall, tucked under the soil at the back of the yard. But she'll check. I know she will, she will find out he was still here on the date on my birth certificate.

Looking away from her penetrating gaze, I lower my head. 'I think there may have been an accident.'

'An accident?'

'Yes. I think Mom killed me, got rid of the body, and replaced me while Dad was away.'

Turner stands up. She walks around the room, her fingers twitching as she leans against the wall behind her chair. Her stare is making me feel even more nervous, so I turn my attention to the desk. I know what she's thinking; this is unbelievable. I'm thinking it too.

'What makes you think there was an accident, that a baby died?'

'I have a birth certificate, photos from the hospital. A baby was born.'

'What age was your brother when this took place?'

I pretend to do the calculation in my head. 'Three years old, I think.'

'You think?'

'He could have been four, depending on what date she abducted me.'

Turner moves back to the table, pulls out the chair and sits down again.

'Rebecca, somebody killed Katie Collins,' she says, staring now like she's trying to hypnotize me. 'Someone lured her to Treehill Park using an untraceable phone. They had her number, which they probably got from the note. The note she left for you.'

I'm guessing she's suggesting Danny, so I quickly interrupt. Danny has always been there for me, protecting me. He's a good man who has had to live with this lie all his life. He was only a baby himself when it all happened, when his mother threatened him with jail if he told the truth. I'm not letting her accuse Danny. It's my turn to protect him now.

'She probably left Danny with her mom when she made the journey to take me.'

'What journey? How do you know she made a journey?'

I'm beginning to lose it. I must remember not to mention any of the details Danny gave me.

'I just presumed,' I say. 'She's hardly going to abduct the neighbor's baby, is she?' I sound cheeky now and I don't want to, because I need this woman to feel sorry for me. *Focus, Becca, Focus.*

'Rebecca,' Turner says patiently. 'Whoever killed Katie Collins was probably trying to keep her away from you. It wasn't your mother, so… who else knew?'

She's zooming back in on Danny. Staring me down, waiting for me to come to the same conclusion.

'What about Bert?' I say.

'Bert?'

'The neighbor who gave me the coat. He knew.' I'm hoping Bert isn't looking down from heaven right now, cursing me.

'Do you think it was Bert?' she says. When she discovers Bert was an eighty-year-old man who could barely walk and was nursing his dying wife at the time of Katie's murder, he'll immediately come off the wanted list.

'I don't know what to think. All I know is, I didn't do it.'

'So it's possible it could have been your fake brother or your fake father?'

This conversation is taking a turn for the weird. Turner is trying to break me down, suspects I know more than I'm saying.

'No, I don't think it's possible either of them did it. I've known them all my life. They're not killers and they didn't know anything about the abduction anyway.'

My voice is getting croaky. The truth, catching in my throat. Danny did know, and he lied to me for twenty-five years about it. But I'm not going to tell her that because I don't believe Danny killed her. I don't believe he'd risk all he has; Joanna, Liam, the perfect house, the perfect job.

I think he would have allowed Katie find me rather than kill her.

Turner stands up and wanders around the room for a bit before suggesting we call it a day. She'll want to talk to me again, she says. I'm not to go far. I wish I could, I wish I could get on the next plane out of here and never come back. Maybe I will.

Chapter Fifty-Three

Out in the lobby Jeff stands up when he sees me. His eyes are full of questions, but I'm too exhausted to fill him in right now. I'll wait until we get home, or out of the building at least.

The sky is completely blue when we step outside, no clouds, they're all hanging around in my head. Sucking in fresh air I look up at the sky, to where my real mom is, and wonder what she was like.

She wasn't very attentive to her children if Danny's story can be believed. But who am I to judge? Maybe she was having a bad day when they passed by. Maybe she was sick, and that's why she left Katie out on the deck looking after me while she slept. Or maybe she was drunk, I'll never know now. Everyone who knows is gone. Unless Katie told her husband something about her, what she remembered of her mom before her mom took her life. What she remembers of that day.

Icy shivers run through my body. The woman killed herself and it's my fault. Well, not my fault exactly, but because of me. It was Nancy Wall's fault. But then my mother left me out in the yard, toasting in the sun with a heavy woolen coat covering my dehydrating body. She left me unattended. It wouldn't have happened if she'd been taking better care of me. *Jesus, Becca. Stop.* I don't know what I should be thinking, my mind is scrambled.

'Do you want to go for a coffee?' Jeff says, nodding towards the Dunkie's across the street.

'I think I should ring him,' I say.

'Ring who?'

'Her husband, Thomas Collins. I think I should let him know Katie was right this time, that she finally found her sister. He should know that, shouldn't he? That she wasn't mad.'

'Relax, Becca.'

'No, I won't relax. And I want him to hear it from me, not Turner.' I'm walking at a ferocious pace now, Jeff struggling to keep up. I don't even know where I'm going. I feel his hand on my arm, pulling me around to face him. I'm looking this way and that, anywhere except at him.

'Becca, stop it,'

My head is twitching now, uncontrollably, but I can't stop it. Why can't I stop it?

'Becca… Becca.' Jeff is still calling my name, at least I think it's Jeff, what is happening to me?

–

I wake to shadows of heads hovering amongst the bright light blinding my eyes, the ground hard beneath me. Amongst the voices I hear Jeff's. He is telling people that I'm okay, that I only fainted, to stand back. Then I see his face. 'Becca, Becca.' I fill my lungs, holding in the air, nervous to let it out. 'Breathe, Becca, breathe.' Slowly I allow my chest to rise and fall. Pain throbs through my head.

'Jeff,' I whisper.

Someone hands him water in a Dunkin' Donut's paper cup. Strange I can make out the yellow and pink logo, most things are still quite blurred.

'Drink this,' he says.

After a few minutes of Jeff convincing the security man on the nearby door that I don't need an ambulance, he lifts me to my feet. Then he flags down a taxi and takes me back to his apartment. This is getting familiar, a bit too familiar for Jeff I'd say. But he's still here, nursing his crumbling friend.

'I'm sorry, Jeff.'

'Don't be sorry. It's not your fault you fainted. You're under a lot of stress, it's a lot to take in.'

'I know, but you're so good, Jeff, thanks.'

'Don't worry about it, you'll get me back someday,' he says, trying to make a joke of things.

After a few minutes of attempting to keep my thoughts away from reality, I dip back in.

'What should I do, Jeff? What would *you* do?'

Jeff rests his arm across the back of the couch and tells me that I shouldn't be wondering what I should do. Just let the reality soak into my mind without trying to fight it. He says I should just get through the next few days absorbing the truth, and then think about what I want to do.

He laughs. 'It's not like you can Google the answer, Becca.'

So I lie on Jeff's couch, numb from head to toe, fear tightening my skin. If Jeff wasn't here to hold my hand, I'd be in the nuthouse by now. I might yet be. Everything seems to be going from bad to worse. I don't think Turner believes I killed Katie, though I can't say for sure. It's hard to read professionals, they're so practiced at maintaining an unreadable face.

Danny, on the other hand, seems to be sliding under her microscope. I hope he didn't fucking do it.

I sleep for almost two hours, and then I'm woken by the familiar call of the outside world beeping in my ear. Picking up my cell from the floor I see Danny's name flashing. For a moment I think about not answering, but then I take the call.

His voice is completely unrecognizable, whimpering between sobs and pleading.

'Please, Becca. Please come and say goodbye.'

'Danny.' I feel his pain. Poor Danny. His spirit is on the verge of collapse.

'The doctor says there's only a couple of hours left, Becca. Pease come, I don't want you to regret staying away.'

He has no idea where my head's at. What makes him think I've anything to regret?

'How's Dad?' I say.

'Not good, he keeps asking where you are. I told him you're down with food poisoning, that you're puking all the time, but he doesn't believe me. He knows something's up. Please, Becca,' his voice is pleading.

I'm torn, ripped, sliced down the middle. If Dad doesn't know what's going on he must be completely confused as to why I'm not there. Why his daughter, who spent so much time with her sick mother, isn't coming in to say goodbye, to be there with him, with her brother, with her mom.

Oh, Jesus, it's not easy being Louise.

'I'll think about it,' I say, then hang up.

'He wants you to go in and see her?' Jeff says from behind the kitchen island.

'I hope you're not thinking of cooking, I can't eat anything.'

Closing the door on the refrigerator, he walks back to the couch.

'What do you think you should do?' he says.

My head drops into my hands. 'What would you do?' I ask.

'Don't know. Would I want to say goodbye? Not really. Would I want to be there? Not really. Would I regret it later in life? Maybe, maybe not… It's up to you, Becca.'

'It's Dad I'm worried about. What must he think?'

'Don't worry about him. He'll understand when he finds out the truth. This is about you, you and your mom, if we can still call her that.'

He's right. This decision is about me, not Danny or Dad. I'm sick of spending my life trying to please other people. No, I'm doing this for me. I'm going to see her.

Chapter Fifty-Four

The room pulses with sadness when I open the door. Curtains pulled, candles flickering. A large vase of fresh lilies sits on the cabinet amongst all the lying photos. Danny is standing at the end of the bed, just standing there, completely still, hands wrapped around the metal bar. He glances up to see who has entered and when he sees it's me, he smiles a little. His eyes brighten as he lets out a sigh of relief.

If he thinks I'm here to play happy families, he can think again.

Dad gets up from the chair by the side of the bed. His face is white like a ghost's, his burnt eyes blinking, making sure it's me he is looking at.

'Becca,' he says. He hugs me, squeezing tightly, afraid I might float away if he lets go. After a few seconds he whispers, 'Are you feeling better?' I nod.

Moving the chair closer to the bed, he tells me to sit down. I'm like a robot, doing what I'm told because I don't really know what I should be doing.

Danny nods, letting me know he's grateful I came, probably praying I won't say anything, not here, not now.

After a few minutes I realize I can't hear their voices. I can see them, both of them, lips moving, heads nodding, tears flowing, but whatever they're saying is floating around the room, landing everywhere but in my ears. All

I can hear is me asking myself, *why did I come here? What am I planning to do? Is Danny the killer?*

Eventually Danny shakes me, then tells me that he and Dad are going to the coffee room to give me time on my own with Mom. Time for what, Danny? But I say nothing, watching as they drag themselves from the room. I haven't looked at her yet.

Slowly I let my eyes travel from her feet up to her face. Her shrunken, unrecognizable face. Her eyes are closed. Short wisps of breath leave her mouth every few seconds, the only sign that life is still clinging on. Her hand is resting on top of the sheet where Dad must have been holding it. Not really knowing why, I put her hand in mine and feel her cold waxy skin against my own. Then I squeeze it, this hand, the hand that fed me, bathed me, brushed my hair. The hand that wiped my tears, soothed my pains. The hand that took me.

I pull my hand away for a moment, breathing heavily, sweat gathering on my skin. What am I doing here? This woman abducted me. I want to leave, run away.

I look at her face again and this time I imagine the smile, the one that greeted me every morning, those big blue eyes. I feel the heat that wrapped itself around my body with every hug. I hear her soft voice whispering that she loves me – hear her singing, laughing, dancing. Why do I still love her?

Suddenly I know why I'm here. I came to tell her that I know.

–

The cross on the bedside locker is flickering in the light of the candle. Jesus, hangs here, hands and feet nailed. I feel like that. Like someone is torturing me. I look at his face, the calm face, forgiving us our sins. Then I look at Mom's. Did she know what she was doing, or was she so distraught from the death of her baby that she just panicked? Was it too late afterwards to admit what she had done? Everything had fallen into place nicely, with Dad being away. She probably sent him photos of me during the year, so I'd look familiar when he returned. Did she spend night after night lying in her bed, sleepless, imagining that knock on the door, the knock that never came?

Glancing away from the dying woman, I let my head sink back into my shoulders and stare at the ceiling. This nightmare belonged to everyone, not just me; Danny and Mom as well, and Katie Collins, and my real mother. One moment of madness rerouting the lives of so many. What were you thinking, Mom? What was going on in your head? I wish I could talk to her now. But I can't, I'll never know what she was thinking that day. Did postpartum depression precipitate her madness, the death of Rebecca, sending her into a frenzy. Or did she act with cold calculation to ease Danny's lifetime of regret? Whatever the reason, and maybe it was all of these things, I'll never know.

Outside in the corridor a trolley screeches as it passes by, reminding me where I am, that Dad and Danny will be back soon. I have only a few moments to do what I want to do. Leaning forward, I move my lips close to her ears.

'I know what you did. I know you abducted me.'

My heart swells as I smell her death closing in on me, her shallow breaths moving further apart. Mom is leaving.

Suddenly I start to shiver all over, my teeth chattering, my hands shaking.

Taking her hand, I press it to my face and feel the dry skin scrape my cheek. I loved this woman, I love this woman. My tears fall onto her face.

'I forgive you, Mom.'

Gently at first, then stronger, her hand squeezes mine. It only lasts a few seconds, but it's enough.

'Mom… Mom!' I cry, letting my face fall onto hers, feeling her last breath on my lips.

–

When the door opens, Nurse Lucy walks in, with Danny and Dad following behind. Danny stares at me, wondering will I burst this bubble of sadness that unites us. He seems more interested in me than his mom.

The nurse moves to the bed and I step away, turning my back on everything and everyone. I'm here trying to blank it all out, but Dad's sobbing follows me. There's no escape.

The nurse's whisper is a small sound, big enough to destroy everything in its path.

'She's gone.'

Chapter Fifty-Five

The two soldiers of grief lean against the wall. Danny with his arm draped across my father's shoulder. Both faces blank with disbelief. She's gone. Nancy Wall is gone.

Nurse Lucy is inside with some people from the funeral parlor, arranging the body so it can be taken away and prepared for the wake. The funeral will take place in two days' time at St. Brendan's. The body will lie in wait at Dad's house the previous night. I've been told all of this and yet it feels unbelievable. Like she got away with it, bowed out just when the shit was hitting the fan. Left the rest of us behind to try and fit all the pieces of her destructive jigsaw into place.

Outside the window a tree sways back and forth, its roots keeping it in place when all it seems to want to do is get away. I am that tree, stuck to this slip proof flooring, wanting to run, my roots keeping me here. Part of me is sorry now that I told her I forgave her. I haven't forgiven her, but something came over me while I was in there by her side. A kind of peace, brought on by the numbing ambience of the room. It seemed to seep into my soul, melt my anger.

But the anger is back now, brewing beneath the surface. How can Danny be so cool about all this?

In the distance I see Joanna rushing down the corridor, preened to perfection as usual, but as she gets closer I see her red eyes, the stress carved into lines across her forehead.

'I'm so sorry, Danny,' she says, hugging her husband before she gives my dad a hug.

Then she notices me standing at the opposite wall.

'Oh, Becca,' she cries. 'I'm so sorry, Becca.' She rushes towards me, flinging her arms out. I hug her back, feeling fake. This can't go on any longer. My mind is telling me to say it now, get it over with; tell Dad I'm not his, that Nancy Wall is not my mother. But something is stopping me. I know that if I say it now, there's no turning back. The whole world will explode around me.

After tossing thought after thought around my head, I decide to wait, to think about it, take control, like Jeff said. Pick my moment.

When Danny catches my eye I give him a hard stare, reminding him of the pain I'm going through. He moves over to my side and whispers in my ear.

'Don't crack now, Becca. Please, hang in there, you're doing great.'

Doing great? What the fuck does he mean?

'I have to go,' I say, walking away from Danny, from Dad, from Joanna.

Barry is standing outside the front door when I rush out with tears streaming down my face.

'Are you okay?' he says, moving to the wall and beckoning me to follow. For some reason I trust this man and without thinking I tell him everything that happened, everything that led to me being stripped of my identity. Barry listens without interference offering his help if I need it. When we're finished talking, I walk away feeling better. But something is niggling at me. Something Detective Turner said. I take out my phone and call her.

'Detective Turner. I need to see you.'

–

She's sitting waiting on me when I arrive, her stiff dark eyed stare displaying unrelenting confidence.

'You wanted to see me,' she says.

'Yes, I wanted to ask you about the DNA sample you mentioned when we last spoke. I have no recollection of giving you any sample?'

Turner stretches her back into the chair.

'Well, Becca, we didn't ask you for a sample, we got Dr. Josie Reilly to do that.'

What? I can't believe what she is saying.

'Was the whole clinical trial thing a set up then?' I say.

'Oh no, that was real, we just asked her to invite you on board.'

I feel my heart thumping in my chest but not in a nervous way. It's anger. How was I played like a fool?

'Don't feel bad, Rebecca, we had to do what we had to do.'

'But you're no closer, are you?'

'No closer to what?'

'To finding the killer. I guess you know by now it isn't me but you don't know who it is, do you?'

'We have our suspects, and yes, you are no longer one of them, but I still need you to answer my questions.'

What the hell is she going to ask me now? I was the one who came to see her.

'Did you ever find the note? This time, before you answer, remember we will find the killer and if we find out you lied to us, you will be charged.'

The bitch thinks she's scaring me, she's not. After what I've been through, it would take a lot more than her threats to scare me.

'No.'

'Did you ask your brother Danny about it?'

'Yes, he didn't see it.'

'Your father, Nicholas Wall, did you ask him?'

'Yes, he didn't see it.'

'Have you seen either of them using a phone that wasn't their usual one?'

'No.'

I'm sitting here listening to this woman ask the same questions and expect a different answer. This woman who insisted I produce an alibi for the night of Katie's murder.

'Did you need the alibi? Or did you know at that point it wasn't me?'

She puffs air out of her mouth while placing both her two hands on the table. 'Rebecca, we had to keep the pressure on you. See what you would tell us.'

'Did you need the fucking alibi?' I say again. 'You didn't, you had it already, didn't you? From the CCTV at Mattie's.' My mind flashes back to Stephen Black shoving me against the wall. The shoe, the belt, the animal.

Pushing my chair backwards, I head for the door. 'Next time you want to talk to me call my lawyer.'

-

My whole body is shaking. I need some water or I'm going to faint. I can't believe I did that. Turns out Louise has a lot more guts than Becca ever had. Heading down the corridor, I stop to get some water from the vending machine. My mind is in turmoil. She thinks Danny or Dad killed Katie. The problem is… so do I.

Back at Jeff's, the room feels lonely. I was hoping he'd be here so I could tell him what happened with Turner, tell him how brave I was. Maybe it's good he isn't here. I've been relying too much on the man over the last few days, I need to do things for myself, make my own decisions. But there is so much to think about, so much to decide, and this feeling of not belonging won't leave me. I feel separated from everyone else, awkward, like I've shown up to a funeral in fancy dress. I need to calm down. *Relax, Louise, relax.*

So I sit on the couch with a coffee from Jeff's fancy percolator. It took me ages to figure out how it worked, but I did. Slurping the foam, I lick my lips and consider doing nothing for a while, even an hour, just nothing.

But it's impossible, my mind is in overdrive. I have to do something, but what? What do you do when you find out your mother who has just died is not your mother? That Becca Wall is dead too, has been for a very long time. And me, what about me? The girl I was last week, where is she? Also dead. A different kind of dead.

With my mind bouncing from me, to her, to him, to what the fuck, it finally settles on Katie Collins. Jesus, the woman died trying to find me, her long-lost sister. Her baby's aunt.

A gust of fear blows through my body. I'm weak and I want to puke. Did I cause all this? No, Mom did. The woman Danny and Dad expect me to bury, standing, in a black coat, shedding white tears beside the coffin. I don't know if I'll be able to do that, if I want to do that.

I make myself another coffee and think about Louise, baby Louise, the little girl whose mommy was killed.

What's going to happen to her, growing up without her mom? Thank God she still has her dad, Thomas. Realizing I haven't called him yet, I decide to do it now. But where's his number? I know Jeff asked him for it when we were leaving the house in Algiers, I remember that much, it was just before I saw the pink coat. But I don't know what happened while I was staring in shock at the photograph.

Hoping that Jeff might have put it into my phone, I grab my cell and flick through the contacts. Thomas Collins. There it is. My hand is shaking, mouth dry. I'm nervous about what he'll say when I tell him Katie was right. Will he hate me? Blame me? Curse me? It doesn't matter, I'll take whatever's coming. He has to know and I want to tell him before Turner does.

Chapter Fifty-Six

'Thomas Collins?'

My heart is thumping. I've never felt this nervous before and I have had a lot of experience of late. Silence floats between us for a moment and I think that maybe he's going to hang up.

'Yes?' he says.

'Thomas, this is Rebecca Wall.'

'Rebecca Wall?'

'Yes. I came to see you last week about Katie. I was the girl she came to Boston to find.'

'Of course,' he says.

I can't read him, don't know if he's annoyed or interested, so I just spit it out.

'Katie was right. I am her sister.'

Thomas says nothing, but he doesn't hang up either, so I continue.

'I'm Louise. I was abducted when I was a few months old.'

It's only when I say these words that it strikes me – I don't even know my own birthday. This makes me want to cry, but I push the tears back. I can't cry now. It's important I stay strong.

'My mother took me. Her baby died, and she took me from my real mom, Katie's mom.'

Thomas remains silent but he's still listening. I guess a guy in his situation gets a load of prank calls. Weirdos, psychos, broken people looking for someone else's pain to play with.

I'm struggling with what to say next because I thought he'd have joined in by now.

'Katie was right this time, Thomas. I'm so sorry she was killed before she found me.'

I want to ask him what was she like, her interests, her hates, the things she laughed at, the things that made her cry. What music did she like? There are hundreds of questions to be answered. But now is not the time.

'Thomas?'

I hear a sniffle. He's crying. Fuck.

'Thomas, I'm sorry if I upset you, but I wanted to be the one to tell you.'

I wait, but still he doesn't speak. He had doubted her and now she's dead.

'I know this is hard, Thomas. I'm going to hang up, and you can call me back when you're ready to talk.'

I picture him nodding even though I can't see him. Slowly I take the cell from my ear and press the screen. End Call.

I'm feeling slightly liberated when I hear Jeff opening the door. He looks surprised to see me standing there smiling.

'You look a lot better,' he says, glancing at the cell in my hand. 'Who was that?'

'That was my brother-in-law,' I say, feeling weirdly excited. Almost ecstatic. I have a real family, one where I rightly belong. It makes me feel so much better now that I know my identity. The last few days had left me feeling like a plastic bag being tossed by the wind – go here, no, here, no here.

'What did he say?' Jeff asks, tossing his leather coat onto the back of the couch and heading straight for the refrigerator. He grabs a handful of leaves and walks over to the rabbits.

'Nothing.'

'Nothing?'

'Not a word.'

Jeff turns to look at me. 'How did that work?'

So I tell him about the call, and it's obvious I'm a little too excited for Jeff's liking.

'Becca, don't get upset if he doesn't ring back. This is all a massive trauma for him. It may be a while before he welcomes you with open arms, if he ever does.'

Jeff has gone all sensible. Trying to prepare me for the worst, I guess. But what if Thomas Collins doesn't want to talk to me, or get to know me, or let me meet baby Louise? I hadn't thought of that.

'One thing at a time, Becca,' Jeff says.

He's right, I know. I need to calm down and not let my new identity fool me into thinking this world is my friend.

I sit at the counter watching Jeff take ingredients out of the cupboards. He's making me eat again. I fill him in on how events unfolded earlier at Oakridge. Jeff assures me that I'd be more likely to regret not saying I forgive her than saying it, and that I shouldn't lose too much sleep, because it doesn't really matter. I'm not sure I agree with him.

'You have to make a decision, Becca. Only you can decide whether to go to the funeral or not.'

'I know. It's so hard, though. I didn't realize how hard until today, when I had to stand with Dad and Danny, pretending... when all I wanted to do was run away. What if I feel that way at the funeral?'

'If you want to run away, run away.'

'What?'

'Becca, you're overthinking this. It's not about how you're going to feel, it's about how you feel now. Do you want to be at her funeral?'

–

Hours later I still don't have a clue what I want to do. I want to be at the funeral; I don't want to be at the funeral. It's like choosing my dress for prom all over again. She was with me that day, standing outside the dressing room, laughing at me. I put the same two dresses on at least four times each, and still couldn't choose. I can't remember how I decided in the end, maybe she did it for me.

My cell rings. Thomas Collins?

I rush to the counter and grab my phone. The number displayed is unfamiliar but I'm pretty sure it's not Thomas Collins. Jeff's waiting on my reaction, so I shake my head to let him know it's not Collins and answer the call.

'Becca Wall?' I recognize the voice, the deep considerate tone. 'Becca, it's Barry from Oakridge.'

'Hi, Barry.' I'm about to tell him I'm fine now, and that he's very good for checking up on me, when he says, 'I shouldn't be doing this, but I got your number out of the client contacts book and, well...'

'Well, what?'

'Becca, I found something, you need to get down here.'

Chapter Fifty-Seven

I didn't think I'd ever be back at Oakridge but here I am, parking my car in its usual spot, heading for the door. A chilly breeze is brewing up into the storm that's forecast. Barry asked me to wait until after eight, said there'd be fewer eyes watching him. It felt like I was waiting for days, mind racing, wondering what Barry had discovered that was so important he wanted me to see it for myself. Something on the tapes, maybe? Or something in Dr. Reilly's room? All I'm hoping is that I haven't come all the way out here to find out something I already know.

I see Barry behind the reception desk as I approach. Seeing me coming, he stands and walks to the door.

'Becca,' he says, pulling the door open. 'Is it still Becca?'

'Becca's fine.'

I walk with him to the reception area where I expect the big reveal to unfold but I've forgotten how Barry works. Forgotten his motto. The slower you go, the quicker you get there.

'How are you doing, Becca?' he says, walking through reception and on towards the corridors where Dr. Reilly's office is. He continues to make small talk, asking about the traffic, commenting on the cold night. But reading my stress levels, which must be clearly on display, he changes his tone to tell me why he called me here.

'When the body was taken away this afternoon,' he says, 'I was called in to supervise the clearing out of Nancy's room. It's part of the job, making sure everything goes back to the rightful owners.'

We're arriving at the entrance to the corridor that leads to Dr. Reilly's room, but he passes by, taking me further on down the corridor instead, stopping to push open a door with a 'Staff Only' sign. He ushers me inside.

'I often lend a hand, packing things or wrapping stuff while the rest of the staff are disinfecting everything,' he says.

I look around the room. There are boxes and boxes on wooden shelves covering the walls on both sides of the room. Every box has a name, ward location and a date scribbled on the side of it.

'Sometimes they never come back to collect their loved one's bits and pieces,' he says, pushing a small ladder out of his way. 'But we hold them here, just in case, for five years, then they're removed,'

I want to tell him to hurry, that I can't stand being in a room full of dead people's things. But I don't want to sound ungrateful, so I keep my mouth shut and listen.

'There's some good stuff in here,' he says, bending over to pull out a box from the lowest shelf. 'Here it is.'

He plonks a cardboard box marked 'Nancy Wall, Room 26' on to a countertop. Then, taking his keys out of his pocket, he chooses what looks like a small knife and slices open the lid.

'What is it?' I say.

'I'll let you see for yourself,' he says, standing back from the counter so I can move in closer. I look at him, nervous, before lifting the cardboard flap and glancing inside.

At first I don't notice anything out of the ordinary, just a bundle of folded nightgowns. The smell is familiar when I pull them out and place them on the table. It's the smell of Mom. Not the fresh flowery scent that used to radiate from her when she lived at home, but the sanitized version I've become accustomed to since she entered this place. While lifting a second pile of clothes out of the box, something catches my eye. It's small and black, lying on top of a bunch of towels.

'I thought you should know,' Barry says, as I turn to look at him.

I'm afraid to touch it.

'It's one of those untraceable ones. When you told me earlier that's what was used to contact the dead girl, I thought you should know. After all, Nancy Wall had no need for a cell phone.'

He's right. Mom never owned a cell phone even when she was capable of using one. 'If someone needs to talk to me they can use the house phone,' she'd say when we tried to coax her into getting one. This cell phone did not belong to her. Someone left it here – no, hid it here. But who would do that? I think I know, but I'm afraid to accept the obvious answer.

'I don't think I should touch it, Barry.'

He nods his head like I've just answered a tough question correctly.

'Do you want to take it with you?' he says.

I think about this for a moment. Should I call the cops? But what will they do? Send it to be fingerprinted and waste another few weeks waiting for the results. No, I can't wait that long for an answer. I need to know who hid this phone in Mom's room.

'I'll take it with me, try to find out what I can before taking it to the cops.'

Barry goes to a nearby sink and removes two plastic gloves from a box hanging on the wall. Then he places the cell phone in a plastic bag and hands it to me. He knows, and I know, that there are only two people who could have put this here. Dad or Danny. Mom never had any other visitors except me.

'Did you open it?'

'No. I tried, but the battery's dead.'

When we pack up the box, I take it in my arms and leave the room. This is all that's left of Nancy Wall now. Just things. Things she couldn't take with her.

'I'll tell the cops I found it when I searched the box at home, Barry. I won't tell them you had anything to do with this.' He nods like he's not particularly bothered whether I do or not, then takes me back out to the reception area.

The thought of driving back to the city scares me. Everything scares me now. I should have let Jeff drive me out here when he offered, but my newly acquired independence decided it would be best to go on my own, for Barry's sake. Arriving with someone else in tow might have unnerved him, made him less willing to reveal his discovery. Fuck independence. Now I'd give anything not to be alone.

Chapter Fifty-Eight

The cold wind seems to have disappeared. Or else I can't feel anymore. My hands are busy carrying the box so I bite my lip to make sure I can feel. Blood seeps into my mouth. It tastes of steel. Am I made of steel now? I hope so.

Driving home in the darkness the black cell phone cripples my mind. It's as if I've found the murder weapon. I know I should bring it to Turner, but I want to see what I can find out myself first, and I want to be sure it's the phone that made the fateful call to Katie Collins. If it is, it means Danny or Dad arranged to meet her in Treehill Park that night. The night she was killed.

–

Jeff rushes to meet me when I come through the door. Taking the box from my hands, he sets it down on the coffee table.

'What is it?' he says. Flopping down on the couch, I watch his face while taking the cell phone from my pocket.

'This.'

'A cell phone?' he says, looking disappointed. Then he realizes what the cell phone represents. 'You mean…'

'Yes.'

'Christ, Becca, what are you doing with it?'

'It was found in Mom's room, at the back of her bedside locker, when they were cleaning it out.'

'Take it to the cops, Becca.' Stomping away from me, he says, 'You know what this means, this is too fucking serious, you've got to protect yourself.'

'Do you have a charger that fits this?' I say, walking towards the kitchen cupboards.

'Becca, don't you hear what I'm saying to you? You can't play games. You need to do the right thing.'

Anger starts to boil up inside me. This is *my* life, Louise Johnson's life. Doing the right thing was for Becca, for the pushover. *I'm* taking charge now.

'I'm going to find out if this is the cell that contacted Katie Collins and if so, who sent the text.'

Jeff places his hand on my arm.

'Don't touch me.' I shout, pulling away from him.

'But Becca…'

'And stop calling me Becca!'

Everything stops. With his mouth open, Jeff stands frozen to the spot. In my hand the cell sits like a grenade ready to be dropped into the dugout where I'm hiding. Hiding from the truth. My mother is not my mother, my father is not my father, Danny is not my brother. One of them is a killer. My sister is dead. Becca Wall is dead. All this and more, and Jeff wants me to go to the cops.

After a moment of silence, I look up at him.

'I will go to the cops, Jeff, but give me a day, just a day. Turner won't know how long I've had the phone, and with the funeral and everything… Please Jeff, I promise I'll go then. Just one day.'

He turns to look directly into my eyes.

'I think you're mad,' he says. 'Completely mad.'

'I don't doubt it.'

'So how are you going to find out who sent the text?'

Considering his question, I walk to the sofa and sit down. Whoever made contact with Katie Collins had to have had her number. The number was on the note, the note she left at Dad's house. If Dad had it, it's long gone by now, I've searched that house from top to bottom. But if Danny was the one who found the note, then there's only one thing for it. I have to search Danny's house. But how will I do that without them knowing?

'I have to find that note, Jeff.'

'And how will you do that?'

'I'll just keep looking. It has to be somewhere.'

Exhaling like he's trying to blow the situation away, Jeff stares at the wall. 'I guess,' he says, in a defeated tone, like he's fed up with me, fed up with all this.

'Look, Jeff, if you want me to move out I will. I don't want to drag you any further into this.'

Shaking his head, he walks towards his bedroom door.

'No, it's okay, Becca. Or Louise, whatever. I'm just exhausted. I need to get some sleep. Stay, go, do what you want.'

–

Outside the window, grey clouds rush across the sky creating shadows and shapes. A man in a cloak, a wolf, a devil, a… a Danny.

The room feels empty again, just me and my secrets. I can hear Jeff's bed creak as he crawls beneath the duvet. On the wall behind my head, a clock tick-tocks, reminding me I'm running out of time. In the middle of the coffee table the cell phone sits, the grenade, the pin still in place.

It's hard to ignore the damage it will do when I pull that pin.

How will I even get into Danny' house without him knowing? Has Dad a key? I don't think so, and I doubt I'd be able to find it, or even recognize it if he did. *Think, think*.

The wake. They'll all be at my Dad's tomorrow night for Mom's wake. With Joanna's parents living in Florida, Joanna's grandma is coming to babysit Liam, to enable both Joanna and Danny to attend.

That's it. That's when I'll get in to Danny's house. During the wake.

Now, how do I get past doddery old Mrs. Cooper?

Chapter Fifty-Nine

It takes a few minutes for Mrs. Cooper to answer the door. At one point I think she isn't going to, that I'm going to have to come up with a new plan to get into Danny's, but then the light from the back room streams out into the hallway. She's on her way.

Earlier, I decided to show up at the wake for a little while, not that I wanted to but the less attention I draw to myself the better. Joanna was serving tea and drinks, keeping the show on the road. I stood in the corner of the room, feigning heartbreak, shaking the hands of a few relatives when Danny approached.

'Thanks for showing up, Becca,' he said. 'I know it must be hard for you.'

'I'm doing it for Dad,' I replied, wondering how the hell he'd know if it was hard for me or not.

When the room got crowded I snuck out the back door and walked the short distance to Danny's house.

-

Mrs. Cooper pushes her face up against the glass pane. Her grey hair is standing on her head like a bird's nest, her skin covered in face powder like a loaf ready to go into the oven. Wrinkles circle her squinting, blue eyes as she strains to see who's there.

'It's me, Mrs. Cooper.' I wave, smiling.

Her feeble hand struggles to unlock the door but eventually she succeeds.

'Becca,' she says. 'Come in.'

Mrs. Cooper is Joanna's closest relative living in Boston. I've met her at a few family events since Joanna married Danny. She likes me because I always spend time talking to her.

'How's Liam?' I say, walking past her into the hallway. The door on my right is where Danny's office is. If the note is anywhere, it's there. He's not going to leave it lying around for Joanna to find.

'Were you sent here to check up on me?' Mrs. Cooper says with a short chuckle.

'No, not at all, I'm just here to collect something for Danny.' Walking into the room she came out of, I wait for her to follow. I want to be sure she's out of the way while I search. 'He wants me to find a photo of Mom that he thinks is in his office. It's for the top of the coffin.' Gosh, twenty-five years living with professional liars has rubbed off on me.

'I was very sorry to hear about your Mom passing, Becca, she was a lovely woman.'

So she fooled you too, I think. The sound of Liam's baby snores echo from the monitor on the table. They must have it on full volume.

Mrs. Cooper sits down and I chat to her for a few minutes before saying, 'I better have a look for this photo.'

'Do you want me to help you?'

'No, I'll be fine, thanks. It's probably best you stay with the monitor.'

'Oh yes,' she says, as if just remembering why she's there.

Out in the hallway I approach Danny's office, hoping he's not one of those men who keep their personal spaces locked in case the little wife messes up what she doesn't understand. Thankfully, he's not. The door opens first try. The smell of fresh paint hits me when I step inside. It's dark, the curtains drawn, so I switch on the light to reveal a desk, a chair and a cabinet. Well, this shouldn't take long. Starting with the desk, I rummage through its drawers but find nothing that resembles a note from Katie Collins. The cabinet takes longer, reams of paper clog every drawer. I flick through everything as quickly as I can but again this yields nothing. With my butt resting on the cabinet, I put my hands behind me on the top and look around to see where else he could have hidden it. My fingers are gripping the edge of cabinet when one of them bumps against something and I hear a click. Turning to investigate, I see that the top of the cabinet lifts up, revealing a secret drawer. My eyes widen, my mouth opens, my heart speeds up.

'Did you find it?'

Shit. Mrs. Cooper is outside, about to come in. Pushing the lid closed, I rush to the door and turn the key, calling out to her that I'm almost done. Her feet shuffle away, and I breathe a sigh of relief. Back at the cabinet I pull on the lid but it's locked and won't budge. Fuck it. What did I do first time? I place my fingers under the edge, tapping every inch like I'm playing a piano upside down, but nothing. What the hell? I get down on my knees and scrutinize every inch but I can't see anything standing out. Back to where I was when it opened, resting my butt on the top, my fingers gripping the underneath, I hear a click. Bingo.

I see a rabbit. Not a real rabbit or even a toy rabbit. It's a picture of a cardboard cut out with a naked girl sitting on it. *Playboy*. October 1971. One dollar. Jesus, Danny. Pushing the magazine to the side, I lift some cards in my hand. Birthday cards, all from the one person with the one message written inside. 'All my love, Hannah.' Oh my God. If Joanna gets her fingers on that elusive secret button, Danny is dead. Hannah Boyd was the girl Danny went out with for years before he met Joanna. I'm not sure who finished with who. At seventeen you don't really care about your brother's love life, but I do remember tears.

Placing the cards back where I found them, I shuffle through the rest of Danny's memorabilia and notice a small plastic bag stuffed in the corner. The soft wool itches my hand as I pull out the contents. Baby socks. White knitted socks covered in old dirt and soil. They can't be, can they? Blood rushes to my head, my stomach lurches. These are Becca's socks. He must have taken them off her little feet while she lay in the ground. But he couldn't have done that when he was three years old. Danny must have returned to the scene of the crime at some point as an adult.

I stare at the socks with the lacy top, gently running my fingers over the pattern. Funny, I never did like socks with lace trimmings. The noise of Mrs. Cooper once again shuffling down the hallway breaks in on my trance and reminds me of why I'm here. *The note, Louise, the note.* But I can't find it. It's nowhere in this, Danny's secret world.

I say my goodbyes and walk out of the house to where the cold night encircles me. I think about Danny, his secrets, his pretending, and I wonder what else he is hiding. The fact that the note is not in his secret drawer, which I've no doubt is where he'd keep it if he did have it, does not mean he didn't destroy it. Having secrets is a way of life for him. The question is, how far would he go to keep them?

Chapter Sixty

'I can't go today, Jeff. I'm going to the funeral.'

'What about afterwards?'

Jeff is not letting go of the promise I made him. He thinks I should be down at the police station now, cell in hand. I didn't tell him about Danny's secret drawer because I know he'll jump to conclusions and he already thinks Danny is the killer.

Asking for help with the zip on my dress, I walk into his bedroom. Jeff is dousing his clear skin with some sort of shaving lotion. It's smells a bit strong for my liking but I say nothing, presuming the overbearing poison will die down after a while.

'Black suits you,' he says, taking hold of the zip and tugging it up.

I can't tell if he's being funny or serious because I have my back to him, so I turn around. 'I'm always in black,' I say, watching him repress his urge to laugh as his eyes look me up and down.

'Well then, dresses suit you.'

I blush, thinking he may have given me a compliment, and leave the room.

My mind is shredded. I can't think, or focus. I know the game is over if I give Turner the cell phone and while I should be happy about that, I'm not. The truth, staring me in the face, is not what I want the truth to be. I don't *want*

Danny to have murdered Katie Collins. So I'm searching for reason after reason for this not to be the case. Like, what if he didn't meet Katie to kill her? Katie may already have been dead before he had a chance to meet her? It's possible, she could have collided with some mad psycho who was at Treehill Park that same night. As soon as this day is over, as soon as Nancy Wall is laid to rest, I'm going to confront him.

-

The black suit hangs on my father like it's still on the hanger. The man has almost disappeared, his skin a mere coat of paint covering his bones. Outside the church grounds with Dad's arm around my shoulder, I listen to his cries as the coffin is lifted out of the funeral car. His body trembles by my side as I hug him tightly. 'It'll be okay, Dad. She's in a better place.'

I think about these words. Ready-made phrases that sound like they were rented from Hallmark. 'She's no longer in pain.' 'She's had a good life.' How does anyone know that she's in a better place? That woman could be in hell right now.

The crowd follow us up the aisle as we take our place in the front row, Danny on my left, Dad on my right. I don't feel like I'm here, not really, it's like I'm in a play or something, detached from it all and yet pulling off a great performance.

The priest performs his role to perfection too, leading us all back down the aisle having convinced us that it's all part of God's great plan. 'Nearer My God, to Thee' rings out from the balcony above. When we get outside a gust of wind shakes the trees circling the churchyard. But

I don't feel it. My body is numb; none of this is really happening.

I shake a few more hands, shed a few more tears, and wait. It will be all over soon, this pretense. The truth is only a few hours away. Dad will know what happened while he was away with the army, and Danny will have to admit if he killed Katie Collins. There's no way out for him. I have the phone. Which I hope has the fingerprints.

–

Three miles reminiscing in the back of a limousine is not what you want when you know the stories are all tainted by the small fact that none of them are true. They may have happened alright, these great memories from the past. But Becca wasn't there. 'That was me,' I want to say, 'That was Louise.' But I don't, instead turning my attention to the everyday normality beyond the limousine's window. We arrive at the graveside, to the best plot in the cemetery according to Dad, under a tree.

'She loved trees,' he says, getting out of the car. But I don't remember that about her. Don't remember too much about her anymore. Everything is fading quickly. I'm losing Becca too.

–

Standing beside the priest, Danny tells everyone how great Nancy Wall was. His words are like gravel in my ears, scratching at my brain. On the opposite side of the coffin, Jeff stands straight, hands behind his back in his black leather jacket. He winks at me, smiling, letting me know I'm not alone. Barry from Oakridge is standing behind him. I didn't recognize him at first without that awful brown uniform.

The priest says a bunch of prayers and the coffin is finally and forever lowered into the ground. Pain shoots through my hand; it's Dad, he's squeezing far too tightly. Watching his wife disappear out of sight is breaking my hand. Suddenly I feel sad – at least, I think it's sadness, though it's hard to describe. Am I letting Louise down if I feel sad?

With tears of confusion beginning to blur my sight, I raise my eyes away from the ceremony and see a cop car driving into the cemetery, followed closely by another. What's going on? Surely Turner hasn't come to hassle me while I'm at a funeral? Doubt swells into fear and I try to get Jeff's attention but he's not looking at me. *Look at me, Jeff.* The cars are moving closer, coming up behind the parked limousines. I glance back to where Jeff is standing and this time he's watching me. Nudging my head to the right, I alert him. Jeff eventually realizes what I'm doing and looks over to see what's unfolding behind him. Stepping backwards, he disappears behind the crowd, and the next time I see him he's walking over towards the cop cars. What's he going to do? Stop them?

The first cop car slows to a halt and out steps Detective Turner. My heart somersaults in my chest. Pulling on her jacket, she glances around the cemetery before fixing her eyes on the crowd gathered by the open grave. As far as I can tell, no one else seems to have noticed her yet, everyone still gaping at the hole in the ground. My mouth fills with water. The contents of my stomach race towards my mouth. If they don't cover that coffin soon I'm going to puke on it. Releasing my hand from my father's grip, I step backwards until I'm out of sight. The vomit jolts from my mouth onto the grave in front of me. *Joseph Best, loving husband and father.* Marble stones and Celtic crosses swirl into a blurred picture like some Gothic movie trailer, so I lift my head upwards and pull deep breaths into my lungs. *Relax, Becca, relax.* Then I feel somebody's arms encircle me.

'It's over, Becca. She's gone.' Danny hugs me tightly, whispering in my ear. 'No matter what happens, or happened, Becca, you'll always be my sister. I love you.' He kisses my forehead, lingering, unable to pull away. His tears drop, mingling with mine as they flow down my face.

'Was it you, Danny?' I whisper.

'Was what me?' he says, pulling his head back, his confused eyes staring into mine.

Behind him, the crowd hushes, everyone standing still as Detective Turner moves closer. 'Was what me? Becca?'

'Daniel Wall, I am arresting you for the murder of Katie Collins. You have the right to remain silent, but anything you say…' Her voice fades to a muffle. Stumbling backwards, his eyes locked on mine, Danny says, 'Becca?'

I'm frozen, unable to move. The sound of handcuffs echo in my head, as they pull him away. And in that moment, in that stare, those searching eyes struggling to understand what's happening, I believe in my heart it wasn't him. Danny did not kill Katie Collins.

Chapter Sixty-One

A shocked silence. Then Joanna screaming.

'Danny! *Danny!*'

Stumbling over a graveled grave, she tries to reach her husband. She's only a few feet away when a cop puts out a thick muscled arm to block her. 'Danny,' she cries, her voice screeching with fear. Danny is saying something; I can see his lips moving but I can't make out his words. Glued to the spot, a human headstone amongst all the granite, my gaze follows his black suit as it moves further and further away.

The buzzing in my head is soon replaced with the muffle of voices, one or two at first, but soon everyone is expressing their shock, their disbelief. Why is Danny Wall being arrested? Did he kill that poor girl? My ears close to their chorus, my eyes still fixed on Danny's black funeral suit in the distance, watching as Turner's hand pushes his head down into the back seat of the car.

A ghostly figure moves towards me. Dad, his face, whiter than before, black rings circling his eyes.

'What's going on?' he says in a hushed voice. Does he think no one else noticed? That he might be able to hide this too? I can't look him in the eye, can't tell him what he wants to know. 'Why are they arresting Danny?' he says.

Choosing to move past him, I walk down the pathway, not knowing where I'm going or what I'm doing. A hundred eyes burn into my back as Jeff arrives at my side to clutch my arm.

'Are you okay?' he says.

Holding on to his arm, his strength, the only life jacket on my leaking boat, I keep my head down and walk past Joanna, who is sobbing into the arms of some unfamiliar woman. She turns to look at me but I ignore her as she calls out, 'Why have they taken Danny away, Becca? Becca?'

The name echoes through the air, floating amongst the dead where it belongs.

I need to get away from here, away from this memorial circus.

–

We're outside the cemetery when the two cop cars pass by, Turner's satisfied face turning to look at me from the side window. It's the first time I've seen anything other than a grim expression on that face. She thinks her job is done, that she has her man. But I think she's wrong. It doesn't feel right. Something doesn't add up.

That can mean only one thing. One sad, bad thing. My father knew about the abduction. It was my one last vestige of hope, the straw I was clutching, wishing he too had been taken in by Nancy Wall's performance. But now I realize my life has been spent on the stage with three, not two, brilliant actors. Oscar performances all around.

'I need to go down to the precinct,' I say, when I finally manage to speak.

'Okay. Have you got the cell with you?'

'Yes.'

With my hand in my pocket, I feel the cell phone, the single flame burning with the truth. Clutching the plastic covering, I hold it tightly in my grip. It was supposed to be a confrontation. I was planning to do it when all the mourners had left the house later this evening. When Joanna was gone back home to Liam. When Danny, Dad and Becca played happy families, telling their stories as they tidied up after the amazing turnout. Dad was supposed to be discussing how beautiful a service Nancy Wall got, just like she deserved. And, as it turned out, she did get what she deserved – cops by her graveside. But Turner robbed me of my moment. My one reason for coming here today. Whatever she has on Danny must be incriminating. I wonder if it's something to do with the jacket they took from his house the day they were supposedly doing door-to-door calls. We'll see how that turns out when I give her the phone, with the fingerprints of whoever sent that text arranging to meet Katie Collins in Treehill Park. I'll have to tell her I only opened the box from Oakridge this morning, before going to the funeral; that I had planned to give it to her as soon as the funeral was over. I don't want her going all fucking legal when she finds out I've had it since yesterday, interrogating me about who else touched it? blah blah blah.

When we get to Jeff's car he puts his hands on my face and tilts my chin so I can't avoid his existence. His eyes are actually quite comforting, lifting my spirits slightly. But only slightly. I still feel like I'm in hell.

'Jeff, I don't think Danny did it,' I blurt out. 'The way he looked at me, the despair in his eyes, the disbelief… I just don't believe he did it.' And I don't, he had too much to lose; his new baby, his wife, his big job. Why would he commit murder just to cover up a secret for his dying mother? Whereas Dad… his wife was already gone, maybe he couldn't face losing his daughter too.

'Well, we'll know soon enough,' Jeff says. 'It'll soon be over.' He kisses my forehead. It will be all over. I don't know about that. For me it's only beginning. Life, real life. Up to now it's been like *The Truman Show*, everyone playing their role in the bubble for Becca, while outside the world continued on. Katie Collins continued on. My real mom continued on, until she didn't. And I, oblivious to everything, played my part unaware of the production. Well, not anymore.

The car pulls out into the traffic, Jeff at the wheel, me at the crossroads of life. To make a turn I must first of all leave the road I'm on behind me. But will I be able to move on? Say goodbye to everything I know or will I want to stay here in the comfort of the familiar? Time will tell.

-

The precinct car lot is full when we arrive, so Jeff drops me off, telling me to go on inside while he parks the car out on the street. I'm not nervous, not like before when everything would shake and shiver like I was dancing through these doors. Going straight to the cop working the front desk, I ask to see Detective Turner. He looks bored, worn out, I'm not sure which, but I can tell he is readying himself to tell me I have to wait. Before he gets to say a word I speak.

'She'll want to see me ASAP,' I say. 'Tell her it's Louise Johnson, tell her I have the untraceable cell.'

Chapter Sixty-Two

The following ten minutes drag like I'm waiting for the results of a cancer test. Seconds, disguised as hours. Unable to sit, I walk around the waiting area hoping I'm doing the right thing, reminding myself I have no choice, the killer's fingerprints are on the cell phone. They have to be. There's no other reasonable explanation for an untraceable phone to be hidden in Nancy Wall's room. I wonder, did they text Katie from Mom's bedside? Did Nancy say something to Dad or Danny, providing the catalyst for them to make contact with her? They may have gone to put Katie off the scent, tell her I left town months ago, or that I was dead, hoping she'd go away and leave their perfect lie intact.

Turner eventually arrives with that goddamn look of superiority on her face. My confidence instantly ducks into my boots, but this time I stand straight and pull it back out.

'Maybe Danny's fingerprints aren't on it,' I say, handing her the plastic bag containing the cell phone.

Turner pauses, inspecting the parcel in her hand.

'Why do you say that? Did you find the note?'

'No. Just a hunch.'

'A hunch.'

Turner's smirk is irritating. She looks from the cell phone to me. Her fringe is longer now, too long for her eyes to pierce, so she has it pushed to the side.

'Becca, we don't run investigations on a hunch. We collect facts,' she says, the condescending tone in her voice making me want to slap her.

'Well, you didn't collect that fact,' I say, nodding at the cell in her hand.

She smiles a little, shaking her head. 'And thank you for bringing it in,' she says, walking away, leaving me here none the wiser.

'When can I see Danny?' I shout after her. 'When will you get the fingerprints ID'd?' I'm beginning to sound like some hysterical mother unable to face the ugly truth about her precious son.

Turner says nothing. When she gets to the automatic doors I get a rush of blood to the head. I can't leave it like that; walk away without trying to find out why he was arrested.

'Detective!' I shout, hurrying towards her.

'Rebecca?'

'Why did you arrest Danny?' I say.

Turner sighs without even attempting to hide how annoying she finds me.

'I can't tell you that,' she says, shaking her head as she walks away. I can tell by her smug smile that she has something big on him. Danny must be guilty.

Behind me, I hear the familiar comfort in Joanna's voice directing my father through the entrance door, telling him she's found me, that I'm in here.

I don't want to turn around. I don't want to see him.

Danny killed Katie Collins. The words are flying around in my head. Danny is going to spend his life in prison. I can't believe it.

'What's happening?' Joanna says, coming up behind me. Will I tell her? Can I turn around and destroy her life or will I wait for the legal team to do it? I'll let the legal team do it.

'They're not saying much. He's inside now with some attorney being interrogated.' I say this not knowing if he is or not. 'We have to wait out here.'

Behind Joanna, Dad stands like a scared puppy, afraid to approach me. Guilt is sticking to my soul. How did I doubt him? How could I think that he was part of this deceit, that he knew about the abduction? The poor man, what a fucking day he's put in. Nonetheless, I'm going to have to tell him the truth about everything, throw one last bomb into his crumbling world.

Jeff pushes through the door searching for me. Seeing him, Joanna pulls me to the side saying, 'We need to talk, alone.'

I'm surprised by how calm she is; her ability to remain in control even though her husband has just been arrested is baffling me. But then again, that's always been a trait of hers, control. The woman is always one step in front of me and everyone else, always ready, knowing what to do, organizing the troops. Nothing seems to faze her. I think that's what Danny likes best about her. Everything gets done. She's going to get some shock when she finds out the truth about our family.

'Erm…' I say. I'm looking at Jeff approaching. He smiles when he sees me notice him.

'*Now*, Becca,' Joanna says.

The waiting area is almost full so we leave Jeff with Dad and walk outside the building.

'He knows,' Joanna says.

'He knows what?' I say.

'Your dad. He knows about you, Becca, about the abduction. I had to tell him, on the way over in the car.'

Anger sweeps through my body like a tsunami, wiping out every other emotion.

'What the fuck?' I shout. 'You told him?'

'I had to, nothing was making sense to him.'

My mouth opens but all I want to do is spit on her. How dare she? And how does she even know?

Holding her hand out as if diverting an assault, she says, 'I had to, Becca. He wanted to know how Danny knew Katie Collins.'

'How did you know?' I growl through gritted teeth.

'Danny told me the week before we got married, said he couldn't marry me unless I knew the whole truth.'

'You shouldn't have told him,' I say, pushing her arm out of the way and stepping in closer until my face is inches from hers. 'You're just an interfering bitch. You had no right, but you had to be the one to tell him, didn't you? Had to be the one taking control.'

'I… I…'

'Shut up.'

The ground below my feet feels like it's shifting. I know it's not, that it's just in my head, but I walk away from her anyway, attempting to calm down. What will I do now? Dad knows I was abducted, thanks to Joanna sticking her nose in. She's still there, by the wall where I left her, staring over at me. My mouth is completely dry, my head burning, I need to get some water.

I wanted to tell him, to assure him that as far as I was concerned, it changed nothing, that he was still my dad. He didn't know anything about the abduction so I have no reason to blame him. I wonder what his reaction was when he discovered his favorite daughter was really buried at the end of his yard.

'He cried,' Joanna says when I eventually muster up the courage to go back over and ask her. 'He wanted to know if you knew but I said I didn't think so.'

'Does he know Katie Collins was my sister?'

'Yes.'

I don't want to continue talking to Joanna about this because she feels like an intruder in our secret. It's *our* secret, it doesn't belong to her. Danny had no right telling her. She must have really loved him to marry him, even after hearing what happened. Weird that, I'd have run ten miles in the opposite direction rather than get involved with such a fucked-up family.

'I'm parched. I need to get some water before I go in and face him or I'll collapse.'

I think of Jeff, sitting in there by Dad's side. I wonder if they're talking, discussing me or Danny, or just sitting there, Dad trying to swallow the truth, Jeff wishing he was someplace else.

'There's a deli over there,' Joanna says, pointing to Jack's Deli across the road. 'Or there's a vending machine inside.'

I don't want to answer her, to make normal conversation with her after what she's done, so I walk in the direction of the precinct. 'Do you need change?' she says, taking her purse from her bag. I grab the purse and walk ahead of her into the building. Dad turns to look at me when he hears the doors open. I freeze.

'It's over there,' Ms. Know-All says, her manicured nail pointing at the machine in the corner. Afraid to take my eyes off Dad in case he disappears, I stand for a moment watching him watching me. *Do something, Dad, say something.* He smiles, just a small one. It forces its shape onto his shrinking face. But it's enough for now.

Joanna walks back over to Dad while I make my way to the vending machine. Two dollars, I need two dollars. Opening the zip on her expensive Gucci purse, I take out a bundle of notes as a young woman pushes past me, cursing and swinging her arms, knocking the purse from my hand. It opens out – credit cards, identity cards, loyalty cards, probably all in alphabetical order, fill the pockets of the wallet. Bending down, I'm about to close it over when I see something that looks out of place. A slip of white notepaper.

I open it.

Chapter Sixty-Three

To Rebecca Wall,

My name is Katie Collins. I need to talk to you. My cell is 1 504 6070143 Email – KatieC10@gmail.com. I'm only in town for a few days. It's crucial we meet up.

I HAVE SOMETHING VERY IMPORTANT TO TELL YOU.

Call me.

Katie

I read it again, this time the room fading from my consciousness. It was her. Joanna. Perfect fucking Joanna, with her perfect eyelashes and perfect house. How could I not have seen it? I knew it was someone in the family but she completely dodged my radar. How could I possibly have suspected Danny or Dad?

Oh my God. Joanna killed Katie Collins. She had the note all along. She is the one who arranged to meet Katie. What does this mean? Poor Liam. Poor Danny. The bitch stood by and let Danny get arrested. How could she do that?

I lift my head. All I can see is Joanna. Dark green eyes open wide, locked on mine, unable to blink. MAC Chili-coated lips, open with fear. Slowly I stand, holding the stare, clenching the note in my hand.

Joanna walks towards me, calculating her next move, I imagine. How to explain this. I cannot let her have one more moment of control. I must get the note to Turner before she has a chance to take it from me and make up some story, manipulate the situation. Lie. Kill me too.

Turner has to be told Joanna is the one who had the note, the only one who could have made that call. I can't believe she was letting Danny take the fall for this. Turning on my heels, I head towards the door. Joanna follows me.

'Becca, Becca,' she calls out, her voice swelled in panic.

'Detective Turner,' I shout, pushing my way towards the door, one hand in the air parading the note. 'Turner, I have it. I found the note.'

'Becca, Becca,' she calls out after me. 'It's not what it looks like.'

It is what it looks like. Everything is spinning into control.

Out of the corner of my eye I see Dad standing up, looking at me with a concerned expression. He doesn't know what's going on. His whole life, he hasn't known what was going on.

The door swings open with one push. Left? Right? I don't know… Go right. Mom always said, 'If you're ever lost, Becca, turn right.' Funny I can think of that now.

'Turner,' I call out, officers in uniforms looking bemused as I pass their stations.

'Can I help you?' one guy says, standing up. I rush past him, Joanna closing in behind me, the clanking of her high heeled shoes on the tiled floor becoming more rapid. Click-clock, click-clock.

'Detective Turner,' I shout again, continuing to hurry as I enter a narrow corridor. Joanna's pleas ringing in my ear. 'Wait, Becca… I can explain.'

I'm going to run out of options if she doesn't appear soon. Where the hell is Turner?

'Rebecca.'

I hear her voice, her dull, unexcited voice. Turner is standing behind me when I look around.

'I have it. I have the note.' I say, holding my hand out. 'I know who met Katie Collins at Treehill Park.' Turner's eyes move to the piece of paper imprisoned in my grip.

Click-clock, click-clock, Joanna is now running down the corridor, away from us.

'You might want to stop her.' I say, gasping for breath while pointing in Joanna's direction. But before my words have an impact, Joanna is apprehended by a man in uniform as she tries to escape.

With the evidence safely in Turner's possession, I walk down the corridor. I have no job, no place of my own. Maybe it's time to make a fresh start. Move away from here and own my new identity. New Orleans is nice. I open the door to where the only other person deceived by this lifelong pretense waits outside. Will I call him Dad? Probably.

Chapter Sixty-Four

Four Weeks Earlier

Slipping out from under the duvet, a shadow in the dark room, Joanna gently pulled on the handle that she had never fully closed when she came to bed. The less noise she made, the less chance Danny would wake up. Out in the hallway, she lifted her feet off the wooden boards with precision. A creak could do it, startle him, put an end to her plan.

The woman was not going to ruin everything. Not now. Not with Joanna's whole world finally moving in the right direction. She had taken a risk marrying Danny. His past kept him awake at night. But it had paid off. Joanna had it all now; the fancy house, the fancy car, the best of friends. And, in a couple of weeks' time, the baby.

She knew if this woman ever got to meet Becca, Joanna's whole world would be destroyed. Danny would be questioned and possibly even arrested for the death of that little baby all those years ago. When she found Katie's note in her father-in-law's mailbox, Joanna knew the past had arrived to taunt the future. Her future. And she was not about to let some trailer trash passer-by destroy that.

At the bottom of the stairs she walked in the darkness to the cloakroom, switching on the small light inside the door. Her heart was beating faster. Anxious? Excited?

Joanna wasn't sure. It was the same feeling she'd had the day she searched Becca's apartment to see if Katie had sent a note there too.

Taking her jacket from the hook, she realized it didn't fit anymore. It wouldn't close over the bump. The night was cold, icy cold, she could feel it sneaking in below the front door. So she took Danny's navy jacket and tried it on. Perfect, it closed all the way up, covering the bump and keeping her warm. With the sleeves pushed up, she pulled on a pair of Uggs, tucked in her pajama bottoms and walked to the kitchen. 1.45am; the meeting was at 2am. Fifteen minutes, plenty of time. Taking the keys from the hook by the door, she stepped out into the dark night, the whistling wind providing a camouflage for the car's engine as she backed out onto the empty road.

Rehearsing her story, Joanna moved through the night's shadows, arriving at the pre-arranged spot. The bridge. '*You can't miss it. It's the only one. It crosses the dried-up river.*' No one else would be there at that hour.

Thinking she was meeting Becca, Katie had agreed to wait until Becca had finished her shift at work. She would have agreed to anything, she was so desperate to meet her. Her sister.

It was never meant to happen the way it did. The push, the fall, the body just lying there, blood flowing from the back of her head. But she wouldn't listen, wouldn't go away.

Joanna had tried to tell Katie Collins that her sister wanted nothing to do with her. That she had sent Joanna to tell her to leave her alone or she'd kill herself, just like their mom did.

Joanna thought that would scare her. That Katie would go away when she heard that. But she was wrong. Katie demanded that her sister tell her to her face. Said she was going to meet her, whether Becca wanted to or not. Katie had spent most of her life searching for her sister and was not walking away now that she had found her.

Joanna recognized Katie's determination, her strength. Her ability to win.

It infuriated her. She was not going to lose everything. Frantically, she moved closer to Katie, grabbed her shoulders and pushed her to the ground, cracking her head off a rock. The dark night disguised the color but Joanna knew it was blood flowing from Katie's head. Bending down, one arm wrapped around the baby bump, she leaned over Katie's face and felt soft breath escaping from Katie's lips. Joanna could sense the life in front of her draining away but there was still time. She could make the call.

With one hand on her back, the other pushing the soil below her, Joanna pulled herself into a standing position, feeling the cell phone in her pocket. She looked down at Katie, the past lying at her feet. She wrapped protective hands over her bump, the future. If she did make the call, what would happen to the perfect wife, the perfect mother, the perfect murderer?

Joanna walked away.

A Letter from Jackie

Thank you for taking the time to read my debut novel, *Familiar Strangers*. If you enjoyed it, and I really hope you have, I would love to hear your thoughts via a review. Knowing what you think of the story is important to me.

The story came to me when I visited my aunt in a nursing home. People who didn't know their own name, or that of their loved ones, could somehow move into their past and live there momentarily, like time travel. It was very stressful for the families, which stayed with me. To lose someone before they are dead must be a different kind of grief and I wanted to portray this agony in Becca's story.

The other thought that played in my mind, was what if one of these patients revealed a dark secret from their past?

I hope you enjoyed this journey with Becca as she discovers the truth behind her own identity, the lies she has been subjected to and the strong woman she proves to be.

The story is not true and all the characters are fictional. Researching the types and stages of Alzheimer's disease, was both interesting and sad. Depicting the loss of a loved one was painful.

Thank you for your support. I would love to have your continued support as I progress on my writing journey.

You are welcome to contact me with any questions or comments any time. I'm available on Facebook and Twitter.

Best Wishes

Jackie Walsh

Acknowledgements

What surprised me most about writing a novel, is how an isolated venture could bring me in contact with so many wonderful people. Without their encouragement and knowledge, I would not have got to where I am today. Amongst these people, some wonderful friends.

Patricia Gibney, who has been an endless source of encouragement during each stage of the process and also my traveling partner.

Louise Phillips, a genuine champion for anyone starting out on this journey.

Niamh Brennan and Grainne Daly, two great writers with whom I laugh a lot.

Declan Burke, who has played an important role in developing my writing.

Conor Kostick at the Irish Writer's Centre, who suggested, that with a lot of work I might get there.

Well, here I am, but not without the support of the most important people in my life, my family. My Dad, my sister and brothers, nieces and nephews, sisters-in-law, without whom nothing is worth it.

And to my Mam, who I know is looking down and loving this, thank you for always encouraging me. The pain of losing you can never be put into words.

To all my friends, my fun, especially Cora Potts who has encouraged and contributed to my dark sense of humor, thank you all for your support throughout my life. To my little nephew, Jason Carr, who is already writing great stories. Keep it up young man.

To Keshini and Lindsey, my publishers at Hera Books, for putting your faith in me and for helping shape my story into something better.

To the staff at Lollipops, wonderful strong women whose dedication to their job has allowed me the space to write.

To Layla my dog, and the reason I get up early every morning, you have changed what I care about.

To Paul, my husband. Your love and support is the rock on which I stand. Thanks for always being there and for encouraging me to follow my dreams. I love you.

To anyone who has taken the time to read my book.

Thank you.